GW00381459

First Edition 2021

Book design by www.Bexandbooks.com

www.rahatton.com

Thank you to my readers, family, friends,
and most of all to my loving husband.

Without you all in my life showing your support,
this book may have never become a reality.

MANUMISSION

'To be released from slavery'

Chapter 1

REFLECTIONS

I was walking through an unfamiliar forest, with trees so tall you could not see the tops. There were only a few stray beams of light making it through the thick branches full of green leaves.

My skin shivered as though an icy wind was caressing the surface of my body, but not from the breeze, as it was a warm day. With each step I could hear the crunching of leaves and the snapping of fallen twigs, forcing me to take every step as lightly as I could, so I would not make so much noise. The forest was unnaturally quiet. No birds chirping, no whistling of the wind or the creaking of branches as they swayed. It was eerily silent.

I continued to walk forward slowly, carefully weaving

through the trunks, conscious of each step, until a strange sight came into view. I froze mid-step and stared.

Ahead of me in the distance, surrounded by a sea of natural greenery, sat a pure white fox; its narrow muzzle turned as it looked towards me. Although visually out of place, it was clearly comfortable with my presence. The fox stretched, and it slowly crossed its front legs as if demonstrating how confidently relaxed it remained. I slowly approached to investigate. The fox did not move as it lazily basked in the soft green thicket, watching me.

Hearing a tree rustling behind me, my hand darted to grab the hilt of my sword whilst I instinctively swivelled to check my surroundings. My breathing was slow and shallow as I listened carefully. I was an intruder here, a prisoner to my surroundings, and the trees were my jailors.

I glanced back to where the fox had been relaxing only to find it was gone. I scanned the forest, my eyes searching for tracks or a sign of a white shape, but there was nothing.

I walked forward once again, with more haste this time. The noise of my steps were no longer a concern as a sense of unease was building within me, telling me I was not safe. Pushing forward, a streak of white flashed in front of me.

The fox had returned, this time with its back to me. It glanced towards me over its shoulder as if inviting me to follow. I decided to humour the creature and comply with its suggestion, maintaining a safe distance.

The fox took off in a sprint, and for a while I matched its speed until eventually losing the animal once again. The flick of its shiny tail was my final sight as it disappeared through a small gap within the thick foliage. The ferns and brambles in my path thickened, wrapping around the trunks, blocking my way forward.

Deciding to continue, I pulled my sword from its sheath on my back and used it to clear a path, swinging the steel blade in all directions. Once my route was open, I picked up speed again and eventually saw the end of the treeline where there was a grass field bathed with sunshine in the distance. My heart skipped a beat at the idea I was nearly free, and I sprinted towards the light.

Just before I reached the perimeter, I halted to a stop as a figure stepped from beside a tree at least a metre in front of me, with their back turned. Reacting defensively, I held my sword forward with both hands, creating a steel barrier of protection between me and this potential threat. As the stranger turned, I gasped in shock when my eyes landed on her face.

She looked identical to me, yet there were some differences between us. We could easily pass as the same person, if it were not for her softer features. While my body was well covered with thick leather clothes and plated armour, hers was on display. She wore a sage green cotton dress, matching the shade of our eyes, that fell just above her knees. The thin, loosely stitched material showed off the attributes of our body that would normally be hidden. She had a narrow waist that was supported by long, strong legs, a toned stomach, and an ample sized chest, the shape of her breasts more visible in this poor excuse for a garment. With thin hide slippers on her feet, and no weapon or sword, she clutched on to a basket full of wild mushrooms.

Her long russet hair, the colour of autumn, was left loose, hanging beyond her shoulders. In the spring and summer months, my auburn hair would be full of flecks of gold, lightened by the sun's rays as I spent hours in the daylight; just as her hair did now, shining in the sun's beams of light between the trees.

"Who are you?" I asked. She did not respond or react to my presence as she gazed in the distance beyond where I stood, as though I was invisible. A branch snapped loudly behind me as someone or something, was approaching me from behind. I swiftly turned and sharply inhaled.

Two cloudy white eyes stared at me from underneath a dark hooded cloak, they whispered my name... "Truda."

~*~

I woke suddenly, my heart pounding, sweat beads rolling down my forehead. It took me a moment to take in my surroundings, thankful to find I was lying on my travel cot. What a strange dream. It was so vivid, like I was really there in that forest. I could still smell the damp shrubbery with a hint of a sweet floral scent coming from the flowers.

Who were the people in my dream? The mysterious cloaked figure with white eyes, and the one that looked like me. I had experienced strange dreams before, but nothing so intense. That had felt real, like I had just teleported back from that place to the safety of my tent.

Sitting up, realising I was still in our temporary camp, I thought of home. The place that gave me my name and rank, the city of Kven. I missed the comfort of a soft bed and a real bath, of which I was currently in desperate need of. However, for now, I was to be content with washing using a cloth and a bowl of water.

At least the water was usually warm. My house Guan was always good enough to heat the water on a campfire before bringing it to my tent. I appreciated this, not that I ever told him so.

"Tobias?" I called, glancing toward the tent entrance. Shortly after I had called, Tobias walked in. The young human in his early twenties, dressed in a plain untanned cloth tunic and trousers, with hide boots which represented his low status, bowed his head in greeting.

He was average in height for a human, but much shorter than I.

I was tall for an elf.

He was of a medium build but had strong defined muscles

on his arms, which could be seen as the tunic he wore was armless and loosely stitched. He had a round face with hazel brown and green eyes, and small lips. His copper hair grew just past his shoulders, but today it was wrapped back in a bun.

He was a Guan of little word and I liked that. Others often asked questions or replied with answers like 'yes my master,' which became tedious after a while. Tobias took direction well, and I never had to ask or explain things twice. He had been my Guan for many years, since he was just fourteen years old.

"Bring me some nuts and fruit, then fetch me a bowl of water and some clean cloth and towels," I instructed. He gently closed his eyes whilst bowing his head, and then retreated from my tent.

With a deep sigh, I stood and walked over towards the table which held my maps. I began to analyse my markings of the valleys and desert domes we had already scouted; we were tracking a band of rebels that had been spotted from the city wall. The queen had sent me to lead a few dozen of our strongest warriors to track them down and eradicate them. I was in charge. My soldiers referred to me by my title, their 'General'.

Queen Cassandra favoured me, we shared a mutual trust and respect. She had been my mother's best friend. They had fought together in battle at the start of the rebellion many years ago, when the beginning of the uprising happened, and rebel numbers were much larger and more of a threat to the city.

Queen Cassandra was princess back then and she was a fierce warrior like my mother, until my mother was killed during a siege.

I was already an adult at this point, and although saddened by my mother's death, I knew it was an honour for her to die in battle. Turning away from my table, I looked to see a plate of food placed on a chair just inside the entrance of the tent. Tobias must have left it there and then retreated to fetch my hot water.

I grabbed the plate with one hand, and with the other I parted the cotton canvas to look out from my tent. I could see the light of morning coming through, my eyes squinting for a moment as they adjusted to the glow emanating from the sun that had not yet fully set in the sky.

By the time I had finished my plate, Tobias walked back through the tent and placed a bowl of water on the rug in the centre of my pitch, and then placed the clean cloth and towels on a stool next to the rug.

"Tend to my horse and saddle him up, I want to be ready to ride out early this morning," I told him. Tobias gave me a courteous nod and left.

Walking over to the ceramic wash bowl, I touched the surface with my index finger. Vapours of lavender oil wafted over my face; it was my favourite scent. The temperature was perfect; not hot enough to burn, but warm enough to turn the skin on my finger a pink hue. I removed my soft cotton pants and cropped top I had slept in and stood naked in the centre of the tent. Bending down, I submerged a clean cloth in the fragrant water and ran it along my body.

Once I was clean, I picked up a towel and padded myself dry. After placing some soothing oils laced with peach nectar on my skin, I walked over to my armour stand and started dressing myself.

First, I wrapped myself in clean cotton under garments, then donned my azure blue, thick leather painted chest piece, which had a floral pattern set into the body of its hard leather. I pulled on my black leather pants and placed my cotton wrapped feet inside my black knee-high boots.

To complete my warrior's outfit, I put on my light metal armour plates covering my chest, shoulders and forearms, pulling at the front lace to secure them tight. Using a strand of stretched leather, I tied my thick, long brown hair back into a high ponytail, scraping the strands past my pointed ears, ensuring it was tight enough to stop it from falling down my face.

I walked over to my weapons and picked up a thick black belt that held two daggers, one either side, fastening the buckle around my waist. I picked up my sword in its sheath which was attached to a belt that I wrapped around my shoulder with the buckle in the centre of my chest, allowing my large sword to sit comfortably against my upper back.

Reaching my hand over my shoulder, I wrapped my fingers

around the swords handle and pulled it from its casing. Opening the lid to my pot of woad dye, I used my sword to reflect the image of my face. I dipped two fingers into the blue paste and smeared rough lines diagonally over from my forehead, across the lid of my left eye, stopping just at the ridge of my cheekbone.

I looked at my reflection, the blue markings conflicting with the colour of my bright green eyes. Like my hair, if I held my sword close enough, I could make out small flecks of gold that sparkled in my eyes. I could see my lids, full of thick lashes that held a natural upward curve. My plump rosy lips, the softest part of my facial features, completed by my prominent cheekbones, connected to the line that shaped my square jaw. Taking one final look, satisfied that I was ready, I walked out of my dimly candle lit tent, into the natural light of dawn.

Outside mingled a few other warriors already awake, beginning to emerge from their partnered tents. I closed my eyes for a second, taking a long slow inhale, smelling the morning fresh air. Despite having my rest cut short thanks to my strange dream, I felt strong and energized, ready to take on the challenges of the day.

I had been that way for most of my life. As a child, I was very competitive, always wanting to be the best in everything.

It was not long before I had surpassed everyone else's skill with any weapon held in my hands. My current focus was to find the rebel base and destroy it. I wanted legendary stories to be told of the great warrior that finally brought an end to all the fighting and restored peace to the Kingdom of Nysa. My thought process was interrupted when Imelda, my captain, walked towards me.

"Good morning General," she said, slamming a closed fist against her heart, showing respect for my rank. It was something we all did to those who were a higher rank than ourselves. I only had to use this gesture for one person; Queen Cassandra.

"And what a good morning it will be Captain," I replied with positive assertiveness.

"Shall I round up the camp to get ready to move?" she excitedly asked.

She was already dressed in full armour, her sword sheathed to her side. She was always up early and ready for my instruction, something I never showed appreciation for. Instead, I expected it of her. Imelda was almost as tall as me, though much leaner. Our bodies were incomparable as she was much younger than I, and had not yet put her body through the vigorous training that would give her the defined muscle and body strength I had. She had a thin face with blue eyes and long brown hair. Despite the beauty of our race, Imelda was plainer than most.

"Yes, fetch the twins and some of the others, we shall take a small group and head out earlier today." With that, she signalled the salute of respect and walked away. I liked including the twins in our excursions. Although young and inexperienced, Shanor and Shanon were at the battle hungry age of eighteen, both recently becoming my shadow, eager to learn. Especially Shanor, who told me she aspired to be a great leader, upholding peace to the kingdom; I held great affection for them both. I looked towards the rising sun and felt slight warmth on my face. It had not yet reached over the hills, and darkness still cast shadows over the camp.

Approaching to my left was Tobias, leading my saddled horse Thio, a large black stallion. Tobias patted the side of his neck and whispered something in his ear as he walked closer towards me along the mud track. I wondered what he was saying. Thio seemed agitated and Tobias was clearly trying to sooth and calm him.

Just then, in the corner of my eye I saw a blurred image run past between the tents to my right, and as I grabbed my sword handle, pulling it from its sheath and raising it in front of me, shouts of 'ambush' rang throughout the camp.

"We are under attack, stay back," I commanded Tobias, who's eyes were darting around frantically in fear.

Ahead of us, I could see figures dressed in old battered armour appearing from the shadows between the tents as they swiftly began to approach and attack my warriors.

Shanor was being confronted by a rebel elf holding a short sword and broken shield. As they swung their sword towards her, I watched as she luckily took a quick step back just in time, allowing the blade to only slice a shallow cut through the side of her arm.

I started to charge towards Shanor to come to her aid, but I was startled when I heard a scream of rage close behind me. As I turned, I saw a ragged elf in shredded clothes run towards me with a dagger in her dirty hands.

I raised my sword, ready to step forward and strike my blow, when another figure stood directly in front of me, blocking my body from the attacker like a shield made of flesh.

It was Tobias. I could only watch as the elf's blade pierced straight through his chest. Immediately, with a frustrated growl, she pulled her dagger from Tobias's body. As he started to fall to the ground, she came at me again, blood dripping from her knife, with determination to strike; obviously I was her intended target.

Without hesitation, I stuck my sword through her chest. A scream of rage escaped my lips as I yanked out my blade, wet with her blood, and rammed it through her neck. With one booted foot, I pushed her lifeless corpse off my blade and watched it crumple onto the mud.

Behind me, my warriors had finished off the other attackers with ease. They searched around the tents for anyone hidden and began checking the fallen bodies, to make sure none were left alive.

On the ground by my feet, facing away from me was Tobias,

looking towards his now dead attacker lying on her back in the mud.

"Stupid boy, why did you do that?" I muttered. Crouching to one knee, I gently rolled Tobias onto his back. Blood soaked through his clothes as his hand feebly pressed on the gaping wound in his chest. I knew there was nothing that could be done, there was too much blood and no way he would survive. I looked up to his face and he was looking directly at me, his breathing sharp and erratic. He looked into my eyes, his lips moving as if to speak, his bottom lip beginning to quiver.

"I... I'm... I... Truda," he began to say, struggling to get the words out as he fought for breath.

"It is okay Tobias," I said, whilst gently placing my hand over his. He gripped my hand, holding it tightly to him as he again tried to form words, my name being the last coherent sound to come from his lips.

"You may rest now," I told him, and he closed his eyes. I kept my hand rested on his until his grip loosened, and he let go. I watched as his arm slumped back and dropped to the floor. Looking at Tobias's lifeless body, an unexpected anger bubbled up inside me. I stood and swiftly turned to grab my horse's reins. Pulling myself up onto his back I cantered closer to my warriors and shouted my instructions.

"Captain Imelda, you and half a dozen others mount your horses now and follow me immediately, we will scout the area for any retreating rebels."

"Yes General," she replied, looking towards the twins and pointing to a few others who quickly dashed off towards their steeds.

~*~

We searched in all directions, at least half a mile around the camp, but found no others. Trying to steady my fury, I thought over what just happened. They must have tracked our camp knowing we were in the nearby lands hunting for them.

They were clever to attack at dawn, when they would be able to still linger in the shadows of the night not yet passed. They knew that we would still be preparing for the day and would less likely be ready for an attack. We trotted back and I saw a great fire blazing a few metres away from the camp.

"Report," I asked one of the warriors as we passed the first tent.

"There were no survivors, we searched their bodies before we burnt them but didn't find anything informative," she told me.

"Good, pack up the camp, we are leaving to return to the city." I nodded at Imelda, telling her to oversee the preparations and disassemble the camp.

I dismounted my horse and walked it towards my tent. The bodies had indeed been removed, and all that was left behind were a few bloodied patches where our enemies had fallen. I looked next to my tent where Tobias had laid. I looked towards the blood-stained ground which still looked damp; his body would no doubt be burning in the large smoke-filled pyre along with the rest of the deceased.

There would be no burial or funeral for the death of a Guan, even one who had sacrificed himself for his master. Removing my eyes from the red dirt, I tied up my horse to a post outside my tent and entered. For a moment, I just stood there, listening to the sound of my own breathing.

I looked down at the dried blood that covered my hands; it was Tobias's blood. In all the years he had been my slave, I had never touched him, I had never yelled at him or punished him, but I had also never been kind. I had never said thank you or given him a gift of gratitude. It was not our way. Men were beneath us, they were our slaves, born into our race of female elf warriors as servants.

The histories told us that a long time ago we had been human once, in a world of constant war because of men, with their natural inclination and tendencies towards violence, until a group of women discovered they could use magic. They rose together and killed all but a few of the men. As the knowledge and power of magic grew, so did we; evolving into something stronger, faster, smarter and more gifted, with longer life.

Men however, stayed the same, never evolving and remaining insentient and imbecilic, the lowest of beings. We used them now for construction, agriculture and breeding. To the higher ranks like myself, we would be granted a Guan to assist with all the everyday things that we were too busy or important to do. Tobias was my Guan. He had been a farmer as a young boy and then was given to me, and now he was dead.

I rushed over to the pot of water that was still in the centre of my tent and dropped to my knees in front of it. Using a cloth, I scrubbed the blood from my hands until all traces had gone. I stood slowly and reached for a dry towel to remove the moisture.

Why had Tobias sacrificed himself? Had he wanted to protect me? I could have easily fought off the elf, there was no need for him to die, he still had many years left. Why did I feel this way? Was I sad that he was gone? Just then, Imelda walked into my tent, distracting me from my conflicting thoughts.

"General, I have spoken with the others who dealt with the bodies, they counted six rebels. We had no casualties, except for a graze on Shanor's arm," she told me.

"Good," I replied. With my hands now dry, I threw the cloth on the floor. "Ensure the camp is ready to leave, send word to the city of what has happened here and that we are returning."

"I will have our Raven Keeper send a message," said Imelda, and before leaving she placed her closed fist over her chest.

I looked around my tent, now standing alone, looking around at my clothes, armour and weapons, thinking about how I would have to pack up all these things myself. Yes, that was it; I did miss Tobias, but only because of the inconvenience of it all, having to make do without a Guan's service until he could be replaced.

Chapter 2

START THE COUNTDOWN

After riding for most of the day, we were finally leaving the desert and reaching the grassland. In the distance I could now see our home, the beautiful sandstone city of Kven. It was still light but soon would become dusk; it looked like we would make it home just in time for supper. I looked ahead while guiding my horse into a quick trot towards the city, with my warriors following behind me, also on horseback, some pulling carts full of our camping supplies.

The white palace looked truly magnificent with its great needle like towers, the tallest out of sight hidden in the clouds. The enormous decadent structure sat animate in the centre of the city. There were other large buildings, such as the Battle Coliseum, Mages Temple, Training House and some larger households belonging to wealthier elves.

From here, all the larger buildings looked like they were connected to the palace, making its size appear more impressive; perhaps that was the intent with the layout design. Most people that lived inside the city had substantial sized homes. The queen, princess and royal guard all lived in the grand palace. My home was a few minutes' walk from the palace entrance, and although not as grand in size as some of the others, it had everything that suited my needs.

Thoughts of Tobias not returning with me clouded my mind. His presence in the house had never offered me any real comfort, as being alone never bothered me, but returning to an empty and unusually quiet home unnerved me.

Looking on towards the city of Kven, I could see its large wooden gate laced with silver; this was the main entrance in and out of the city. As we got closer, I saw the gates open and a single rider galloped on their horse towards us, stopping directly in front of me.

"General. Welcome home, for we are pleased of your safe return," she said while signalling the salute of respect.

"Thank you," I said, wondering why this young warrior had saddled her horse and passed the cities stone walls just to welcome me home. Of course, I did not have to wait long before this was explained.

"Queen Cassandra has sent me to fetch for you my General, she has asked that you urgently present yourself upon your return in the great throne room."

I nodded that I understood, and she steered her horse to gallop back towards the main gates. I was looking forward to a hot bath and some proper rest; however, it was a small price to pay for being the general and duty to my queen always comes first.

~*~

I walked down the corridor heading towards the throne room and as I turned the corner, I saw Acqueline walking towards me.

"Tru, you're back!" she exclaimed, dashing towards me with a beaming smile.

"Acqueline, it is good to see you," I said, and I meant it. She was my lifelong friend and sparring partner, and despite her being a few years younger than me, we had always been close. Since childhood, we had been in constant competition with each other when it came to fighting skills and the use of weaponry.

Acqueline's favourite weapon of choice was a bow and arrow, whereas I preferred the up close and personal range of a sword. We used to fight against our enemy side by side, until Acqueline got promoted to head of the royal guard, close protectors of the royal family. Now she spent most of her days walking around the palace and escorting the queen when she chose to travel around the city. It was a great honour, and I was happy for her. Where I would describe Imelda as plain, Acqueline was far from that. She had long chestnut coloured hair, lighter than mine, half tied up, half left loose with its natural waves covering her shoulders. She had a soft oval face, with a pointed jaw that matched the symmetry of her petite pointed nose. Her lips were a natural rose in colour, her bottom lip larger than her top. She had small hazel brown eyes, and small lids covered in full lashes. She was shorter than I and had retained much of her childlike figure.

"I heard you got into a bit of trouble, let some rebels catch you off guard?" said Acqueline with a playful smirk.

"Hardly a surprise attack, just half a dozen lucky few that managed to get past my scouts; they were dealt with quickly," I replied curtly. I knew Acqueline did not mean to insult, but the morning attack was still fresh in my thoughts. I was not in the right frame of mind to talk about it as though it was a game or a laughing matter. Acqueline must have detected my mood as she quickly added, "were there any casualties?"

"Shanor got a nasty scrape on her arm. It looked deep enough to get a scar, so that will please her," I replied.

"Oh yes, the young ones do like their battle scars," replied Acqueline with a snigger. I did not tell her that I had lost Tobias. The loss of a Guan did not mean much to us in the higher ranks, and she would not understand my feelings on the matter. I would be granted a new one, but it would not be the same. Tobias and I had built up an understanding, he knew how things needed to be, and I was content with him in my service.

"The queen has requested your presence, she seems agitated. I think she was worried for you after hearing about the ambush."

"Well, the throne room is where I am headed now, so I will be able to put her mind at ease," I responded. She nodded, placed her closed fist over her chest and started to continue walking forward. Just as she was about to walk past me, I turned towards her.

"We should have a sparring session soon. I am keen to see if your new duties have made you careless and slack." This lifted her spirits as she almost jumped in excitement at the challenge.

"Ha, you wish. I look forward to proving you wrong," she finished with a bigger grin, making me chuckle at her eagerness. After Acqueline showed the signal of respect, I turned to continue my walk down the long corridor towards the throne room.

My spirits had lifted from seeing my friend after a weary day's travel. Her light and pleasant character always managed to put a smile on my face. Unfortunately, my amused mood was not to last, as a figure appeared from the shadow of an unlit doorway.

"And so, the queen's favourite warrior has returned." Her voice croaked as if someone had left scratches at the base of her throat.

"Freyja," I said with a frustrated sigh, knowing the sound of that voice only too well. She was an elder from the Mages Temple, a group of magically talented elves, who at a young age were discovered as having the power to manipulate nature. They were excluded from fighting and instead were encouraged to practise their magic skill through chants, and imbuing liquids or other items with special abilities. Most of them were quiet and kept themselves locked away in the temple, focusing on their skill.

Freyja, however, was a member of the council. She spoke on behalf of the Mages Temple and reported their progress to the queen and her advisors. I had never trusted her. I could not tell exactly what it was; she had never done anything that would warrant my mistrust, but it was there. I felt it in my gut, there was something about her that was dangerous. Freyja reciprocated my dislike, usually having something foul to say, or even when she said anything nice, it was always over exaggerated so that I knew she did not really mean it. She moved closer towards me from the shadows and spoke in a dry and sarcastic tone.

"I am so pleased you have returned safely. When I heard about the ambush, I was worried that something awful may have happened." There was no doubt in my mind that she would get pleasure if I were injured or did not return. If an elf's appearance could match a personality, then Freyja should have been so unsightly that her image would haunt the nightmares of children. In reality, she was actually very beautiful. With much paler skin than most, probably attained by the fact that she spent most of her time hidden from the sun, the contrast between her skin and mid-length black hair was striking. She also had perfectly small symmetrical facial features and a perfectly shaped body. She was wearing a black leather fur lined tunic, with a hood covering most of her face. The material fell just below her knees and underneath I could see her black leather pants and boots.

On her shoulder was her pet raven. It was an ugly looking deformed creature, large in size for a bird of its type, with great sharp talons and a razor tapered beak that curved slightly at the end. It glared at me with its garnet eyes that matched Freyja's red face paint that she used to decorate her eyelids and lips. She called the creature Jetta.

Choosing not to reply, I stepped to walk around her.

"I am very much looking forward to our next council meeting," Freyja muttered. Our eyes momentarily met as I reached her side. She grinned at me, enjoying my silence, then she saluted half-heartedly as I walked past. I did not have time for Freyja's nonsense; right now, I had more important places to be. As I continued, I imagined two sets of eyes burning into my back.

~*~

I reached the large arched double doors that were the entrance to the throne room. On either side of the doorway was a guard. As I approached the doors, they both nodded their heads in unison to let me know I was free to enter, gesturing the salute as I passed.

Inside the great stone hall, the walls were covered in large hand threaded tapestries of various colour and size, some laced with silver cotton, so they shimmered in the sunlight. The large windows encased in metal frames that held the stained enamelled glass of painted flowers and vine, allowed the sun to illuminate every corner of the grand hall.

At the end of the monumental sized room was the throne of dignitary itself, an enormous wooden chair painted entirely in silver. Chiselled into the arm rests were patterns of trailing vines and blossoms with a single red cushion placed on the flat centre. Next to the Throne was another impressive silver painted chair, with a single pink cushion at its flat centre.

Behind the two prestigious chairs on the floor lay smooth stone slabs that worked as steps leading to a small door, which I knew was the royal entrance for the queen and princess, leading to their own private chambers. This door was guarded by an elf warrior of the royal guard.

As I walked towards the throne, the small door opened, and my queen entered. As soon as I saw her, I knelt on one knee and placed my clenched fist up to my chest, just above my heart.

Queen Cassandra was tall and beautiful, her hair was champagne blonde and cascaded down past her waist. Flowing freely except for a few small plaits that were randomly weaved in through her hair and tied at the ends by silver silk strands.

Upon her head she wore a gold tiara that was embellished with sapphire gemstones. On her body she wore a floor length ivory silk dress, with thick straps over her shoulders. On her feet were golden flat sandals that made no sound as she gracefully walked from the royal chamber door to the throne in the centre, which was where she sat when being approached by her subjects.

The smaller chair that mimicked the throne in design, was for her daughter, Princess Callidice, who was very rarely present for council meetings. Today was no exception as Queen Cassandra entered the hall and took her place in her seat, without her daughter by her side.

"You may rise my dear Truda, let me look upon you," she said in a gentle tone. As I rose, she smiled at me with endearment.

"My Queen, I bring good news. We found some rebels, or rather they found us, but they were vanquished quickly and easily." I reported proudly, with my head held high; I wanted her approval and respect. I always wanted her to see me as a strong warrior that would defend her kingdom and her life with my own.

"Truda, it brings me great joy to hear of your victory. It

brings me even greater joy that you are here before me, telling me the news yourself."

She tilted her head towards me, making me smile. She had always been so kind to me, even more so after we lost my mother. I had lost my parent, but she had lost her best friend, and because of that we had formed a bond, finding comfort in each other.

Queen Cassandra asked me more questions about what had happened in the days of my absence, asking if I had discovered any information of the rumours behind a rebel base, hidden beyond the deserts. I told her my soldiers had searched the bodies of the rebels we came across but found nothing. Thinking of the bodies brought me back to thoughts of the pyre where Tobias had burned.

My face must have frowned as Queen Cassandra looked at me with concern.

"Was anyone badly injured?"

"No, my Queen." My eyes looked to the floor, and when I looked back at her she was watching me as though waiting for me to finish my sentence.

"One of the twins, Shanor, was badly cut on her arm and…" I paused for a moment. "And I lost my house Guan. He was stabbed in the chest by one of the assailants."

I looked directly at the queen when I spoke, hoping that she did not see my hesitation, as conflict of my emotions regarding Tobias's death began to resurface. I was relieved when Queen Cassandra smiled at me sweetly and nodded her head as though she understood.

"I will send for a healer to visit Shanor, ensuring she gets all the care she may need, and I will have a new Guan delivered to your home."

She did not seem phased by me talking about Tobias. I assumed she thought my hesitance and concern was for Shanor as she knew I was close with the twins, recognising their great potential as warriors.

"If you please my Queen, if I am not needed for anything else, I am weary from travel and would like to retire for the evening." I also longed for that hot bath, and a night's sleep in the comfort and luxury of my own bed covered in soft furs.

"Of course Truda, I understand you must be exhausted. I have called for a council meeting first thing tomorrow. I would like you to report your recent events to the council and…" she paused before she continued her next words, "we have some other important matters to discuss."

"Of course, my Queen. I will see you then." I saluted towards her and headed home.

~*~

At first light the next day, I headed back towards the palace for the council meeting. Once inside the throne room, I saw it was the same as before except for one difference; the usual large rectangle table now sat in front of the queen's throne and around it were four other chairs.

One meant for me, as general, and the second for Acqueline, my closest friend and head of the royal guard. The third chair belonged to Peril, she was considered master of Guans and the Breeding House. Finally, in the last seat was Freyja, ambassador of the Mages Temple.

As I walked forward towards the table, I could see Acqueline and Peril were already there, just about to take their seats. Hearing me enter, they both looked towards me and smiled.

As I got to my seat, they sat in theirs, and we struck up conversation while waiting for the others. We did not have long before Freyja entered, who quickly made a grimacing face to me before taking her seat. Then the queen appeared from her private entrance and walked towards our table. We all stopped in our conversation and respectfully looked towards her, watching as she took her seat.

"I would like to make today brief if we can," said Queen Cassandra.

"We have two things on the agenda this morning," she said, scanning across the table to all of us. I nodded in respect when her eyes reached mine. I could see her serious gaze soften for a moment, although she did not smile.

"General Truda, please can you report to the council on yesterday's events." She gestured her hand for me to speak. I stood from my chair and looked around the table as I reported on my scouting efforts and the ambush.

"Did you find out anything about the rumoured secret rebel base?" Peril asked.

"I am afraid not, but I believe I am getting closer," I replied. That was not exactly true, but I had certainly searched out enough lands in the kingdom to rule out many places, meaning I must be closer to finding it, if it even existed.

With that, I nodded my head to the council members and sat back in my seat. As Queen Cassandra prepared herself to speak again, I glanced towards Freyja who, to my surprise, was glaring at me with a huge grin. Why was she staring at me like that? Had I said something amusing?

"In light of this news, I think we can agree that the rebels are not currently that much of a concern, or threat to the city. Despite not knowing the location of this rumoured base, their numbers are low, attacks are infrequent, and after taking advice from other members of the council, I think now is as good a time as we shall have."

She then looked directly at me. What was she talking about? I glanced over to Acqueline, who was looking at the queen puzzlingly; she obviously did not know what was going on either.

"General Truda. We have decided now is a good time to place you into the breeding programme." My mouth dropped open. I blinked and gasped in shock.

Chapter 3

WEEK ONE

"You are entering me into the breeding programme!" I exclaimed.

"General Truda, I understand your feelings on the matter, but I have discussed it at length with other members of the council. It is a requirement of all our strongest to pass along their knowledge and skill to the next generation. This is how we remain an unassailable race," Queen Cassandra said, talking to me more sternly than she would have if we were having this conversation in private, for the councils' benefit I had no doubt.

"My Queen, I understand our traditions, but I have to argue against this decision, especially the timing of it. I am so close to wiping out the rebels for good, and finding the rebel base, do not put me on the side-lines now. If you put me in the breeding programme, you put me out of service for the next year," I argued, slamming my fist into the table. This was unbelievable, after I had worked so hard, especially in the last few months. That is when I noticed Freyja's mocking face, grinning at me. In that moment, I knew she had something to do with this.

"We will still allow you to assist in training until you are with child. You may also advise us during council meetings. Aside from that, all other duties will be passed over to your captain. You are here by suspended and forbidden to leave the city," said the queen, showing no sign of regret or compassion for the anger she knew I now felt. I held my gaze at the queen for a moment longer, with an expression on my face that most likely conveyed the anguish I felt.

The room had fallen silent with everyone clearly on edge with what I would do next. Queen Cassandra looked away silently. Realising I was not going to get any further explanation, I abruptly stood from my chair and gave an over-exaggerated salute before storming out of the throne room, not bothering to wait for everyone to salute me.

~*~

Slamming the door to my bed-chamber, I paced around the room. I was not angry, I was furious. Letting out a scream, I kicked over the table, spilling its contents. Books, parchment paper and ink went flying, scattering over the floor. I did not care, I needed an outlet, something to curb my rage. I felt betrayed.

How could the queen do this to me? I was a general, a warrior, and I had no interest in an elf's ability to create life. I had tried to argue against her decision; it had been a short and frustrating attempt. Clearly there was nothing more I could have said, nothing that would have made a difference. This is how it had been for hundreds of years. This is how we had kept the strong genes of our humanoid race in existence; by breeding the strongest of us. That, and a little magic.

I would just have to think of a way to get out of it without having to blatantly go against the queen's orders. It was not just that the queen wanted me to bear a child that infuriated me, but that she was also excluding me from my duties.

I was a warrior, born and trained for battle!

Breeding was beneath me.

Now I was to be trapped within the confines of this city, unable to search for the rebels or their secret base.

I threw off my day clothes and armour, opting to wear something a little more casual for the evening. I needed to put plans in place. However, to do that, I required a better understanding of what I was about to come up against, there were questions that needed answers. I knew the programme lasted a maximum of twelve weeks. If I was then to get pregnant, that would last for nine months, potentially adding up to a whole year excluded from service.

Well, there was no chance I was going to get pregnant, so I just had to figure out how I was going to get out of this situation. I decided I needed to pay the Breeding House a visit. I had walked past the flat, one story building many times, but never stepped through those doors. I needed a better understanding of its layout and guard rotation, as well as learning what was expected.

I chose some faded cherry red leather pants, and a tan hide cropped top with one strap that ran across my breasts and over my right shoulder. I left my hair up in its high ponytail, tucking a few loose brown strands behind my arrow-like ears. Lastly putting on my ankle leather boots and walking towards my bed-chamber door, I needed whoever was on guard in the Breeding House to consider my visit tonight as a social call. I would need to leave my sword behind. I turned back towards my small weapon rack on the other side of my armour stand, instead picking up a bronze dagger in a belted leather case and buckled its strap around the top of my thigh.

Feeling better and less naked with my weapon, I walked out of my bed-chamber and headed towards my front door.

~*~

I looked up towards the large plain rectangle building in front of me, it was characterless in comparison to all the other buildings within the city. Although still colossal in size, it had no windows, just small gaps of missing brick on the front of the structure to let the breeze in and out.

I walked up the steps that were at the left end of the building and opened the metal framed wooden door, immediately seeing a woman I recognised, council member Peril. She was in her red guard uniform, standing behind a wooden pedestal. On the stool was a book and quill. She looked up as I walked towards her and smiled, recognising me immediately. Although I saw her regularly on the council, I had never noticed her beyond that. I was aware that most of her time was spent here, making breeding arrangements and organising Guan placements throughout the city.

"General, let me be one of the first to congratulate you, for I have just received the good news." I looked at her puzzled for a second. She was present during that council meeting, she was there when the queen gave her orders, there was nothing good about it, not in my opinion, anyway. What good news could she possibly have to share with me now?

"I just received word you are to have a daughter." Her smile then dropped as she said, "although, I don't have you scheduled in for tonight."

"I am just here to familiarise myself with protocol. Unless you're too busy? I can come back another time," I suggested, trying to sound less commanding but instead, friendly and innocent, failing miserably.

"Not at all, it's actually a slow night tonight. Let me show you around and explain a few things," she replied, excited of my presence in her domain.

Peril was the oldest member on the council. Although I had been informed she used to be a warrior, I had never seen her in action as she was considered too old to get involved in battle anymore. Small lines appeared on the sides of her eyes and mouth, and she had silver mid-length hair that was twisted back in a bun. The pigment in her hair and her wrinkles were the only real signs of her age, as aside from that, she looked to be in perfectly good health. Scooting out from behind her pedestal, she stepped closer to me and began a motioning action with her hands.

"When you arrive, you will be greeted at the door. Your name will be ticked off in the book, and the attendant will check against your name to see whether you had been registered to have a daughter or a Guan, then the relevant potion will be given to you."

I nodded at Peril that I understood about the potion; it was one of the things the mages had developed. In the early years, a baby's gender was still randomised by the luck of genetics and to keep the male population down, most male babies were killed upon birth.

Eventually, the mages had found a way of manipulating the cells in an elf's body for a short period of time. If a potion was consumed before the breeding took place, then the gender of a baby conceived could be controlled. However, the effects wore off after a day or so, meaning a woman would have to take a potion every time she came for a session to ensure the gender of an offspring could be controlled. Conception never happened beyond these walls, so there were never any unwarranted pregnancies without the control of the Breeding House master and the potions.

"Then, along with the potion, you are given the key to your designated room. Would you like to see one of the empty rooms?" Peril asked me.

"If it is no trouble," I replied.

However, before she had the chance, another elf entered the building.

"Excuse me," Peril said as she walked around me to greet the elf. I took a step back and took the opportunity to watch the process that Peril had just explained. She led the woman over to the pedestal and must have said something funny, as the newcomer giggled.

She asked for the elf woman's name and placed a mark on the parchment of her book. Then, reaching behind her on a shelf, she passed her a small glass bottle that was filled with blue liquid. Opening a small wooden cabinet underneath the pedestal, she reached for a key. Embossed in the metal was a number that had been painted in black; number twelve. The elf woman took the key and looked at it.

"Don't worry if you lose it, we have a master key for each room. If you need anything, don't hesitate to call for me,"

Peril said to the young elf with a smile.

"Thank you," she replied. She placed a closed fist over her chest and nodded towards Peril. Then, turning slightly to face me, she did the same before walking down the long corridor towards her door number.

"Such a shame," Peril said with a sigh, dropping her smile.

"What do you mean?" I asked.

"Oh, it's just I always feel sorry for the ones that have to bare a Guan child. Most who come here to be part of the breeding programme, do so voluntarily. Others are selected because of their skill or lineage. Those who choose to be here want the experience of being a mother. However, for those who are selected to conceive a Guan, they will carry it for nine months and then it will be taken. It must be somewhat degrading." Peril scrunched her nose as though she had smelt something horrible.

"Of course, if they really wanted to be a mother, she would just be granted access back into the breeding programme to conceive a daughter," she continued with a smile. Not that this information was any use to me. If an elf volunteered to be in the breeding programme then clearly, they did not have a role within the city of great importance and had nothing better to fill their time with. After a few moments of awkward silence, I thought of something I was interested in knowing.

"How many rooms do you have here?" I asked, looking down towards the long corridor with heavy wooden doors every few metres.

"We have thirty rooms. Only seventeen are currently occupied with breeders," replied Peril. Then she looked back at her book, and using her finger, moved it down the page as though looking through the names. After wetting the tip with her tongue to turn the paper, she continued looking through until she stopped by one name.

"Ah, here you are. You have been paired with the Guan in room number twenty-three. Would you like to inspect it? I could then show you the room as well?" she finished, looking up towards me.

I paused for a moment and looked back down towards the corridor. I scanned the door numbers written in the centre of the wood but could not make out anymore after door number six. Beyond that, the corridor looked dark with only flickering light coming from the odd wall torch. Somewhere down that long corridor was room number twenty-three, and in it was a breeder slave, a Guan that I had been selected to pair with.

"No, that will not be necessary. Just tell me when my first session is scheduled," I said, feeling a bit uneasy and out of my comfort zone. I was anxious to leave this place and get back to the fresh air.

"One moment, let me just go and have a look," said Peril, once again immersing her face into the pages and using her finger to direct her to the correct information.

"You are scheduled for sessions four times a week, every

other day, starting tomorrow night." She looked up at me, and gasped.

"General, are you alright? You look ghostly."

I felt nauseous. Four times a week, for the next twelve weeks! I had to be careful as I did not want the astonishment of my thoughts to show on my face. This was not going to be as easy as I first thought. The frequency of my visits for the duration of the programme gave a lot of opportunity for me to get caught. I was going to have to be careful.

More importantly, there was one other factor that I had not thought of until now. Looking down towards the black stone corridor of flickering lights full of doors, I could not help but wonder how I was going to keep the Guan from talking about what would not happen in that room.

"I am fine, just a bit shocked at the frequency of my sessions."

"Well of course, that's only until you conceive, which could easily happen in the first few weeks. Then you won't need to continue the visits," Peril said with a smile.

"You have been very helpful. I thank you for your time," I said, eager to get out of that place as soon as possible.

"Oh, and one other thing General."

"Yes?" I replied, turning to face her.

"We don't allow weapons in here, only the guards are allowed to carry them," she said, pointing towards the dagger strapped to the top of my thigh. I looked down at my dagger then back at her with a puzzling look.

"We had an incident once, where a slave managed to get hold of a knife and took it to his own throat," Peril explained dismissively. Then she saluted before tilting her head back down towards the book.

~*~

The next day I found it hard to focus. After a restless night's sleep and no duties to distract me, I spent most of my day wondering around my house. In less than an hour I would be back at the Breeding House to fulfil the only duty I had been given for the moment. My only option for now was to act normal and as willing as possible around the elves.

Once alone with the Guan, I would use my position of power to intimidate him, threatening his life if he spoke a word to anyone about our 'sessions'.

Looking out my bedroom window I sighed, wishing I could delay, but knowing I might as well just go and get this over and done with. Once again wearing my casual clothing, with my hair tied up in a high bun, I went to leave the house. This time I did not bother to fetch a weapon, knowing it was not allowed in the Breeding House and I was quite safe within the city walls.

Walking around in civilian clothing always made me feel uncomfortable. I wanted to be wearing my armour and have a large sword at my back, that to me was what felt normal. I walked through the Breeding House entrance and was greeted politely once again by Peril.

"Good evening General Truda. Come, let me sign you in." As I walked over to her, she marked against my name and reached behind her, passing me a small glass vial filled with red liquid. She also gave me a key with the numbers twenty-three painted within the indented metal.

"Let me know if you need anything," she said, and gave me a quick salute before looking back down towards her pages.

Turning to peer down the corridor, I started slowly walking forward, reading the door numbers as I went. When I reached door number seven, I heard what sounded like voices, and paused for a moment. I instantly regretted that I had, as I heard moans of pleasure coming from within the room. I hastily continued on until I reached my destination.

Room number twenty-three.

Lifting the key in my hands and placing it into the lock, holding my breath for a second, I closed my eyes as if reaching for a moment of strength, composing myself for what was to come. I opened my eyes and pursed my lips as though to look angry. Briefly, I looked back down the corridor to ensure I was alone, and then unlocked the door.

Twisting the handle, I walked inside the room, immediately locking the door behind me. I slowly stepped back from the door and looked around at my surroundings. The room was fairly small and had little in the way of furnishings.

I first noticed a small circular table, holding a single candle already lit, its flame giving off a faint orange glow that only partially lit up the room. Aside from the table was a large bed, with a few scattered cushions and a blanket. The room smelt musky and damp, reminding me of a prison. Aside from the luxury of a table and a bed, this room could certainly pass for a cell in the Coliseum.

I walked over to the small air gap in the brickwork and pulled the cork stopper from the small glass bottle. After peering through the gap to check no-one was there, I emptied its red liquid contents out on the back-alley street. Turning towards the table, I placed the empty bottle next to the lit candle.

I froze when I heard a noise behind me.

It was the sound of rattling chains. I spun around quickly and instinctively reached for my sword, only to remember I had not brought it. Scanning the room, in the opposite corner I saw a large figure emerge from the shadows.

Without making eye contact, the Guan slowly took a few steps towards me. As he slowly appeared further into the light, I could see him better.

He was tall, over six foot, was pure muscle with broad shoulders and thick arms. He was bare chested and wore nothing on his feet; the only item of clothing was a slightly torn cotton loin cloth.

He had short chains connected to the metal cuffs on his

hands and feet. Keeping his head down, his black, messy, shoulder length hair covering most of his face, he shuffled forward slowly as the chains prevented his large feet from taking a full step.

"Stop," I said with authority as he got closer to me.

"Take a few steps back and stand quietly, do not look at or speak to me. We will stand this way until a considerable amount of time has passed, then I shall leave, and you will speak nothing of what happened tonight. Nod if you understand."

The Guan nodded once, keeping his head to the ground.

"Good," I replied, facing away from him and looking towards the door. After I felt a significant amount of time had passed, I walked towards the door and left, locking it behind me. Walking quickly back down towards the corridor, I saw Peril look up towards me.

"That was quick!" she exclaimed whilst reaching towards my outstretched hands that held the room key and empty glass bottle. Not knowing what to say, I had not actually thought about how long these sessions were to last. Should I have asked?

"Sometimes that happens on the first experience," she followed. I felt relieved but would clearly have to spend more time in here in the future to make things seem more natural. How long would that be I wondered, an hour? Three hours?

"I will be back the day after tomorrow as scheduled," I

immediately replied and looked back to her as she signalled the salute. I left the building.

Chapter 4

WEEK TWO

After that first session, I had been concerned that my inaction would immediately be discovered. I worried that they would search the room for evidence, or interrogate the Guan, but my first week passed and nothing had happened. The breeding Guan had followed my instruction and had kept that same position standing still with his head to the ground. I did not have a long-term solution, but for now my tactic seemed to be working.

The next morning, I was up early. I had scheduled a meeting at my home with Captain Imelda and I was not looking forward to it. She was a strong fighter, but I was hesitant of her ability to be able to competently perform my role.

I was glad to be back in the comfort of my own home. It

certainly was not the largest of houses, a family would have struggled with space, but for myself it was perfect.

With a large entrance hall that split at either end, one route took you into a comfortable lounge area with a big stone fireplace with animal skins placed in front of it. The room had a large settee accompanied by two armchairs, with small tables at either side of them.

On the walls hung the occasional painting or tapestry, most of which were gifts; others had been hand crafted by my house Guan, Tobias. Decorations were not a necessity to me, and I had never collected them myself. In the centre of the great hall was an elegant spiral stone staircase that took you to the next floor, which consisted of a training room, two bed-chambers and a bathing room.

The other end of the entrance hall took you into a well-stocked kitchen and pantry. The back door from the kitchen did not lead you outside like you would expect, but instead took you to a small living space that held an old wooden chair, a side table, and against the wall a small cot bed; this room was where Tobias rested and slept.

Had rested and slept.

I had never entered that room, nor did I want to now.

The new Guan, when they arrived, would clean it, and I would permit them to reposition the furniture however they wished.

When Imelda arrived, we sat in my kitchen.

"I apologise for not having fruit and drink available. As you know, I am currently without a house Guan," I said dismissively, not really caring if she was insulted by my lack of refreshments. Opening some of my maps, I stretched them over the dining room table, using daggers as weights to hold down the corners.

"There's no need General Truda," she replied, taking a deep breath before continuing. "I know you think I am not ready for this, and I confess I did not expect it to happen, not yet. I want you to know I take this new responsibility very seriously." She held her head high, trying to show me her strength.

"This is only temporary," I replied, making it clear that she was not filling my boots, just borrowing a pair for a short time. Her agreeable and apologetic nature irked me.

"And I want you to report back to me regularly," I added, curtly. I knew she wanted me to tell her I had full confidence in her, but the truth was I did not. I knew the only person for this job was me. Imelda was undeniably skilled in combat. She was one of the best in our myriad of warriors, which was one of the reasons she had been promoted to captain at such a young age. She just did not have the years, and her experience was sorely lacking.

When she nodded, I saw a flicker of disappointment in her expression, clearly as a result of my words, or lack thereof. We continued our discussion, talking about the guard rotation in the city, looking over maps and discussing scouting strategies. While showing her the areas of the kingdom which I had planned to search next for the rebels, I marked out the routes I would have taken. After a few hours Imelda left, taking some of my maps with her.

~*~

I got myself ready to leave for the Training House. I had arranged to meet up with Acqueline for a sparring session, and after my frustrating meeting with Imelda, I needed to let off some steam.

I should not have become so frustrated with the captain, I realised that now, but the situation was more than a little difficult for me. I did not want to explain how to do my job to someone who clearly was not ready for it. Not to mention the fact that she had looked confused and completely out of her depth when I tried to explain my strategy for scouting the lands for the rebel base. In the end, I told her not to worry about it and just to focus on the protection of the city. Luckily, my suspension would only last another eleven weeks, then I could continue my search for the rebel base myself.

It was still early when I left, and the streets were quiet as I walked along the smooth white path. We had collected the sand from the desert and melded it into stones, laying them together to form solid rivers of white paths, which flowed throughout the city.

The Training House was one of the only buildings in the city that was made mostly of wood, and the contrast was beautiful against all the other buildings made of sandstone. It was largely a square structure with a curved wooden roof, each meeting in the centre creating a large point towards the sky, embellished and supported with tall iron beams.

I walked through the entrance and out onto the training court. There, Acqueline stood leaning against one of the pillars, her eyes beamed in delight when she saw me.

"Finally. I was beginning to think you weren't coming," she said.

I knew she was joking, we always teased each other like this. I would have liked to reply with something witty about being busier than a royal guard, strolling around the palace all day. However, that was not the case, so instead I merely raised my eyebrows at her. She laughed and walked towards me with a sword in her hand, unsheathed. Wasting no time, I walked towards her, pulling out my sword, displaying my readiness.

She charged at me, lifting her sword high above her head, and quickly slashing it down towards mine. I side stepped and lifted my sword to hers. Hearing the clang of steel on steel as they vibrated against each other, I rotated my wrist and swung my sword down and around the back of my body. With half a turn, I brought my sword back down towards her. Acqueline jumped back and again we heard the sound of our swords clash as she raised her sword to hit mine defensively.

Stomping my foot forward with a grunt, I attempted another blow matched again by the clang of her sword. We toyed like this for a few minutes before Acqueline raised her shoulders and pushed her sword horizontally towards my chest. As I raised my weapon to stop her sword's path, she tried a sneak attack by pulling out a small dagger from her back and pressed forward, directly aiming for my throat.

Anticipating this move, I used my free hand to grip her wrist, and forcefully swung my leg to kick under hers, whilst manipulating her upper body strength to cause her to lose balance and she fell to the floor.

After a few moments she leaned back on her elbows and started laughing.

"I was sure I almost had you that time," she said, still amused. I held out my hand to help pull her up.

"Perhaps one day you will," I said smiling, using my strength to pull her from the floor. Acqueline's beautiful chestnut hair was tied back in a single long plait hanging down her left shoulder. She was wearing her standard guards' uniform; a silver breast plate sculpted with floral patterns, emphasised over a plain black leather outfit consisting of trousers, a top and a pair of boots.

"Are you on duty today?" I asked her.

"Yes, later this morning at the Palace." She turned to me, and with an earnest expression, she continued. "Tru, I wanted to tell you that if I knew of the council's plans to place you in the breeding programme, I would've told you."

"I know that, and although it is unfortunate timing, I will fulfil my duty as expected." I lied without particular tone or expression.

"I know it's not what you wanted, but it does seem logical. You are one of the strongest warriors."

"I was just hoping that my position would exclude me from having to take part," I replied with a sigh.

It was a ludicrous assumption considering the queen herself had been through the programme twice, and was obligated regardless of her own preference. She had lost the first offspring, trying again a few years later, successfully giving birth to Princess Callidice. If royalty could not be excluded, it was foolish of me to believe I would be.

"What you mean to say is that you thought being in your position, and the queen's favourite, would grant you the luxury of choice?" she asked.

"Yes," I replied honestly, realising Acqueline had a point.

"Tru, it's probably because you are in her favour that she has ordered you to do it, knowing that you wouldn't volunteer on your own," Acqueline suggested. "Besides, you are getting on a bit now, I guess the queen wants you to crack on before you get too old."

I tutted and punched her lightly on the arm. I was not considered old for an elf, not even close. They say that when a human body reaches a certain age, the slow journey of its decay begins. Skin would wrinkle, wounds would take longer to heal, and they would lose their strength.

We however, had evolved differently. From the first women who had tapped into the earth magic, and changed the makeup of our genetics, not only had we evolved into beings that were faster, smarter and stronger, but we had also slowed the ageing process. I had lived for thirty-two years, but my body looked no older than twenty.

~*~

Later that week, whilst in my living room watching the flames dance in my stone fireplace, I heard a light tapping sound on my front door.

"Come in," I huffed, and a young boy entered. He looked really young, around the age of ten if I were to guess. The boy walked through the room and stood in front of me.

"I am Castor your new house Guan," he said with a high-pitched shaky tone, his eyes looking down at the floor.

"Go run me a bath boy, it is upstairs on the left." I must have spoken harshly, as the boy nodded quickly and almost ran as he exited the room. The arrival of this new Guan frustrated me. For starters, he looked too young and would be inexperienced. Secondly, it was only another reminder that Tobias was gone, and I would have to move on from no longer having him in my service. After my bath, which was not filled with my usual favourite lavender oils, I ate some food and changed my clothes, ready to head to the Breeding House.

When I arrived, I was greeted by Peril. Looking back at her book and placing a mark on the page, she reached down and collected a key from inside the pedestal. Whilst turning, she picked up a red liquid filled glass bottle from the shelf behind her and handed both items to me. She saluted and smiled as I turned to walk down the corridor.

Pausing in front of room number twenty-three, I slowly inserted in the key and turned the handle. Walking into the room, I saw him immediately, standing with his head down as before.

I glanced his way briefly before walking over to the gap in the brickwork and tipping out the contents of the glass bottle as I usually did. Keeping the bottle in my hand, I turned and faced towards the door.

After that first session, I had been dragging out my time here; the longest I had stayed was almost two hours. Two hours of silently staring at the door was almost as tiresome as sitting at home staring into the fireplace. This was my life now.

It was not long before I already felt like I had been standing for hours. It was so quiet, with the only interruption being the occasional rattle of chains.

He must have been situated closer to the door today, because I could hear him breathing. I turned my head slightly in curiosity and looked towards him. I could see his muscled chest moving as he drew breath, his arms remaining by his side, his shackled hands in front of him.

From here I could see the callous rough skin on them. I assumed he must have been a heavy labourer before coming to the breeding programme. There were scars on his hands and forearms, with light white lines that looked like deep scuffs or scratches. His skin was tanned, making the marks more visible.

I could not help but to continue my gaze, he was actually very impressive. I had not seen a Guan so large before. Looking down at his legs, he had strong muscles on his calves and thighs with thin black hairs covering the most part of his lower legs. My eyes scanned up, until I reached the loin cloth, surprisingly I found myself wondering what was concealed underneath. I visually traced every muscle of his legs, past his thighs, analysing his tight abs, the definition of his broad muscled shoulders and noticed a circular branded mark on his chest, the number twenty-three at its centre.

I had seen branding used on Guan's before, the same way we would brand cattle on the farms with a hot poker, with its end shaped into a number, placing it in hot coal until the metal absorbed enough heat to sear its mark on flesh. The numbers on this Guan's chest looked fresh, like he had been branded recently.

Finally, I looked up towards his face. His jet-black hair that was usually loose around his shoulders was tied up in a short ponytail, his square jaw with a short black beard surrounded his full lips.

As I looked further at his facial features, I gasped, suddenly finding myself looking straight into a pair of deep blue eyes.

He was observing me. How long had he been watching? Had he seen me scanning his entire body with my own eyes? Breaking eye contact without saying a word, hoping enough time had passed, I hastily unlocked the door and stormed out of the room, locking it behind me.

I stood for a moment just outside the door, instantly regretting my actions. I should have scolded him for daring to look at me, but instead I had felt my cheeks go red with embarrassment for looking at him, and in my panicked state, I had decided on a quick exit. I waited with my back against the door until I could feel my cheeks cooling, an indicator that the colour in my face was returning to normal.

Walking down the corridor without looking back on room number twenty-three, as I got closer to the desk my pace slowed, allowing me time to think. What had come over me? Why did I react in such a foolish manner? I had not done anything wrong. I was entitled to stare. I could do whatever I wanted with the Guan and no judgment would be passed on me.

"Can I take those from you?" asked Peril from her stool. When had I reached the entrance? I was in such a daze I had not been paying attention, still clutching at the bottle and key tightly in my hands.

"Yes, thank you," I said, handing the objects to her. Saying our goodbye's, I left. Arriving back home I heard a gasp as I entered the front door. Looking over towards my kitchen, I saw Castor on his knees, scrubbing the floor. Clearly startled, he started scrubbing faster.

I had given him a few chores before I had left, and he was obviously worried I would scold him for not completing them. After glancing his way, I said nothing as I walked up my stairs towards my bed-chamber.

It bothered me that he was so frightened, not that anything could be done. I would just have to endure it. I missed the simplicity of life with Tobias. Castor would just have to learn that, as long as he kept the house in order, scrubbed my armour and weapons, no harm would come to him. Thinking of Tobias, I remembered his first day. He was so scared of me he had over worked himself cleaning and working through the night. The next day he had looked so exhausted, I thought he would drop at any moment. I had not said anything, instead I gave him a few lighter chores for a few days, allowing him the opportunity to rest and regain his strength.

He became less nervous around me over time, able to perform chores and follow instruction without fear of repercussions. This was about respect and trust. Once I had gained his trust, respect followed, and in my opinion, it made the relationship between master and Guan much more productive, rather than inflicting constant punishment. Tobias had been the most perfect Guan and I wished for a moment that I could memorialise his death. Not the same way as an elf of course, but it just did not feel right that he had died, and nobody would do anything in honour of his life. He was just gone, and that did not seem to bother anyone else other than me. I was to live with the constant reminder of his absence through a young child scampering around me in fear. I wanted to forget about Tobias, to move on from the memories I had of him.

I just had to be patient with the new Guan. If Tobias could learn, then so could Castor. I could ease him into his chores, it certainly would have been better for the boy if I still had my duties as General. I could be out on a scouting mission right now, leaving Castor to settle in my home, without feeling the pressure of my presence. Well, there was nothing I could do about that for the moment, so I laid down on my bed and slept.

~*~

The next few days I avoided Castor as much as possible, only speaking to him to give instruction for serving food or providing a few light chores. I was sat in my bedroom, following another visit to the Breeding House, thinking about the slave with the crystal blue eyes.

After the day I had caught him looking at me, I was more than prepared to return and speak my mind, as I should have the night it happened. However, this seemed unnecessary. When I walked back into room number twenty-three, he had kept his face to the floor for the entire time, not looking in my direction once.

I had tried to keep my eyes straight, but every now and again, as though they worked against my will, my eyes would wander and look at the Guan. Looking him up and down, I saw his strong arms and large hands. I saw his chest with a few strands of black hairs in the centre, his abs that seemed as solid as a rock, and just below his muscles, I saw a distinguished V shape, like an arrow pointing towards the only hidden part of his body.

This was ridiculous! Clearly being stuck in this room all day had given me nothing better to think of. I needed to find something else to occupy my time and mind.

Chapter 5

WEEK THREE

Approaching the Training House for a workout session, I heard noises inside of grunting and shuffling of feet, making me smile. Perhaps I would find someone to spar with today.

My visits here had become more frequent, usually daily. The more time I spent off duty, attending the Breeding House, the more I did not feel like myself. Here I could focus, work my body, and relieve tension. This was the only place where I still felt like General Truda.

Entering the building which opened into a large square space, a few fighters were in training. To the left, a young elf flung knives at her haggard, body shaped target, straw protruding from most of the seams and gashes. To the right was a warrior elf with a crossbow, pulling back the string with ease, releasing arrow after arrow, hitting her ringed target. Next to her on some steps, sat a petite elf wearing a loose fit, ankle length purple linen dress. She was watching the archer and occasionally clapped in encouragement when she had made a good shot.

In the centre of the training square were two very familiar faces, the twins, Shanor and Shanon. They were fighting close combat, currently wrestling each other onto the ground. When the door closed behind me, everyone stopped and looked in my direction.

"General Truda!" exclaimed Shanor in excitement. She scrambled from under her sister, running over towards me. The other women in the room nodded and saluted in respect, before returning to what they were doing. Shanor and Shanon looked almost identical, aside from a few very small differences. If you were to speak with them, you would easily be able to tell them apart, not just from the way they spoke but because their personalities were just so different. If, however, you were just looking at a painting, they would both be portrayed with such likeness, you would not be able to identify them individually. Both were lean and tall, with ash blond long hair, usually plaited or in a high ponytail. Both had round faces with wide eyes, the colour of the sky filtered by clouds.

"Hello to you both. Shanor, how is your arm?" I asked, pointing towards her clearly bandaged bicep.

"Oh, it's fine, my sister tells me it's a deep cut, but it doesn't even hurt," she smirked.

"Good, then how about we have a little sparring session together?" I suggested. Both of their eyes lit up.

"We would like that," said Shanor.

"Who shall go first?" asked Shanon.

"How about both of you?" I said with a grin. Taking on the twins together was just what I needed to work up a good sweat.

The twins looked at each other in amazement.

Taking a few steps back, they nodded in agreement and walked to the centre of the training square, waiting for me to be ready. I walked over to the edge of the room towards some shelves along the wooden wall which held oils, lotions, gauze and bandages. I picked up two thick bandages and unravelled them, then started wrapping my knuckles. I repeated the process on my other hand, clenching my fists to make sure they were secured tight so I could close a hard grip.

I looked back towards the twins; they were talking quietly to each other while stretching their bodies, perhaps talking strategy on how to work together for my defeat. They were clearly excited; I could see this in their expressions as I approached them.

"Ready!" I said, my tone serious now. I wanted the twins to know I meant business and did not want them to hold back. Shanor looked once more towards her sister who nodded in confirmation. She slowly walked around to flank me.

So, this was their plan, a pincer attack! They were hoping

my focus would remain on one while the other could strike.

As my gaze followed Shanor standing at my back, Shanon charged towards me from the front, swinging her fist towards my face. I leaned my body to the side, avoiding her attack and swiftly grabbed her wrist, twisting it behind her back, forcing her to the side, and kneed her hard in the stomach. Shanor charged at me from behind. I did not need to look; my trained ears heard her footsteps. I spun around, my foot slamming into her chest.

She stumbled back but did not fall, stepping towards me again. She swung her arms at me, grunting with frustration as I deflected punch after punch, pushing away her arms.

Spotting an opening, I jabbed and hit her directly in the face. She grunted in pain and stumbled back looking behind me. Her sister Shanon had recovered and jumped on my back. She now had her arm wrapped around my throat, squeezing with her forearm, trying to cut off my airway.

Thrusting my elbow back into her gut, feeling her grip loosen, I grabbed her forearm wrapped around my throat, and lurched her body over my shoulder, throwing her to the floor.

She laid there, holding her stomach where I had elbowed her. Shanor came at me once more, throwing punches into the air. I grabbed her fist with lightning precision, a high pitch growl in frustration escaped her lips as she swung her other arm at me. Grabbing her second fist, I jumped into the air, and kicked her in the chest with full force, causing her to fall right beside her sister.

Landing on my back, I rolled my knees up towards my chest, my hands turned backwards either side of my head. I thrusted my legs in the air, giving my body the momentum it needed to stand up straight once more.

After a few seconds of me looking at them on the floor, I outstretched both of my arms with a kind smile. They each took one of my hands and I grunted as I helped pull them up.

"That was a good technique. However, it may have been more effective if you had both taken me on from one angle at the same time." I said. I frowned as I looked towards Shanor's bandaged arm and saw blood. Shanor looked at her arm and winced; clearly it hurt more than she wanted to say.

"Let me help with that," said a voice from across the room. I looked up to see a pair of eyes watching us, they had obviously stopped what they were doing to watch the fight. The woman in the purple dress stood and walked over towards us.

"I'm Lelane," she said in a sweet girly voice.

"I'm a trained healer, so I can help with her injury," she added, looking towards Shanor's now bleeding arm.

"Please do," I said, crossing my arms whilst following Lelane as she guided the twins over to the wooden shelves. I watched as she slowly and carefully unwrapped the blood-stained bandage from Shanor's arm. The cut had been deep, and small trickles of blood were now flowing down her arm.

"Looks like you have re-opened your wound, it will need

a few stitches," Lelane told Shanor.

"Just do what you need to do," replied Shanor, clearly frustrated at the fuss she was getting.

"Could you fetch me some clean water, some thread and a needle?" Lelane asked Shanon, who nodded and quickly sped off to collect the things that Lelane required.

"How long have you been a healer?" I asked Lelane.

"Oh no, I am a warrior, but I have had training from a healer to help deal with injuries in the battlefield," she answered sweetly. I was puzzled by her outfit, looking at the loose, long, purple cotton dress.

"I was in the breeding programme," she continued, noticing my gaze at her attire. "My girlfriend insists I wear more comfortable clothing while our daughter grows."

"You are pregnant," I said, now understanding.

"I'm approximately four weeks and not yet showing, but the mages test confirmed that I had conceived." Just then, Shanon returned with the items that Lelane asked for.

I stepped back, giving Lelane space to do her work. She washed her hands in the water, dampened a cloth and gently cleaned Shanor's arm. Using her fingers, she slowly covered the gash with a lotion, which must have soothed Shanor, as her scrunched face relaxed and her shoulders dropped. Lelane doused the thread and needle in an ointment and began stitching Shanor's arm. I stood patiently and admired Lelane's skill; she obviously had a natural gift that complimented her caring and attentive personality. My mother was like that, a fierce warrior skilled in the art of healing. I remembered my mother's caring touch as she patched up my scrapes and bruises from training. Her words of endearment with a kiss to my forehead.

"So brave, my little Truda. To never shed a tear is to let your enemies know that they can never hurt you."

"There, all done," Lelane stated, rubbing her hands clean. Then, after nodding towards me and placing a closed fist on her chest, she walked back over to the elf practising her aim with a crossbow.

"I am sorry if we disappointed you," said Shanon, looking at her sister and then down to the floor.

"Not at all. My position should never be taken lightly, and you must not forget that I have many more years of fighting experience than you do." Reaching out my hands, I placed one on Shanon's shoulder and the other on Shanor's uninjured shoulder.

"I am very proud to watch you both gain skill in your fighting abilities. Time will only make you stronger, and one day, I have no doubt you will both be a force to be reckoned with," I encouraged with a smile. "Now go, take your sister to rest. I think you have done enough training for today." The twins both nodded and after saluting, they walked towards the exit.

I looked behind me and saw Lelane, now at the other

side of the large square. The woman next to her had stopped using her crossbow, placing it on the ground so she could hold Lelane in her arms. They hugged and held each other as Lelane placed cute kisses on the elf's nose. They were smiling, clearly very happy and in love, which was a beautiful sight. Although we knew that we had to keep Guan's in order to breed, they were never more than that to us, they were never to love. We would seek companionship with our own kind.

I had never been interested in a relationship with anyone. I was too busy to think of such things, fulfilling my duties as the general. For the first time, I looked at these two and wondered what it would be like to have the love they shared, for someone to look at me the way that Lelane now looked at her partner.

~*~

Three weeks in and I already felt like I would be driven mad with boredom. At home, spending yet another afternoon reading and re-arranging my maps, I was now getting ready for another 'session' at the Breeding House. He had not looked at me again, keeping his face towards the floor, acting like nothing had happened. I was finding it more difficult not to think about those crystal blue eyes, especially on the days I was due to attend the Breeding House, like today.

I found myself thinking about what he did before he was sent there. Unlike Tobias or Castor, he was not a boy, he was a man, probably close to the end of his life. Curiosity was getting the better of me and I wanted to know more. What would it hurt to find out some things about him?

I walked to the Breeding House and was greeted by a smiling Peril.

"Good evening General, I will just sign you in." I nodded to her as she saluted, then walked down towards the room. Unlocking the door and entering, I saw him. This time, he was sitting on the bed, and he did not look up as I locked the door behind me, walked over to the table and placed down the key and glass bottle.

For a moment, I just stood there, hesitating, knowing that trying to talk to him was not a good idea. Elves did not strike up conversations with Guans, and I should just turn towards the door and stare at it as usual. Then, I glanced over to the slave and stepped closer, unable to stop myself as my mouth opened to speak.

"What is your name?" Instantly, I regretted the moment the question escaped my lips. Folding my arms, I stood in front of him where he sat. For a long while he did not say anything, and I wondered if perhaps he was a mute. Then, keeping his head down, I heard him speak.

"You want to know my name?" his voice was deep, but smooth.

"I would not have asked otherwise," I said, more sternly.

He looked at me, then he spoke. "Erik." And there they

were again, those crystal blue eyes.

"You are a builder?" I asked. Still looking at me, he frowned slightly as if now confused with my questions. I suppose that made sense since I had just spent the last three weeks ignoring him.

"I was."

"Before you were sent here you mean?"

"Yes," he replied. Then he looked down again facing the floor, leaving us in a moment of silence. He was obviously not eager to talk to me, giving me short or one worded answers. Unfortunately, that only seemed to make me more curious about him.

"You miss the outside, being stuck in here all day and night?" It was not really a question I needed to ask, because looking at him I realised the answer was already clear. It was like looking at a stallion horse that had been cooped up in a stall all day, not being able to stretch his legs by galloping across open fields of grass. He looked up again, those blue eyes capturing me.

"Wouldn't you?"

He had no idea how much that question was the right one. I had spent so many afternoons procrastinating because I had nothing else better to do, and I already felt like I could go mad, yet I still had my freedom. How would I have coped, being locked in the same room all day, every day? We remained silent after that. When some time had passed, I walked over to the table, emptied the contents of the bottle out the window and left the room, locking it behind me. I walked back down towards Peril and handed her the bottle and key, and she smiled at me as she took them.

"You know he is very big and strong that one. A builder perhaps?" I asked Peril.

"Yes, I believe he was," she answered.

"Seems like such a waste, keeping him locked in here all day when there is plenty of work to be done in the city," I said in a disappointed tone. Then I left, leaving Peril to consider my words.

Chapter 6

WEEK FOUR

I met up with Acqueline in the Training House for another sparring session. When I arrived, it was clear to see that she was buzzing with excitement.

"You must come and look at this," Acqueline said with wide eyes. She grabbed my arm and pulled me to the nearest pillar. From behind it, she pulled out a large redwood bow; its wingspan was huge, like that of a giant bird. She handed it to me, and I was astonished at how light it was. I studied the wood, discovering the stunning markings and engravings. Within the wood, flowers resembling the royal throne had been carved, although none of them appeared to be in full bloom, as only the shapes of buds appeared at the end of the vines.

"It is beautiful," I said, stroking my fingers along the wood, admiring the orange gem that had been recessed in the centre.

"Wait until you fire an arrow from it," she said, grinning with glee whilst leading me over to where the target practice boards were.

"Go ahead, take a shot," she gestured with a wave of her hand towards the circled target that was a little way in front of us.

"Well, for that I will need an arrow," I quipped, looking at the bow, and looking around for Acqueline's quiver.

"Didn't I tell you? This weapon was a gift from the Mages Temple, you don't need arrows," she grinned at me.

I looked puzzled for a moment, then turned towards the target. Lifting the bow up towards me, I used my right hand to touch gently along the string, pulling my elbow back with my finger still lightly attached. I lifted my other arm, which was holding the bow, and I pointed it towards the target.

At first, nothing happened. Then, a few seconds later, just as I was imagining an actual arrow in my fingers, one began to materialise. It was gold and entirely made of magic. Its shape flickered as it formed, like little sparks of light coming together as one.

Aiming its arrowhead in my line of sight, towards the target, releasing my fingers, I watched in amazement as the arrow flew from the bow, and hit the target right in the centre, as intended.

"Isn't it amazing," Acqueline exclaimed. "And the reload speed gets quicker the more you practise," she beamed proudly, obviously meaning she had mastered using it.

"It sure is impressive, but I think I will stick with my sword, even if it is not a magical one," I replied.

"I am surprised you still haven't let the mages gift you with a weapon, or you know, they could probably enchant something amazing onto that giant sword of yours."

"I do not trust those in the Mages Temple, you know that," I replied.

"It's Freyja you don't trust. I agree she's a bit creepy Tru, but she has always been loyal, and besides, not all the mages are like her," she finished.

"I know that, but Freyja is their leader, she controls all that happens in the temple and is ambassador between the queen and the mages."

Freyja was always the first to pipe up in council meetings, reporting of the invention or improvement of a new potion, something she most likely had not achieved herself, but was happy to take credit for. It made me curious as to what other experiments were going on in the temple, and if led by Freyja, were they all honourable?

"Besides, as I have already proven, I do not need a magical weapon to be the most skilled warrior in the kingdom," I sniggered, smiling coyly at Acqueline, making her laugh. For a moment we were both quiet, just enjoying the moment in each other's company, until Acqueline sighed from her own thoughts and spoke.

"I'm worried for the queen," she said in a quiet voice.

"What do you mean?" I asked.

"She seems troubled. I think it's because of the princess."

"Why, what has she done now?" I asked, rolling my eyes.

"Nothing, that's the problem. She never attends the meetings or her private lessons. The queen asked me to help with her combat training and when I see her, which isn't often, she acts bored and doesn't pay attention to anything I try to teach her."

Acqueline's voice got louder as she spoke, clearly wanting to scream in frustration at the situation.

"Actually, I was wondering if you could help in that department. Maybe it's my training strategy, you were excellent with the twins training, maybe you could help me out with the princess?" she asked, raising her eyebrows. I had to admit, I felt sorry for my friend. I was not exactly a big fan of the princess either. She was a spoilt brat and was clearly not taking her responsibility to the Kingdom of Nysa seriously.

"Sure, since I am already spending so much time in the Training House anyway. Although, I cannot guarantee that my methods would be more effective." The princess was still young, and I was not exactly the type of character to take it slow. The twins already had all the basic fighting knowledge, lucky for them, as they had to be quick on their feet when training with me, and if they were not, they would be left with bruises.

"Maybe a hard hand is exactly what she needs," said Acqueline with a smile.

~*~

At the Breeding House, I was greeted by Peril who handed me the required object and I made my way down the corridor. As I entered room number twenty-three, Erik looked up, watching me as I placed the items on the table. I turned to look at him and moved closer to the bed where he sat.

Erik stood and shuffled to the side, his heavy chains making his movements slow. He walked over to the wall and slid to the floor, he nodded to me and then the bed, letting me know he had moved so I could sit comfortably. However, I did no such thing, and chose to remain standing with my arms crossed. After a moment, Erik spoke.

"I've been allowed outside this week to help with repairs, was that you?" he asked me.

"No, it was the woman who runs this house. I just merely suggested to her that we had a lot of repairs in the city, and you were wasted in this room."

"Thank you," he said. I did not know what to say to him, I had never been thanked by a Guan before. It made me feel uncomfortable. After a long, uninterrupted silence, I guessed I would just go back to staring into nothing, and that is how

I should have left it, but talking seemed to pass the time a lot quicker than studying the shapes and curves on the wooden door, which I am pretty sure I could probably draw from memory now. Although I would never admit it out loud, I liked the tone of his deep voice and wanted him to talk with me again. Against my better judgement, I decided to give him my name.

"I am Truda."

"I know who you are," he replied.

"You do?" I pulled back in surprise.

"You're the General, the strongest of all the queen's warriors." All the elves in the city knew, of course all the human slaves would know too.

"I suppose you would know who I am, but I admit I do not make a habit of talking with Guan's." Erik looked at me, realising he must have thought me to be very strange. Weeks of silence one minute, and now I was trying to talk to him. I walked over to the table, deciding to fill the awkward silence with something to do.

Picking up the glass bottle, I emptied its contents through the small gap in the brickwork, then I placed the empty bottle back on the table. I felt Erik's eyes watching me the whole time.

I began talking again.

"My first house slave Tobias was probably the most I had spoken to a Guan over the years, although he was not really one for speaking either. My new house Guan Castor is too afraid of me to utter a single word," I said, thinking of the little boy that was probably scurrying around my home as we spoke.

"I imagine many people are scared of you in your position," he replied, watching me walk back towards the bed.

"You do not seem to be afraid," I challenged.

"I don't have much reason to be afraid anymore," he looked at his hands. He was sat on the floor, resting his feet with his legs bent, each arm resting on his knee.

"What happened to your first house servant?" asked Erik.

"He died," I said quietly.

"How?"

"I did not kill him if that is what you were implying," I answered in an angry tone, infuriated at the insinuation that I had, but it was known that some masters were very cruel to their servants, deaths happened. Erik did not respond, but instead looked at me, waiting for me to continue.

"He died during a battle. He was nearby when we were ambushed. As I was about to be attacked, he jumped in front of me and took a knife to the chest." I shivered as I remembered all the blood and scrubbing my hands clean.

"He sacrificed himself to save you?"

"I believe so, though I do not know why," I replied honestly.

"Hmmm," was the only noise he decided to make at that moment, and I found myself getting frustrated by it.

"What?" I asked.

"He must have held some affection for you."

"Why do you say that?" I asked, looking at him in shock.

"We serve our masters; we don't protect them. I don't know a single one of us who would die for one of you," he said, looking back down at his chains.

'One of you'. It was a fact; he and I were of different worlds. A human Guan and an elf general, and here I was trying to have a normal conversation with him.

~*~

The next day, I was summoned to see the queen. Walking into the throne room, I immediately noticed the princess's absence. Standing before the queen, I offered her my salute of respect.

"You summoned for me?"

"I wanted to see how you were getting on," she replied. After looking at my confused face she questioned, "I have been told that you have not yet asked for a test in the Breeding House?" A pregnancy test I soon realised, and of course, why would I ask for one? This also meant that I was being watched, or someone was reporting on my visits.

"I heard some of the women say that you feel different when you are with child. I feel no different so did not see the need to ask for a test," I said, thinking quickly.

It was not a lie, I had heard other women talk of how

their body changed during the pregnancy. Although, they had already known they were pregnant, so maybe it was just something they said.

"I understand, but you need to get tested regularly," she replied.

"And I was not just asking after your physical health Truda, I know this is not what you wanted, but you must understand that I would be a very appalling queen if I did not select my best warrior to help create the next generation of fighters." I looked up at her and she was smiling, but still held concern in her eyes. Was she really worried about how I felt?

"I understand your reasons, and can only apologise for my reaction, it was just an unexpected shock," I said, more honestly.

"I do not want any ill feelings between us Truda, you know I have always shown you affection, loving you like my own daughter after your mother died." I thought back to the stories Queen Cassandra had told me of my mother. Not just the battle stories, but also how they trained together and studied together.

"Your mother never wanted to enter the breeding programme either," she told me.

"Really?" I asked in surprise.

"Of course not. You are so like her Truda, she always thought of herself as a warrior, and nothing else, until you were born." Her eyes smiled as though she had just remembered a memory from a long time ago.

"She told me then that she realised you were more important to her than anything, she loved you so much. Her family legacy did not end with her and it should not end with you." I saluted with a nod, wanting to show her that I understood and appreciated her words. Then, looking towards the princess's chair, the queen sighed as she noticed me looking.

"I do not see my daughter much these days. I have heard rumours she spends her time in the underground Pleasure House."

I knew what the queen was referring to. Apparently, somewhere in the city, slaves were being used for pleasurable physical acts. It was not permitted, but we had been unable to find its location or who ran such an establishment.

"I think she resents me for the obligations I put on her. I know she is struggling with combat training, and rarely attends her academic studies with me." She told me honestly.

"Acqueline has asked me to help with the princess's training, she thinks my methods might help with her progress."

"Well, that is good news Truda, for this I thank you." She stood, preparing to leave, but before she did, she added, "I did not just place you in the breeding programme for myself, or for the good of our people. You are doing this in honour of your mother's memory, and someday soon you will have a daughter whom you can love as much as she loved you."

Then she left, leaving me kneeling with one leg as I

digested her words. She was wrong. I would not be doing this in memory of my mother, for we were not alike; she was willing to do something she did not want to do. It saddened me to think that the queen would consider my behaviour as an act of betrayal, but I just did not agree. The best place for me was on the battlefield, defending her kingdom, and I would be doing that again soon.

"I am sorry mother," I murmured quietly under my breath. I stood and left the throne room.

Chapter 7

WEEK FIVE

As I was working out in the Training House, Lelane and her partner entered. They were talking and smiling at each other. After meeting with the queen, it now concerned me that someone was obviously reporting on my activity, and I was desperate to know who.

Initially, my suspicions linked straight to Peril, since she was the head of the Breeding House and a council member. However, I could not understand why she would be following my actions so closely, and I could not exactly interrogate her, it would only raise alarm as to my true intentions. This couple however, presented a good opportunity to get an insider's perspective. Perhaps they would be able to tell me something that I did not know. Noticing me approaching, they took a step away from each other but still held hands.

"I wanted to thank you Lelane, for showing such kindness towards Shanor the other day. I feel I may have been too rough with her and should have considered her recent injuries." Lelane was wearing another dress made of purple linen, although this time she had a leather belt around the centre, one she would not be able to wear once her stomach swelled, I thought to myself.

"It was my pleasure General, glad I was able to help." Beaming a smile towards the woman holding her hand she said, "this is my girlfriend Terra." Terra nodded towards me and her mouth curved into a half smile.

"She's not much for words," continued Lelane, "but if she was, she would say I speak enough for the both of us anyway," she giggled.

I looked towards Terra and respectfully nodded. She was clearly a tough warrior and had a much harder edge to her appearance than Lelane. She had short, dark blonde hair, shaved off on one side, with the rest almost swept at the parting to fall on the other side.

She was just shorter than me, her bare arms showing strong muscled biceps, the rest of her covered in thick brown leather. She was clearly a fighter and not someone to mess with, but when she looked towards Lelane, her eyes noticeably softened, clearly holding a lot of love for this woman.

"I also wanted to congratulate you both properly on the

news of your pregnancy," I said, hoping this would stir up a conversation in the area I was most interested in.

"Thank you," said Lelane, smiling down and briefly holding her stomach with her free hand.

"It is something we both very much wanted."

"So, you volunteered?" I asked.

"Oh yes of course. Terra wasn't as keen at first, but she knew it would make me really happy, and now that we know I am with child, I believe she is just as excited as I," she said, whilst squeezing Terra's hand and smiling at her. Terra returned Lelane's smile.

"So, you had no trouble with the procedure then?" I asked, prying for further information, not wanting to hear more of the couples clearly happy, and slightly annoying relationship bliss.

"No, our sessions went really well, it was in the fourth week that we had confirmation that I was pregnant," chirped Lelane.

"Our sessions? Did you both take part together?" I asked. Lelane giggled and looked lovingly towards Terra who looked a little embarrassed.

"Well, not exactly like that. I was the only one that you know, performed 'the act' with the Guan, but Terra was always in the room with me," she finished.

In that moment, I imagined a naked slave lying on the bed, with Lelane giggling as she straddled him and Terra's serious eyes watching, guarding the whole time. Noticing Terra's blush, I wondered if perhaps it was more intimate than that. Had the slave male inserted himself from behind while Terra could stand in front of her to caress and kiss her lips? I decided to leave that firmly in my imagination, knowing it was something I most definitely was not going to ask questions about.

"I see." Thanks to my vivid imagination, I felt the conversation had suddenly become awkward.

"I was thankful to have Terra with me, to share in that special moment," Lelane broke the silence by saying, confirming my theory. Their time together in the Breeding House had most definitely been more intimate for them.

"Besides," she said, "the Guan they paired me with was huge, the tallest and broadest slave I had ever seen. I think I would've been too nervous to go through with it if Terra hadn't been with me."

With this, I snapped my eyes up to her. Could it be, was the slave she was talking about the one I had been paired with?

"What was your room number?"

She replied with the words that confirmed my thoughts.

"Twenty-three."

I wanted to ask more questions, but decided not to. I congratulated them and took my leave to process this information. On my way home, my mind ran rampant. The slave in that room knew his obligations, he had done it before, he had watched me spill the contents of the bottle out of the window.

I started to feel nervous. It was stupid to think my tactic would work, all of this relying on the silence of a Guan. He would most likely report me to the guards, he had to protect himself also. As he said before, no Guan would ever sacrifice themselves for one of us. After reaching my house and barely being able to stomach my dinner, I got myself ready and headed over to the Breeding House.

~*~

On my way, I felt angry at myself for being so naive, but for some reason, I also felt angry that someone else had been in room twenty-three before me. After collecting my items at the Breeding House desk, I walked into the room and immediately began questioning Erik.

"Why did you not tell me?" I asked, angrily.

"Tell you what?" clearly confused by my sudden anger, he was stood in the middle of the room looking at me.

"You did not tell me that you had already been paired with someone before me," I said, waving my hands at him like it was obvious what I meant.

"You never asked," he simply said. I glared at him and started pacing the room.

"You knew how this all worked, what was supposed to happen," I stated. He did not reply with words, but nodded.

"Then you must really wonder of my behaviour," I said without turning. After a moment he replied.

"It's not my place to question." I turned towards him then, calming myself.

"So, you have not spoken to anyone about what happens here?"

"Who would ask me? No-one cares to ask for a Guan's account of things." That I knew to be true, even if someone was watching my movements within the Breeding House, it was unlikely they would come and question him. Walking past Erik, I sat on the bed. I wanted to ask him about his experience with Lelane and Terra. How had it all happened? Did he enjoy the women's company?

What was wrong with me, why did I even care?

I let out a frustrated sigh. How different my life had become; a few weeks ago, I was planning battle strategies and organising hunting parties for the rebels, and now I had been reduced to what? An elf looking over her shoulder and getting jealous of a Guan spending time with other elves! After a few moments, Erik walked over to the wall next to the bed and, leaning against it, he slid down to a seated position.

"How is your new house Guan?" he asked, changing the subject, for which I was grateful.

"The situation is frustrating; he still cowers in my presence."

"Then you must do something for him to put his mind at ease," he told me. I could not hold back a laugh. His eyes lit up.

"You find that funny?"

"No, I find it funny that you are giving me advice on how

to treat my house Guan, but I am curious to hear your view, so continue."

"We are given good reason to fear your kind from a young age. Some of us are lucky to find masters that treat us well, others aren't so lucky." His tone turned serious as he looked at his hands again. For the first time, I really wondered what his life had been like; was he talking from experience, had he had a master who treated him badly?

"You are close to the end of life, are you not?" I asked him.

"I am twenty-nine years and nine months." It was another of our traditions and a way of keeping the Guan population in control. A slave was not allowed to mature past the age of thirty. It was thought that at this age, they had outlived their usefulness, never allowed to live beyond those years.

"You are to be terminated after your time here?" I confirmed. Saying nothing, he solemnly nodded.

"Then I am sorry that this is your last experience of life." I had never said I was sorry to anyone, let alone a Guan, but I looked at his situation and pitied him.

"I'm not sorry," he said, looking at me deeply with those crystal blue eyes again. Not knowing what to say, I stood up and walked over to the table and picked up the glass bottle full of red liquid.

"And you don't need to worry," he said to me before I poured the content through the gap in the brickwork.

"Worry about what?" I asked curiously.

"Even if someone did ask, I wouldn't tell them."

~*~

As I walked through my front door, I could not see or hear Castor, so I assumed he was in the room next to the kitchen. I walked upstairs towards my bed-chamber and went straight to bed, not bothering to remove my clothes. Laying down, I fell straight to sleep and dreamt.

I was standing at the door of room twenty-three, and inside I could hear the moans of someone in pleasure. I twisted the handle on the door and heard the latch lift, echoing as the door swung open in slow motion.

The room was exactly as I had seen it before with the small table holding a single candle. I looked over to the bed and saw Erik's huge naked body on top of a small naked woman. She was holding his arms, moaning as he rhythmically moved his hips, connecting their bodies.

Next to the bed I saw Terra standing, watching the two figures. As I walked towards her, she obviously had not heard me, her eyes never once looking in my direction. She just stood there, frozen, with her arms crossed and her gaze locked.

I walked past her towards the bed. I could not see their faces but could hear Lelane's quiet moaning as Erik's body kept moving down on top of her in slow movements.

Except, as I got closer and could see past Erik's broad shoulders, their faces came into my view, and I could see that it was not

Lelane under his naked body… it was me!

I gasped and woke up suddenly in a sweat. What was that all about? I put it down to my recent talk with Terra & Lelane, and the shock of realising they had recently taken part in the breeding programme with Erik.

Looking towards the window, the sunlight only just peeking through the curtains, I realised it was morning and I got out of bed. I thought about my last meeting with Erik and the advice he gave me regarding Castor. I needed to do something to put his mind at ease. In that moment, I thought of Tobias. 'That is it!' I thought to myself, realising I knew the answer on what to do.

I called for Castor, and after a few moments he appeared without making eye contact. Looking at his hands, I saw his fingers winding and twitching around each other, still clearly nervous in my presence.

"Run me a bath and fetch me some breakfast," I said. Just before he left, I added, "you will come out with me today, as I have someone very important to introduce you to." He looked at me, still clearly afraid but also curious, then swiftly turned to leave.

I walked over to my armour stand, and looked at my sword leaning against the wall. Stroking its handle, I thought about the last time it had been used. When I had struck down the woman who had tried to kill me, the woman who had killed Tobias. He had jumped in front of me, sacrificing his own life to save mine and, according to Erik, it was because he held affection for me. If that were true, then today I was going to do something for Castor, in memory of Tobias, and in doing so, I hoped it would put Castor at ease around me more.

Castor returned, placing down a bowl of fruit, then he slowly backed out of my room, turning to walk faster along the hall towards the bathroom. A few moments later, I heard him filling the bath.

After eating my breakfast and taking my bath, I got dressed. I donned my light armour and placed my big sword on my back. I might not be able to battle for the moment but walking through the city, I still wanted to look the part. Walking down the stairs towards my front door, I saw Castor waiting for me, his hands still twitching. This would be the first time he had left my house beside me, and he was clearly nervous of where I was taking him.

I walked out the door, looking to Castor, instructing him to follow, and continued down the smooth sandstone path. I was walking away from the larger buildings towards my destination, which just so happened to be towards the great city gate.

I looked behind me and smiled as I saw Castor; he was wide eyed, looking around in all directions. We soon reached our destination, and I lightly tapped Castor's shoulder, gesturing for him to look at the structure in front of us. It was the huge city stables. I continued to walk towards the stable entrance towards the posted guard. As I approached her, she saluted.

"Good morning General, are you going for a ride today?" clearly not everyone had yet heard about my restrictions to remain within the city.

"Not today, I am simply introducing my new house servant to my horse and giving him instruction on his care."

"Of course, step right through," said the guard, who was now looking rather menacingly at Castor.

"Come Castor," I ordered as I walked into the stables. When we both walked through, we could see a few slaves here already; some were mucking out stalls, others were moving hay. I continued until we reached the stall holding my horse.

"Castor, I would like you to meet Thio." I watched as the boy slowly walked forward towards my huge black horse. Castor looked so small in comparison, so much more like the child he was. I leaned over him, making him jump.

"You must not be nervous Castor, horses can sense your fear, it makes them agitated and unpredictable. A kick from a horse can be lethal," I said looking down at him. Opening the gate, I stepped towards my horse Thio, smiling while gently stroking his nose.

"Grab that brush and stool and come over to meet him properly." He did as I instructed, and walked nervously into the stall, placing the stool next to me, and then he stepped onto it. Thanks to his assisted height, he was almost as tall as me now, and for the first time I could see his features better.

He had small lips but huge innocent looking, pale green eyes. He looked at me and then back to Thio as he lifted the brush and started stroking it down the horse's hair.

"All you need is patience and a bit of understanding, he will soon come to trust you, and you won't need to be so nervous around him," I said to Castor quietly. He stopped and looked at me.

I gave him further instructions to keep his stall clean, give him fresh food, water and brush his fur, telling him he was to do this every morning after serving my breakfast. Castor nodded that he understood, and with that, I left him to better acquaint himself with Thio, without me watching. As I left the stables, I hoped that Castor would understand the lesson I was trying to teach him. I wanted him to put those same principles I spoke of towards me, to not be afraid and trust that no harm would come to him as long as he performed his duty.

He did not need to attend to my horse every morning, we had stable boys for that, but I thought it might help him. Tobias had always been at ease around my horse. He would often stroke his nose, and whisper into Thio's ear, like he had done the day of his death.

Chapter 8

WEEK SIX

I was at another council meeting, with the queen addressing us on some urgent business.

"We have heard rumours of a woman in the outer edges of the city, who gives aid to the rebels and may know something about their hidden base beyond the sand cliffs," she relayed to us. "What action would you advise we take?"

"Simple," said Peril. "Have the woman strung up and beaten until she tells us all she knows."

"And what if she's innocent?" replied Acqueline. "After all, they are just rumours, we don't know if she knows anything about the rebels."

"Then we send someone to talk with her, find out what she knows," I replied.

"And who will we send?" Queen Cassandra responded. "Captain Imelda is out on a scouting mission with our best warriors." Well, this was certainly news to me. I thought I had made it clear to Imelda that she was to check in with me regularly before making important decisions, like going on scouting missions. Speaking up, I looked directly at Queen Cassandra.

"Allow me my Queen. A visit from the General of Kven will intimidate the woman enough to let me know if she has secrets to hide, and if she does, I will learn them." The queen smiled, clearly liking that idea, until Freyja interrupted.

"Don't forget my Queen, that General Truda has begun the breeding programme and therefore is excluded from these types of tasks." Freyja gave me a menacing smile, knowing the idea that I could not perform the simplest of missions for my queen would make me angry, which it did.

"Then how about I take the twins?" I added, raising my voice. "That way they can carry out your orders, but I will be there to supervise and add impact to the situation." I finished, raising my chin, looking up towards the queen, ignoring Freyja's or anyone else's glances. I did not need permission or approval from them.

"Very well Truda, take your young warriors to the edge of the city and find out what you can about this woman."

I chose this moment to look towards Freyja. She looked like she had just bitten her own tongue. As she turned to look at me, I gave her a coy, triumphant smile.

"Now, moving on to the second part of today's agenda," said the queen. She looked towards the empty chair where her daughter was supposed to sit and then turned to Acqueline.

"How is my daughters training coming along?" Queen Cassandra asked, her face a picture of concern.

"Her training sessions are coming along nicely my Queen," replied Acqueline, clearly not wanting to tell her that Princess Callidice continues to hardly ever turned up for training, and when she did, she was disinterested. "With your permission, I have asked Truda, to come supervise. I wanted her input on how I could improve our training sessions," Acqueline added whilst looking to me.

"Of course," the queen replied. "General Truda has already mentioned this to me, and I certainly see nothing wrong in that," she smiled, then turned towards Freyja. "And how are the princess's private studies coming along?" I was shocked to hear this news. Why was Princess Callidice getting private lessons from that snake of a woman?

"She is a quick study my Queen, attending every session eager to absorb all the knowledge of our histories and legends," said Freyja, looking up excitedly towards the queen. She did not make eye contact with me as I glared at her from across the table.

"Then if there is nothing else to discuss, we shall meet again in a week," Queen Cassandra said, addressing all of us. With that, she rose from her chair, slower than usual, using the chair arms for support as she lifted her body from her seat. We all signalled the salute of respect as she nodded then left through her private entrance.

I watched as Freyja quickly got out of her chair and turned to leave. Swiftly, I followed her out of the throne room. Before she could get too far, I grabbed her arm and pulled her back, pinning her against the wall.

"Why are you giving the princess private studies?" I asked calmly as my hand pinned her chest to the wall, grateful that she did not have Jetta on her shoulders who may have been tempted to peck at my fingers.

"None of your business, warrior," she spat.

Grabbing a clump of the material on her top, I pulled her towards me slightly, then pushed back harder so that she hit the back of her head against the stone wall.

"You will tell me!" I added sternly, making Freyja briefly wince, then glare at me.

"If you must know, the queen came to me and told me that she was struggling with passing on her instruction to the princess," she retorted, straightening herself from the wall, brushing down her clothes as I let her go. "I simply suggested that perhaps the princess needed to hear these things from a different perspective and offered to take the queens place as instructor of the histories."

"And why did you lie about the princess's attendance?" I

added, taking a step back and crossing my arms.

"Oh, I didn't lie. I know the princess has not been attending her training sessions with Acqueline, but she comes to me most days," she finished with a smile.

"Then on your next session, you will teach the princess the importance of being able to fight and defend herself. If she does not, I will go to the queen and tell her that your words of poison have stopped her from becoming the strong warrior she is meant to be." Freyja looked shocked for a second, almost as though she was worried of what would happen if I did.

"Why of course, I would never deprive the princess of any kind of knowledge," Freyja added, pursing her lips. Under her breath she muttered, "even if it that knowledge is how to wave a pointy stick."

"You will find that pointy sticks can be quite effective when used with enough force," I added. I wanted her to feel threatened, and although she did not act scared, I could clearly see she was taking tiny steps back from me, keeping her distance.

"I'm sure they can," she said, whilst quickly saluting and walking away from me. I needed to find a way to keep an eye on her I thought, she was clearly up to something with the princess. It was tradition for the queen to instruct her in our ways and teach her the histories. It seemed odd that Freyja had now taken over that role. Acqueline stepped around from the corner.

"Well, I have to admit Tru, that all sounded a bit suspicious to me," she said, standing next to me whilst also folding her arms, matching my stance. We watched as Freyja's figure seemed to slither off into the distance.

"We need to keep an eye on her Acqueline, there is something strange going on, and you were right about the queen, she does not look herself."

"Agreed," she replied. "Shall I arrange one of the royal guards to follow and watch Freyja?"

"Not yet, I do not want to raise suspicion, we just need to keep a close eye on things, especially for the princess and queen's welfare."

"That I can do," she replied in a much cheerier tone, then asked, "I am due to train the princess again the day after tomorrow, will you join us?"

"Of course, besides it is not like I am going to have anything better to do these days," I sighed.

"Oh, cheer up Tru, the queen granted your quest today, didn't she?" A smile spread across my lips as I nodded and began to walk down the corridor. Acqueline followed and we continued to make small talk until we parted ways from the palace. Acqueline was right, I would always be able to find ways to make myself useful; my position in the city was too important for me not to be. Besides, I would not have to wait up to a full year like everyone thought I would.

I only had to wait another six weeks.

~*~

Later that day, I collected the twins from the Training House and took them with me to the outer edges of the city. As it was a much longer journey, too long for a casual walk, we decided to go by horse and carriage. The twins talked quietly to each other while I sat silently opposite them, looking out the window. Glancing over to the twins, I smiled. Physically they were almost identical, but as I had learned over the last year, they were very different in character.

Shanor was more excitable and talkative. She was faster than her sister but not as strong, she was also the sweeter one, with a caring and tentative nature.

Shanon was the tougher of the two, slightly stronger built and much more reserved; I saw a lot of myself in Shanon. She sometimes had a short temper and would act before thinking.

Both had become somewhat understudies of mine and I liked playing the role of mentor. They had lost their mother during childbirth and had been raised by the women of the royal guard. They had joined the queen's army just over a year ago and I had taken a liking to them from day one.

I looked back out the carriage window, watching the large buildings slowly turn into smaller ones, now seeing the beginnings of our fields of crops and flowers, noticing the occasional Guan with baskets, harvesting fruit and flowers. The closer to the castle you lived, the more important you must be, although looking at the much smaller sparse houses now surrounded by sheets of green, I thought how much of a blessing it must be to be a nobody. To not be important enough to be forced into breeding the next generation.

"Are you worried about our quest?" Shanor asked me. I looked at her and realised I had must have been frowning as I lost myself in my own thoughts.

"Actually no, I think it is more likely we will discover the rumours were false," I replied. I was not lying, we had heard rumours before, and they usually amounted to nothing.

"What if we find out they aren't rumours, but the woman won't speak?" asked Shanor.

"Then we simply punch the answers out of her," replied Shanon, while slamming a fist into the palm of her other hand, displaying a wicked grin. I nodded towards Shanon with a smile, because she was right; if the woman was found hiding something, then the chances of her getting a beating were high. A few moments later, we stepped out of the carriage and looked at our destination.

It was a stone farmhouse situated right next to a lavender field. It looked so peaceful and the fragrance of the flowers was wonderful. My favourite scent, bringing back thoughts of my lavender baths, something I had not experienced since Tobias's death. Realising now that he must have known lavender was my favourite, perhaps he really did care for me.

Pulling myself back from distracting thoughts of sentiment,

I looked at the twins and then tilted my head towards the front door. They were taking the lead on this one, I was here merely to intimidate as a known authoritative figure. They walked ahead of me, and Shanor knocked heavily three times on the wooden door. A woman with long strawberry hair tied into a side plait opened the door and looked at us.

"Can I help you?" she asked, her eyes widening when she saw me, clearly recognising who I was. "General, I apologise, please come in, you and your warriors are welcome, of course."

The twins followed the woman inside the house, and I remained close behind them. Inside was well furnished with an open plan kitchen and living area. In the corner were bare wooden stairs that I guessed would take you to the bedroom and bathroom. Glancing over the woman, I briefly eyed her appearance. She was not wearing anything fancy or luxurious, not even anything with colour. Just plain hide trousers and an armless top, with a light dusting of flour across the front. The smell of fresh baked dough filled the house. I walked over to the large dining table and took a chair, the twins looked at me as if asking for permission. I simply nodded once.

"So, you live alone?" asked Shanor.

"Yes," replied the woman. "Can I ask what this is about?" she asked, dusting her hands on her top to remove the remainder of the flour between her fingers. Shanor paced around the room, touching things with vague interest. Shanon stood, staring at the woman. They were trying to intimidate her, and it was clearly working as she kept looking nervously between the twins and me.

"The palace has heard some rumours about someone in this area providing aid to the rebels," said Shanon, not moving from her spot.

"I don't know anything about the rebels. I don't get involved in such things," said the woman nervously, beads of sweat breaking from the elf's forehead. I looked at her puzzlingly; was she nervous because of the twins? Or was she hiding something?

"So, you don't know anything about a hidden rebel base?" Shanor pressed on.

At this, the woman laughed saying, "why would I?"

I closed my eyes briefly, knowing she should not have laughed as I saw instantly the moment Shanon's face turned to pure rage. She charged at the woman, pushed her against the wall and held a dagger to her throat,

"You find this a laughing matter?" Shanon spat into her face.

"Please, I meant no disrespect," said the woman in a shaky voice, holding up her arms to show she was no threat.

"I am sure the woman speaks the truth," said Shanor, now placing a hand on her sister's shoulder.

"She better be, or I will gladly return with this very blade and cut all the way through her neck," Shanon said with a menacing grin, still looking at the woman.

"Enough," I said, standing from my chair. "It is time to leave," I told them. This was another dead end. She did not know anything, and we were wasting our time. The twins nodded towards me as I started to leave. Shanor stepped away and came to me, whereas Shanon took one last glare at the woman, still holding the dagger to her throat. I turned and left, stepping back inside the carriage and waiting for the twins to join me. A few moments later, they both climbed into the carriage and once again sat opposite me.

"Well, that wasn't exactly fruitful," said Shanor with a sigh.

"We should've questioned her further," said Shanon.

"She didn't know anything," argued Shanor.

"But she was sweating and twitching. I think she was hiding something," said Shanon. I was inclined to agree with Shanon. Something did not seem right in the farmhouse, everything was too neat and organised for someone of her stature, and she looked far too nervous, but I kept these thoughts to myself, knowing it was better to wait for a greater opportunity to present itself. We would have ample time to question the woman again if new evidence came to light.

"I think it is entirely possible that she was terrified of you two," I said with a slight giggle.

"Do you think we did okay?" asked Shanor.

"I think I did not need to come along for intimidation purposes, because you two questioning her together was the most threatening thing I have seen in a long time." Hearing me say this, the twins locked arms with beaming smiles, clearly happy to receive my compliment.

~*~

When we returned to the centre of the city, I said goodbye to the twins and headed to the palace, wanting to catch up with the queen and give her a report. I told her about the woman at the farmhouse, that I believed the rumours were false and she did not know anything. I told her how well the twins had acted, how fierce and intimidating they had been.

Later that day, I found myself mostly wandering the house considering what to do with my time. After eating some food and changing my clothes, I walked towards the Breeding House. I did not know if it was my imagination, but Castor seemed less nervous around me. He twiddled with his fingers less, and barely stuttered on his words, and when I spoke to him giving him instruction, I was almost positive he nodded and smiled. I was looking forward to telling Erik, finding myself walking faster than usual towards the Breeding House. When I entered, I smiled at Peril who greeted me as she always did.

"General, it is good to see you," she said. "However, I am afraid I have some bad news."

"What is it?" I asked, frowning with my arms crossed.

"Slave number twenty-three was punished today for going against orders. I am afraid he may not be able to perform.

Would you like to return another night?" she asked me.

"That will not be necessary Peril, I will just take my potion and key if you please." I held out a hand, eager to get to the room as soon as possible to find out what had happened.

"Of course," she replied, handing me my items and saluted as I turned away from her. After looking back to check I was far enough from sight, I quickened my pace. Reaching the room, I quickly unlocked the door, walked in and locked it behind me.

"Erik?" I called. I could not see him at first, then I heard the movement of his chains coming from the shadows at the other end of the room.

"Stand before me," I demanded, getting frustrated he was hiding in the darkness. He walked forward, and from the expression on his face, I knew he was in a great deal of pain. I looked down at his body as he approached but could not see a mark. Looking confused, I waited until he reached me, then he dropped to his knees.

At first, I still could not see anything as he faced me, not able to look up, then I saw a small patch of blood on his shoulder. Walking around him, I gasped as I saw his back.

Lash marks.

He had at least a dozen deep lash marks, criss-crossing his back. Beneath them were more marks. Some were pink, some were much older and had now become white scars; he had been lashed before, many times it seemed. Erik reached out his hands towards my leg and then fell to the floor, passing out from the pain. Placing the items on the table, I grabbed a cushion from the bed, and immediately walked back towards Erik.

I knelt down and gently lifted his head, placing the cushion underneath. Using my fingers, I moved the hair from his face; he looked so innocent lying there unmoving as my eyes rose to his back. I felt anger, instantly wishing I was in the coliseum right now with whoever decided to dish out this cruel punishment. Rising to my feet, I walked back to the table and collected my items. I left the room, locking it behind me, and stormed down the corridor towards Peril, thrusting the items towards her.

"You are right, the slave is useless tonight, I will return tomorrow."

~*~

The next night, I returned with a healing kit that I had snuck out from the Training House. They never searched me when I entered, clearly only concerned for weaponry.

After greeting Peril, she saluted, and I turned, walking down the corridor to the room. As I walked through the door, Erik was still slumped on the floor. He had not moved from the position I left him in, making me wince.

Hearing me enter, he looked up in surprise

"You're not supposed to be here today," he said, as he tried resting his body on his forearms so that he could see me better, hissing from the pain he was in as he moved. Leaving the items on the table, I walked over to him and bent down grabbing his arm.

"What are you doing?" he rasped as I slowly helped him to his knees and put his arm around my shoulder.

"I am helping you," I said as I used my enhanced strength to help lift him carefully off the floor. He inhaled sharply as he struggled to get to his feet. Then, as he caught his breath from the pain, he murmured, "why?"

"Because, despite what you think, we are not all monsters. Now come, let me help you to the bed." Taking most of his weight as we slowly stepped towards the bed, I did not look at him but instead concentrated on where we were headed. In the corner of my eye, I could see him looking at me.

"Lie face down," I said, nodding towards the bed, removing his arm from around my shoulder but keeping hold of it so I could still help him. He climbed on the bed to lay down, his feet hanging off the end as I studied his injuries.

Looking just as bad as I had remembered, the thick gashes ran from his shoulders down to his hips. They had not healed much, except the blood had dried and the skin had swollen. They looked so deep I was surprised I could not see bone. He would need stitches I thought. Perhaps I should have called for a healer, or someone like Lelane to come and help, but what would they think of me showing such thoughtfulness for a slave? No, I would have to do this myself.

Looking around the room, seeing a small bowl of water and some cloths in the opposite corner on a chair, I walked over and grabbed them, I would use them to help clean up his wounds. Sitting carefully at the edge of the bed, I paused a moment, asking myself if I was really capable of doing this, knowing that I had no other choice but to try.

"I have brought some things to heal you, but it is going to hurt," I told him. He tilted his head to look back at me and simply nodded. Opening my kit, I pulled out the ointments, lotions and finally the thread and needle. It was time to get to work.

Chapter 9

WEEK SEVEN

The next session that followed, I returned with more healing lotion. I was impressed with what I had done. Perhaps once this was all over, I would opt for some healer training as it could not hurt to get a bit more experience under my belt. As I entered, I saw Erik leaning sideways against the wall. After locking the door and placing my items on the table, I turned to look at him.

"Sit on the bed," I instructed. Erik moved and sat on the bed facing away from me. After pulling out a tin from the pocket of my trousers, I walked over and sat behind him. His back still looked terrible, but it was much better than before. I was confident that his wounds would heal nicely but would still need plenty of ointment to help with the healing process.

"This will sting but it will help you heal faster," I said while removing the lid. I placed my fingers in the lotion that was inside.

"Couldn't hurt more than the stitches," he replied. His speech was much better today, meaning his pain must have lessened.

I reached my hand up and carefully began to massage the lotion onto his back. At first, he jumped and tensed his shoulders with a hiss on his breath. Looking down at his hand, he grabbed the edge of the bed, his knuckles turning white as he squeezed tightly. I continued to work my fingers, moving slowly and gently so as to cause as little pain as possible.

"Tell me what happened," I said, trying to distract him from the pain.

"A younger worker had been caught stealing food," he told me. "He was being lashed and I knew he couldn't take anymore, so I stood in front of his master to protect him." I pictured Erik standing tall in front of someone like Castor to protect them from punishment. "The other worker was spared, and I was to take double the number of lashings in his place."

"Well, from the looks of your back that is something you do often," I said in a disapproving tone, still lightly massaging the lotion onto his wounds. His grip on the bed frame relaxed, and I realised it must be the lotions numbing ability along with its healing.

"Ten years ago, I got into trouble with a guard. I challenged her, and I was punished with lashings. However, during my punishment the guard got carried away and continued to lash me, clearly enjoying herself. I was close to passing out from the pain when another elf approached her. Commanding her to stop, that she had taken it too far, the guard was relieved of her duty. She was a captain, the one that saved me, and I would remember her face for years to come. Although, she would not know me. Not until six weeks ago."

He glanced around towards me. I had stopped what I was doing, frozen in the memory of that day, and the flashback immediately entered my mind.

It was a beautiful morning during a hot summer month. I was on my way to meet with Acqueline for a sparring session, one I was not particularly looking forward to due to the heat.

Walking through the city, I saw a crowd of people gathered in the open square where our market opened their stalls for the early morning trade. The streets were bustling with elves.

I headed towards the crowd to find out what was attracting the mass, and that is when I saw it. A Guan covered in blood, barely able to sit up on his knees, while a guard dealt out lashings as punishment across his back. She cracked her whip and I watched as the leather sliced into the Guan's skin, splitting it open like a knife cutting through bread. He screamed in pain.

"This is what you get for stepping out of place Guan!" she shouted through his cries. I stepped forward through the crowd, pushing myself past the bodies that had gathered around the scene.

Another lash followed by another scream of pain. I looked at the guard and she was smiling as she prepared her arm for the next lash. The Guan was huddled in a half kneeling, cradled position, his back shredded beyond being able to see the colour of his skin. Whatever he had done wrong, he had received his punishment, this was now pure cruelty.

"Stop!" I shouted as I stepped forward and walked towards the guard. Pausing mid flow of her next strike, she looked at me perplexed.

"Captain Truda? Is there a problem?" she said, confused at why I had stopped her.

"I think you are done. This Guan has clearly received his punishment, so I suggest you take your leave."

"Captain, I am merely punishing a Guan." She smirked, finding my comment humorous. I stepped closer to her so that I could speak quietly, not wanting the crowd to hear.

"Actually, you are embarrassing yourself. A crowd has gathered here to watch you and your obvious twisted enjoyment at causing pain," I whispered in a stern tone, looking towards the elves who were all glaring at us both. She looked past me at the crowd, then towards the Guan, then back at me. Dropping her whip, she spoke.

"Of course, Captain, you are right. I apologise for my behaviour." She signalled the salute of respect and walked off, passing through the crowd, not once looking back at me.

Looking over towards the Guan, I saw two other slaves step

116

forward and begin helping him to his feet. They paused when they caught me looking. I nodded to them in approval, and as they stepped forward and each took an arm to help carry him. For a split second, I saw the injured Guan look towards me.

Now, here I was with that same Guan, healing him of another lashing punishment.

"I remember that day. I am sorry that you received a punishment so cruel, it should never have happened," I told Erik, who was looking back at me with curious and innocent eyes. We paused for a moment, just looking at each other.

"Thank you for helping me. Not just now, but all those years ago," Erik said kindly, looking intently into my eyes.

"You are welcome." I looked away, feeling confused and embarrassed at his gratefulness. Ignoring his gaze, I continued to focus on rubbing the ointment onto his injured skin.

~*~

For the rest of my time that week at the Breeding House, I continued to take in lotions and ointments to help with his healing. He would tell me stories of his years as a slave while I used my hands to massage lotions into his back. I would tell him stories of my battles against the rebels. It was not long before I discovered he loved listening to my stories, the excitement, the danger, always asking more questions. I was scheduled to see him that night, and I realised I was looking forward to it.

It was morning and I was heading to the Training House, as promised, to help with the princess's training. When I arrived, Acqueline was already there, moving some weapons around and placing some human shaped targets into the centre of the courtyard; she obviously had some structure to her lesson.

"She's already late," said Acqueline in frustration. "I am hoping she will at least bother to show up today after your threat to Freyja."

"And I meant it," I replied. Just then, the princess walked in, and followed closely behind her was a Guan. He was quite well built, not as large as Erik, but he looked strong. He had kind facial features and short blonde hair. I had seen him a few times before, her newly acquired pet. Sometimes he was on a leash, sitting beside her on his knees at council meetings; the ones she could be bothered to attend. He did not appear to be on a lead today as he slumped behind her, keeping his head to the floor.

"Let's make today quick Acqueline, I have better places to be," she said in her spoilt tone, looking at Acqueline. She had not yet seen me, and as I stepped into her view, I saw the surprise on her face.

"And what better places are those?"

"General Truda, what are you doing here?" she said, looking annoyed.

"I am here to assist with your training, Princess Callidice."

"I don't need your assistance; I am doing just fine with

Acqueline."

"Then you show me. Pick up a sword," I challenged.

"What!" she coughed out as a pretend laugh. "You're not serious. I'm not fighting you."

"And why not? If you do not need my assistance, then prove it. If you can cut me once, I will leave you to your training with Acqueline and will not interrupt your sessions again," I said, keeping my face straight and serious.

"Fine," she said whilst stomping over to collect a sword from the rack. I looked over to Acqueline who was smiling at me. She knew the princess could not beat me and was about to learn a hard lesson.

Princess Callidice walked further into the courtyard, turning and raising her sword as a signal she had accepted my challenge. Walking towards her, I pulled my sword from my back and waited for her to make the first move. She lunged at me hopelessly, stumbling over her own steps as I stepped back to avoid her swing. She repeated this pointless process, swinging and stepping, and I kept dancing around her as she kept missing.

The sword she had selected was clearly too heavy for her and every time she swung it, she would step and stumble like a child who had just learned how to walk. As I let her frustration build, I waited for the next swing. This time, instead of stepping out of the way, I lifted my sword to hit hers. With my strength behind my sword, I pushed, making her stumble but not fall. Then, thrusting my sword towards her, I grazed the blade along her arm, leaving a shallow cut.

"Ahhhh!" she screamed in anger. "You can't do that! I will tell my mother," she snarled at me, dropping the sword and wrapping her hand around her injured arm.

"Please do," I said, putting my sword on my back and crossing my arms. She looked at me with a shocked expression.

"Go tell the queen about your graze, and I will tell her it happened because you do not attend your training, and fight like a baby," I added.

"I don't fight like a baby!" she shouted. "I just don't like using swords. Here, I will prove it." Princess Callidice walked over to the weapons rack and picked up a batch of small knives.

Walking back towards one of the stuffed targets, she threw one knife, hitting it in the chest area, then looked back at me, hoping for a reaction. Of course, I did not display one, keeping my stoic expression. Did she think I would be impressed?

"Not good enough?" she asked. "Then how about I demonstrate using a different object as my target, a real life one perhaps." An evil grin spread across her face.

"Phoenyx!" she called. Her Guan walked nervously towards the princess and bowed his head. "Go and stand over there," she pointed at a nearby pillar.

Phoenyx looked up at the princess as if he was about to plead, but then looked down and walked forward, standing still in front of the pillar.

Princess Callidice threw the first knife and it landed in the wooden pillar next to Phoenyx's right arm. She threw another one and it landed close to his left ear. Phoenyx was looking down to the floor, trembling with fear, flinching every time a knife landed near him. The princess threw another knife, and Phoenyx yelped in pain as the blade hit him, landing right at the top of his thigh. Princess Callidice walked towards me, tilting her head up so she could look at my face.

"Now I think I've proven my point," she said quietly. "So, I don't ever want to see you at my training sessions again!" she spat at me and turned to walk away.

"Actually princess, I would not count on that," I replied. She stopped and turned towards me, her eyes glaring with anger.

"Because if that poor demonstration showed me anything, it is that it took you three attempts to hit an unmoving target." Acqueline burst into laughter, making me smile in response.

Princess Callidice looked at me as though she wished she could melt me to death with her eyes. She stormed out of the room, shouting at Phoenyx who was struggling to follow her while limping. After they left, Acqueline approached and placed a hand on my shoulder

"I've got to hand it to you Tru, I don't think I would've had the courage to do that."

"Do what? I barely grazed her."

"No, but you definitely humiliated her, probably for the first time in her life," she laughed.

~*~

I was in room number twenty-three, sitting on the bed with Erik. I noticed him shuffling about, trying to get into a more comfortable seated position around his chains.

"Is your master cruel to you?" I asked.

"My old master was cruel. She owned quite a few of us and helped organise the repairs on the city. When we outgrew our usefulness, she sent us away to other areas. My friend and I got separated on the same day. He was sold to some secret organisation and I was sent here, to be locked away in this room, until you got me outside again." It surprised me that Erik had a friend. I always looked at slaves as loners, not able to connect with anyone.

"Who was your friend?" I asked him.

"His name was Nyx. He was a few years younger than me and I looked out for him."

"Against your master you mean?" I asked.

"Not just the masters, sometimes slaves could be cruel, picking on the younger and weaker ones." Well, I knew that would not likely apply to Erik. No slave was going to pick on a man of his size.

"Wait, earlier you said your old master was cruel?" I stated, looking at him confused.

"That's because I have a new master now, but I'm not sure about her yet," he said with a smile. I could not help but stare, his face was more beautiful when he smiled. In that moment, I instantly wished I could see it more.

"Do I know your new master?" I said, clearly playing into his hands as he replied.

"Yes."

"You are referring to me." I realised, looking down briefly.

"And you are not sure about me yet?" I asked, meeting his gaze and making him laugh. "Erik, I am not your master, I have just been paired with you for a short time," I frowned with a sigh. For some reason, I did not want him to refer to me as a master. After what I had seen today with Phoenyx and thinking about all the punishments that Erik had gone through, masters were cruel, and I did not want him to think of me like that.

"If you're not my master, then what are you?" he asked. I did not know what to say as my reply, deciding after a moment of silence to change the subject with other small talk. I asked Erik what he had been doing during the daylight hours, noticing again as he shuffled his position to get comfortable sitting with his chains.

Shortly after, I left room twenty-three. Leaving Erik's intimate question unanswered, I returned to Peril, who was situated behind her sign in pedestal.

"I want the chains removed from the Guan in room number twenty-three. I will not be needing them for my sessions," I told Peril, while returning the key and empty glass vial.

"General Truda, I don't think that is wise. I understand the chains may be inconvenient, but you are paired with a large Guan, a known troublemaker. The chains are in place for your protection," replied Peril, nervously.

"I think we can all agree that I am in no danger, especially where a single Guan is concerned." I stated, showing my annoyance of her unwelcome concern for my safety.

"Of course, General, my apologies. I will see that it's done," she nodded politely. I left the building, feeling satisfied with the knowledge that I would no longer have to watch Erik struggle with the weight of those chains.

Chapter 10

WEEK EIGHT

I was in the Training House one morning; it was so early outside it was still dark. Not long after, Acqueline entered, clearly having the same idea as me of an early morning workout. We decided to spar together, going hand to hand as we wrestled around the room, dancing. That is if you considered dancing a form of trying to hit each other with our fists or kicking each other to the floor. Afterwards, we both leaned against pillars, drinking water and catching our breath.

"I'm not on duty until later. I was thinking of walking the wall, would you like to accompany me? Unless you have more important things to do?" she asked.

"Actually, that sounds like a great idea," I replied. Spending some time with Acqueline would do me some good, help clear my mind. I always liked walking along the wall of the city, you could see the green valleys of lush grass. Beyond that, you could see the great and vast desert and finally, in the furthest distance, your eyes could just make out the mountains.

"If we hurry, we'll see the rising sun, and what better place to witness the beautiful start to the day than on the wall?" Acqueline chimed.

Walking along the wall we reminisced about old battles and childhood memories; a time long before my responsibility as General weighed so heavily on my shoulders, or the conflicting emotions I was beginning to have about the treatment of a certain Guan.

When we stopped to rest, we sat on the wall edge like we used to do as children and looked over the beautiful city of Kven. From here you could see most of the buildings surrounding the palace, the wooden Training House standing out in contrast to the rest.

I could see the temple clearly from here, it was the fourth largest structure, its huge domed roof of sparkling gold that reflected the sun. Within it housed the Great Library, and many rooms where the mages could practice their magic. It even had living quarters for the women, so they very rarely had to leave their dwelling.

"Have you seen much of Freyja?" I asked Acqueline.

"Not much, although the queen tells me the princess is

still attending all her lessons with her." That made me angry, the thought of what that foul witch was teaching the young princess.

"What's it like?" Acqueline asked.

"What is what like?"

"Being in the breeding programme," she asked, and I looked at her confused.

"Why? Are you thinking about signing up?"

"Not yet, but I suppose one day I might apply, and wondered what it's like," she said, while we looked over the city.

"It can be difficult," I replied. "Not being able to fulfil my duties at full capacity, it is boring, sometimes I struggle with what to fill my days with."

"Tru, I didn't mean that. I meant what is it like to, you know, do 'the act' with a human Guan?" she asked me, now studying my face.

"Acqueline, that is not really something I want to talk about."

"Of course, I understand," she said, clearly a little disappointed. Even if she wanted me to open up and share my experience, I would not know what to say, as I had never actually performed 'the act' in the Breeding House.

"Well, at least tell me what the Guan is like," she replied. I laughed at her clear determination to get information out of me.

"He is very big and strong, probably the largest I have

ever seen," I replied.

"Well, it makes sense that they would pair the strongest warrior with the most impressive of them," she nodded. "Gosh Tru, think how big and strong your daughter will probably be, I can't wait to train her." Excitement sparkled in her eyes.

"I think you are getting ahead of yourself here, I am not even pregnant yet. Besides, if someone was going to train her, I think that would be me, you know, considering I am the strongest warrior," I teased. We both laughed, deciding to walk down from the walls edge and walk street level. I felt slightly guilty for teasing Acqueline about training a daughter that I knew I would never have. She had seemed genuinely excited for me.

As we walked by the wall on ground level, we could see some workers repairing a section up ahead. It did not take me long to recognise Erik.

At first, I was surprised seeing him outside of the Breeding House, but of course thanks to my meddling, I had ensured that he could still come out and work during the day. He was certainly the largest, lifting a stone bigger than my chest plate, sweating from the work.

His huge muscles were solid and ridged from moving the weight. I watched as he lifted the stone and threw it in a cart before walking over to the damaged wall to collect another piece.

"Looks like they are finally repairing the top of the east

wall," Acqueline said. Part of the wall had crumbled a few weeks earlier during a construction incident, a few Guans were crushed and had been lost. I pretended to look, taking an interest in the structure of the wall, but as we got closer, I could not help but watch Erik. When he turned and saw me, our eyes locked, stopping what he was doing. A strange wave of panic overcame me, as thoughts of him getting caught not working entered my mind.

"Is that him?" Acqueline asked curiously.

"Yes" I replied, looking away from the wall.

"You're right Tru, he is huge, the biggest Guan I've ever seen," she said in astonishment. I did not reply. As we walked forward past the workers, Acqueline did not seem to take much of an interest and soon changed the subject.

~*~

Later, when I got to the Breeding House, I was furious. I stormed into the room, and Erik, who was sitting on the floor, looked up and smiled.

"Do not do that," I said to him sternly. He looked at me confused.

"Do what?"

I glared at him.

"Do not look at me like we are friends," I snapped.

"You are angry with me?"

"Of course I am angry with you, you should not have

looked at me like that in public." I yelled. He watched me pacing back and forth in the room.

"I will not get caught because of your stupidity, do you understand? You are a Guan, used for building work and breeding." We were lucky that only Acqueline noticed the looks shared between us when I had walked past him earlier that day. In my position I had no doubt that I was being watched by someone who was clearly reporting back to the palace. What I did not know was whether that person was just someone from the Breeding House, or if all of my movements were being watched.

"Then use me."

"What did you say?" I stepped towards him and he stood from the floor. Even though I was a tall elf, he was easily almost a foot taller than me and standing this close I had to look up slightly to see his face.

"I said use me, if I am just a Guan to you, in this room for one purpose," he said, looking down at my face. We stayed like this for a moment, challenging each other, at a stand-off.

"You think you can talk to me like that because I have spoken to you a few times?" I glared at him.

"I think we both know there is more to it than that," he said, stepping closer.

"You are forgetting your place," I said as I took a step back and turned away.

"Like you have forgotten yours?" he countered. Anger

washed over me. I turned and grabbed him by the throat, shoving him back against the wall. I could feel him trying to struggle from my grip, but I was strong, and he was still weak from his injuries. Our breathing was heavy from mutual fury and we glared at each other.

I had never felt anger build up inside me so quickly. What was it about him that made me lose my focus, made me behave out of character? I should never have spoken to him or asked him his name. I had taken things too far, made him feel comfortable in my presence, comfortable enough to challenge me, and I could not bring myself to punish him for it. Did I care about his well-being?

I loosened my grip, moving my hand away from him slowly as he gazed into my eyes. In that moment, I felt my anger drain, disappear and change into something else, something new. I felt nervous as my breathing became heavy and I could feel my heartbeat in my throat. I inhaled his musky scent, moving my hand down gently to touch the chest that I had been staring at for weeks. I just wanted to feel his skin, just once. Was it soft? Was it smooth? Was it warmed from a day working in the sun?

Staring at my hand as I placed it onto his chest, right above where his heart would be, I felt the vibrations from his pounding heart, and my fingers spread as my hand pressed more firmly onto his body. I looked up at him. I should take my hand away and leave, I told myself, knowing as I looked into his perplexed eyes, that what I was doing was wrong. I slowly dropped my hand, leaving my fingers to linger a moment longer before removing my contact. I left his gaze and started to turn away. Suddenly, Erik stepped forward, grabbed my face with both hands and roughly pressed his lips to mine.

Shocked, as I heard a moan escape from my own lips, my hands rushed to trace the lines of his firm chest. He deepened his kiss as his tongue met mine, kissing me more softly, like the urgency had faded and he was now trying to savour the taste of my lips. I dug my fingers into him as I instinctively pressed my body forward against his.

Wait, what am I doing?

"Stop!" I yelled and pushed myself away from him. "How dare you touch me!" He did not say anything but just looked at me with a shocked expression, still breathing heavily. Was he surprised at his own actions, or was he surprised that I pulled away?

"You might be experienced in things that happen in this room, but I have made myself very clear that I want no part in it," I said. I thought about his lips and hands on Lelane, and instantly felt angry again. Why did this get to me so much? He is just a Guan, and this meant nothing. Looking at him harshly up and down, I stormed out of the room.

~*~

I did not return the next night as I was scheduled, instead I

132

sent Castor to pass on a message that I was not feeling well. Of course, this resulted in a healer turning up at my house. They checked me over, examined me, taking my temperature and performing the blood test to see if I was pregnant, confirming a negative result. In the end I got rid of them by telling them all I needed was to be left alone and allowed to rest.

Once they had gone, I sat on the bed. The truth was, I had avoided going to the Breeding House because of Erik. Feeling confused, during our last argument, I had tried to put him in his place by telling him he was nothing but a slave. I had not been angry in fear of getting caught looking at him, I was afraid that Erik would get punished for looking at me. Thinking of those large scars all across his back, I did not want him to suffer because of me.

Images of his scars haunted my thoughts.

What I had not expected was for him to challenge the status of our relationship. Worst of all, I knew he was right. In the last few weeks, we had gone beyond the relationship of master and slave, but what did that make us, friends?

Why had he kissed me? Why did I kiss him back?

All I knew was that I had started to look forward to our time together and tonight, I wished I had gone. When I first entered the breeding programme, I had been shocked at the number of visits I was required to attend over the twelve-week period, now that time had become too short. Only four weeks left.

Four weeks until I had my freedom back and could once again be 'General Truda'. But, that also meant that Erik only had four weeks left of his life. Tonight, I had left him alone, letting him think I was angry at him. I resigned to never do that again. No matter what happened, I was not going to miss another scheduled night.

~*~

When I returned to room number twenty-three, Erik was sitting on the end of the bed with his head down.

"I thought you weren't coming back," he said without looking in my direction.

"I had to," I replied, instantly regretting the way it sounded, like I did not want to be in this room with him but did not know how to tell him any different.

"I was ordered by the queen to enter the breeding programme," I admitted to him, "and I think you already know I have no intention of entirely following through with those orders." He looked at me then, letting me know he was really listening to what I was telling him.

"My whole life I have trained to become the best and strongest warrior of Kven, to command its warriors and stand on the front lines of all battles. I had never wanted or thought of having a child, that is why I was ordered here, I would have never volunteered."

Facing his head back towards the floor, he nodded that he

understood where I was coming from, but in his face he still looked sad. I walked over to the bed and sat next to him. I wanted to tell him I was not angry anymore, that this was my fault, not his.

I lifted my hand slowly and stretched it out to reach for his, but before our hands even touched, he looked up at me confused. Before he could say anything in response, we were startled when we heard a key go in the door.

Erik did not hesitate as he quickly grabbed me at my waist, pulling me further up the bed and twisted my body so that I was under him. With his other hand, he grabbed a blanket and pulled it over us so that the bottom half of his body was covered. The door opened and Peril half stepped inside the room.

"Apologies General, but you have been summoned to the palace for an urgent meeting," she said, looking towards the bed where I was under Erik's large body. I hoped that it looked like I was doing what was expected.

"Thank you Peril, just give me a moment and I will follow you shortly," I replied. She nodded and left the room, closing the door behind her but not locking it.

I sighed with relief and put my head back on the pillow closing my eyes, then I remembered I was under Erik's body and he had not rushed to move off me. I opened them to find him staring at me, his crystal blue eyes looking over my face. My heart was pounding, and my breathing became heavy.

He was resting on his elbows to hold his body weight from crushing me, but I could still feel his warmth. He moved a hand slowly up to my face and tucked a loose strand of hair behind my pointed ear, then, looking back directly into my eyes, I saw his head move down slightly as though to get closer to me. I started to panic, finding my voice again as I pushed at his chest to get him off me.

"I have to go now," I said with urgency. Erik closed his eyes and nodded, moving off me and returning to a seated position at the end of the bed. I got up, straightened my clothing, walked to the door, and picked up the already empty bottle and room key.

I looked at him one more time before I left, my heart still pounding. His eyes were still fixed on me, his chest rising up and down more quickly than before. It was obvious that we had both been affected by what had just happened.

"Truda," Erik called to me before I walked out the door, it was the first time he had used my first name. I turned to look at him, his crystal blue eyes were looking into mine.

"I am sorry for last time, if I upset you," he said sincerely.

"I know," I replied quietly, then left.

~*~

After passing the items back to Peril, who apologised again for the interruption, I rushed to the palace.

When I entered, the queen and all the other council

members were already present. To my surprise, I also saw Princess Callidice sitting in her chair next to the queen. I could not remember the last time she attended a meeting.

"General Truda, please take your seat," ordered Queen Cassandra. She looked angry.

"What is going on?" I asked, sliding onto my chair.

"Rebels have crossed into our city and broken into some homes, they attacked the household masters and have freed a few slaves," she replied, her attention on me.

"What? How has this happened?" I said, raising my voice.

"It appears your captain didn't leave enough guards covering the wall before she went out on her scouting mission," spoke Freyja, clearly trying to direct the blame.

"It is not my fault that you committed me to the breeding programme, leaving my responsibilities to the captain," I said, looking over to all the council members, and finished by glaring at Freyja.

"But she left the city because of your maps, didn't she?" said Princess Callidice. So not only was she unexpectedly at this council meeting, but now she was speaking on it!

"That's what the council were just discussing before you came in, that you had given her maps to continue the search for the rumoured rebel base," she continued in a mocking manner.

I did not miss the moment she exchanged a smirk with Freyja. Obviously, they were trying to pin the blame on me.

My hatred towards Freyja, and the princess's clear dislike towards me, had brought them closer together, how sweet.

I now had two options; either continue to fight my corner which would likely fail, confident they would have other ammunition against me, or I could accept defeat, temporarily.

"I can only apologise, my queen. I obviously overlooked this fact, not realising that Captain Imelda would ignore her other duties when searching for the rebels." The queen looked angry, but her expression softened after I spoke; she clearly did not blame me.

"She should be punished," said Princess Callidice.

"I agree with the princess," said Freyja. "Because of General Truda's poor instruction to her captain, we had rebels cross into our city for the first time in years."

"You must be joking! The only reason our city has been kept safe for so long is because of General Truda's past actions. She is off duty for less than three months, and the city gets attacked, do you think that is a coincidence?" yelled Acqueline, jumping to my defence. Peril nodded in agreement with her statement and I smiled at my friend, thanking her for her words.

"That is enough," said the queen. "Of course, General Truda cannot be blamed. I suspect it was actually the damage to the east wall, which has yet to be repaired, that allowed the attack to happen."

"We should organise more workers to get the wall repaired

faster, doubling the guard until it is finished," said Peril.

"I shall talk with Captain Imelda when she returns," I added. After the meeting, Queen Cassandra and the princess immediately left, the other council members shortly after. Only Acqueline and I remained.

"Now I do smell a rat," she said.

"Yes, a rat and a snake, clearly working together. Perhaps now it is time to have Freyja followed," I said to Acqueline.

"Consider it done," she said, then saluted to me as she left.

Leaving the throne room, I bumped into Princess Callidice, with her Guan standing behind her.

"Well, if it isn't the favourite," she spat at me.

"Princess," I said, standing with my arms crossed. Despite her behaviour in the meeting, I had nothing to say to her, she was just being manipulated by Freyja.

"Clearly my mother favours you enough to not punish you, even when you deserve it," she said, glaring at me.

"Perhaps she would not favour me if her daughter was acting like the royal she is supposed to be," I simply replied. This made her visibly angry, and I could not deny the smirk that crept to my lips.

"How are you enjoying your time in the breeding programme General? I hear you're not pregnant yet, perhaps you are having performance issues?" she said, mockingly. As my face frowned, she burst into laughter and as she started walking away from me, she continued speaking, "perhaps you should visit the Pleasure House, the slaves there will show you how to properly perform."

"I suppose you would know all about that princess," I said, no longer able to hold back my anger. It was stupid and petty; I should not have lowered to her standards by feeding into her antagonistic behaviour. She turned and glared at me.

"Perhaps I did, but I no longer need to bother with such things, not when they gifted me with my favourite Guan whom I can use however and whenever I want." Then walking away, she shouted, "come Phoenyx!"

I looked at her slave, and just as he walked past me, the realisation kicked in. I said his name out loud quietly to myself, "Nyx." Suddenly, he turned, looking towards me confused.

So, it was him. Phoenyx was Erik's friend. He had obviously been sold to the Pleasure House before the princess had got her hands on him.

"PHOENYX!" The princess screamed. Turning away from me with sad eyes, Phoenyx hobbled quickly down the corridor on his injured leg.

Chapter 11

WEEK NINE

On my next session at the Breeding House, I asked Peril to arrange a test. Getting closer to the end of my time in the programme, I wanted to make it seem like I was more eager to find out if I was pregnant.

She nodded to me and said she would have one ready when I had finished my session. After picking up my potion and key, I walked down the corridor.

When I walked in, Erik was once again sitting on the bed, looking more comfortable with the absence of his heavy chains.

"I'm nervous to smile when you enter, considering what happened the last time I smiled at you," he joked. Laughing lightly, I poured the red liquid out of the gap through the window. I walked over and sat on the bed beside Erik.

"You're in a good mood today," he said to me softly.

"I should be in a bad mood, so much has happened in the last few days."

"Do you want to talk about it?" he asked.

"Not really. I would much rather talk about happier things, to keep me in my good mood." Although I did not really know what that would be, there was nothing positive going on in my life, except for Erik; visiting him was the only thing I looked forward to.

"What was your mother like?" he asked. I smiled thinking of her.

"She was strong like me, a warrior who fought closely with the queen in the early rebellion battles. She had kindness in her heart, caring for others, helping and healing them."

"Then you are more like your mother than you think, for you have a kindness in you." I shook my head as though to disagree, but he reached for my hand.

"You have shown me kindness, caring for me when I was injured."

I looked down at my hand, now being held by his much larger hand, then I looked up towards him, his beautiful eyes looking at me like no one had ever looked at me before, like he cared for me. I removed my hand from his, feeling awkward, and stood up, walking to the other end of the room.

"I think I met your friend the other day," I said in an attempt to change the subject. It worked, as Erik now looked at me with keen interest.

"I have met him before, but did not know at the time it was him. He is the princess's Guan now, she calls him by the name of Phoenyx," I said.

"Yes, that's him," he replied. "How was he?" I thought of Phoenyx and the punishment he had received in the Training House after I humiliated the princess.

"I will not lie to you Erik; the princess is cruel, and I do not think he is being treated kindly."

"Is there nothing you can do?" he asked.

"What could I possibly do? No-one cares for how slaves are treated." He stood, clearly angry and worried for his friend.

"But you're the General, surely you could tell the queen of the princess's abusive behaviour," he said, raising his voice.

"Do not be ridiculous. If I tried, it would only raise suspicion about me, and I am already being watched."

"So, you won't try to help him because you are worried for yourself?" he said, his voice still raised.

"That is not fair," I countered, my voice also rising. Erik looked at me once more and then sat down at the end of the bed. Minutes passed, and we had not talked to each other.

"Erik?" I said. He did not reply.

"So, you are ignoring me now?" I said and laughed. His face was still looking to the floor, clearly lost in thought and angry at the news I had shared.

"Fine, I think enough time has passed and if you do not

want to talk to me, then I shall leave." I stood for a moment facing the door, giving him the opportunity to speak to me, which he did not. So instead, I unlocked the door and left.

What had just happened? How had I ended up being the one receiving the silent treatment? Calming myself, I thought about how I would feel if I found out that Acqueline was being hurt, and I could not save her. Knowing Erik's past of clearly standing up for his friends, he probably felt useless and frustrated that he could do nothing to stop it. When I reached Peril, I handed her back the key and empty bottle.

"As requested, General, I have your pregnancy test," she said, lifting the small bowl of water and handing me the sharp needle. Knowing it was not a bowl of plain water but in fact a mages mixture, that would change to match the colour of a breeding potion if I were to be confirmed pregnant. I took the needle from her and pricked the end of my finger like the healer had at my house, when I claimed to be ill. I watched as a drop of blood landed in the water and nothing happened. Of course, I knew it would not, but I still pretended to have a look of disappointment on my face for Peril's sake.

"Don't worry General, you still have three weeks left. I'm sure it will happen before that time has ended," she said kindly, obviously believing that I cared.

"Thank you Peril, I hope so," I said and turning to leave.

~*~

144

Once I heard that Imelda had returned, I sent a message for her to come to my house immediately to give me a report. When she arrived, she was not expecting the fury I unleashed at her.

"You left the city unprotected!" I yelled, slamming my fist on the table, making her jump.

"General, I didn't leave the city unprotected."

"Do not lie to me Imelda, you depleted the forces by taking a large number of warriors out with you, leaving too few behind to be able to watch all areas of the city!" I said, my voice still raised. She looked down, her eyes moving frantically as her mind raced to figure out what she did wrong.

"You are dismissed Imelda, get out of my sight," I said sternly. Looking angry, she saluted and swiftly left. For a second, I thought perhaps I had been too harsh, after all it was not really her fault, it was the council's decision that had put us in this predicament.

Infuriated by my confrontation with Imelda, and my heated conversation with Erik yesterday, I decided to train. Instead of going to the Training House, today I wanted to be alone, not wanting to show signs of the true rage and turmoil I felt inside. I headed to my training room upstairs. Castor was out, collecting items from the market.

Opening the door, I walked in to see a display of apparatus and weaponry shelved along the wall. In the centre of the room was a wooden dummy, a poor representation of the body; with one long thick stump as legs, a rounded large chest, and two wooden arms that had been slotted into grooves on the sides of the sanded wood.

Standing in the centre of my training room, I closed my eyes, breathing deeply, trying to calm myself, beginning by slowly stretching my body. Placing my palms together, I raised my arms high above my head. However, the moment my lids closed I was instantly flooded with unwanted thoughts. Visuals of all the troubles I held deep inside flashed through my mind, starting with Erik's soft lips kissing mine, then Tobias's lifeless body on the ground, followed by Freyja's evil grin. Erik's half naked chest, Princess Callidice throwing knives at Phoenyx, finally I saw Erik's bloodied scars on his back. I was drowning as the wave of unwanted images attacked me, racing through my mind.

I screamed in rage and lunged at the wooden dummy in the centre of my room. Thrusting my arms to punch its chest repeatedly, until I began to feel the sting in my knuckles, damaging the skin, my hands now bleeding. Finally, taking a large stride backwards, I then kicked with full force, watching as the wooden dummy split in half, splinters of wood scattering all over the floor.

Holding my hair up from my face and shoulders, I felt like I was unravelling, like the shell of 'General Truda' was cracking and something new was creeping through.

Leaving the training room confused, I decided to run a

bath, filling it with lavender oils as Tobias used to, hoping it would calm my mind.

~*~

The next day, I was in the Training House with the twins, sparring. I had taken them on one at a time, showing them techniques on how to block my moves.

"Watch my footwork," I instructed Shanon. "It can give you an indication of my next move, allowing you to act defensively or aggressively, depending on your position." I looked over at Shanor who was watching me spar with her sister, bright beaming eyes, absorbing all I had to teach them.

When we were finished, I sat with them while we drank some water.

"Did you hear the news?" Shanon exclaimed.

"What news was that? I asked her, looking at Shanor who was also beaming and fidgeting like she was struggling to contain her excitement; it made me smile.

"The queen has declared that we are to be promoted to the Royal Guard," Shanor said proudly.

"That is excellent news ladies," I said, smiling proudly at them.

"There's going to be a celebration at the Coliseum where we can demonstrate our skill to the whole city," Shanor added nervously.

It was always a happy affair when someone was promoted

to such a high honour and we usually celebrated these things in the Coliseum. Both Acqueline and I had done the same when we were promoted, her to the head of the Royal Guard and me to General. I remembered that day. There was some pre-entertainment, some kind of show involving horses, and then I was the main event.

I was in the centre of the grand circle facing the audience, our people were seated in the large semi-circle of benches. Behind me was the queen's balcony where she could look at the whole arena and address her people. I was given three challenges. The first was my skill with a bow, as various targets at different distances were placed in front of me; I hit the bullseye on every shot. The second was hand to hand combat with a very skilled opponent; I had won without too much difficulty.

The last was a sword fight with three strong warriors, it was the most challenging of the three. We each had a sword and shield, and after knocking out one of my opponents, the other two ambushed me and I lost my sword. I remember the audience gasp, thinking I had been defeated. Of course, this was not to last long as I defeated the other two women using my shield for defence and as a weapon.

The crowd had cheered and screamed my name. I remember looking up at the queen who was smiling proudly at me.

"You will come to watch us, won't you?" said Shanor, looking at me with such hope.

"Of course. I will be standing on the queen's balcony to watch you both shine in front of the whole city," I said with a smile. "When is the celebration to be?"

"In three weeks' time." Shanon replied.

~*~

Three weeks. That seemed to be the countdown for a lot of things now. Three weeks until the celebration of the twin's promotion at the coliseum. Three weeks until I would finish in the breeding programme and be able to go back to performing my duties.

Three weeks until Erik was to die.

Trying not to focus on the last part as I headed to the Breeding House, feeling guilty after our argument, I had decided to surprise Erik with a gift. When clearing out my bed-chamber, moving some maps and books out of the way, I stumbled on a story book that my mother had read to me when I was a child. It was full of short stories, tales of heroes fighting monsters, and warriors travelling across great seas.

I hoped it would bring Erik some amusement and give him something to do on the nights that I was not with him. Stuffing the small book down my top, hoping it did not stick out too much, I hurried to the Breeding House, collected my items from the guard there, and rushed to Erik's room.

Before I entered, I pulled the book from my top and concealed it behind my back. When I walked in, I smiled, unable to contain my clear excitement about my surprise of what I had brought for him.

I locked the door behind me and, after placing my items on the table as I usually did, I went over and sat next to Erik on the bed, one of my hands still behind my back,

"I have brought you a gift," I said excitedly.

"A gift, why?" he questioned.

"Because I wanted you to have something to amuse you when you are here alone, but you must be careful that no-one catches you with it, promise?"

He looked at me curiously. "Yes, I promise."

I pulled the book from behind me and handed it to him. He took it, looking at it with confusion.

"It's a book," he said, looking up at me with a puzzled expression.

"Of course it is a book," I laughed. "It is filled with stories of adventure and monsters."

"So, it's a children's book?" he said, still looking at me confused, but now smiling.

"Well, if you do not want it," I said, holding out my hand ready to take it from him.

"No, I didn't say that." He pulled back his hand, keeping the book out of my reach. "It's just, I…" He did not finish his sentence and looked down at the book in his hands.

Of course, how could I be so thoughtless.

"You cannot read," I said, realising my mistake.

"Actually, I can read a little, but I am self-taught and have never read anything so complicated as a story, even a children's one," he told me honestly.

"Then I will help you," I said. Sliding further up the bed, rearranging some cushions and pillows so that I could use them to sit at the head of the bed more comfortably, I patted the space next to me indicating to Erik that I wanted him to come up here and sit by me.

He hesitated for a moment, looking to where I now sat, then he shuffled over next to me. Our skin did not touch but he was so close it made me nervous.

Without speaking, he handed me the book. I did not look up at him, but I could feel the warmth of his body. I was worried how close his face must now be to mine. Instead, I focused my attention on the book, opening it up to begin reading the first story. It was a tale about a warrior who had found a magical sword giving her abilities she did not have before. She used her power to rescue people all across the land.

I remembered this story being read to me as a child by my mother. I would often have dreams of finding my own magical sword, which was ironic now, considering I could have a magical sword, if only I trusted the mages enough to let them gift me one.

~*~

On my way home, I approached my front door. It was

late, as I had stayed in the Breeding House much later than I would ordinarily.

The streets were empty, and everything was quiet, the cool evening breeze being the only sound as it whistled through the buildings. I reached for the handle on my front door, and suddenly I heard a thud of an object landing in the wooden frame, not far from my face; a dagger. Pulling the knife from the wood, I turned and saw three masked elves, approaching me with weapons in hand, ready to attack. I turned to face them, considering my options. I did not have any other weapons and knew I would not make it inside my house before one of them reached me. Besides, I did not want Castor to get caught in the crossfire. I did not recognise them, but I did notice they were in city armour. Clenching my fists, I took a step towards them.

"Alright then ladies, ready when you are," I said with a coy smile.

They rushed me, and I jumped to the left, rolling on the ground. By the time I was on my knees, one of them jumped on me. Wrestling with her body on the ground, I held back her arm that held a dagger, now directed to my chest. Twisting it out of her wrist, gripping the knife, I sliced her shoulder and pushed her off, pausing in a crouched position as I waited for the other two to approach. Now, holding a blade in each hand, my heart was racing. Despite the surprise, I was unafraid, feeling excited at the thought of a challenge, especially without armour to protect my skin.

Keeping a smirk on my face, I leapt forward, throwing one of the knives at the elf in front of me. Dodging my throw, she swung her fist towards my face. I pushed it out of the way and, using the palm of my hand, I smacked it up, hearing her nose crack. As she squealed in pain, the last woman charged at me. She had a short sword and was swinging it to the left, then to the right. I avoided each attack, stepping back and tilting my body each time she swung it.

Thrusting the second acquired dagger, I watched as it penetrated in her gut. Then the one with the injured shoulder came at me again with another dagger she had pulled from her side. I quickly spun around and kicked her across the face.

As she steadied herself, I gave her no time to retaliate, I punched her multiple times in the chest, feeling a burning sensation from my hands as I re-opened my wounds from my aggressive training, the cuts now mixed with dirt and sand from the ground.

Standing back with my fists up ready, my hands now covered in blood and peeled skin, I watched as the elf with a bleeding nose went over to help the one holding her bleeding gut. The elf I had just kicked and punched, stumbled back with them, and after sharing confusing glances at each other, they retreated, grabbing their injured friend by each arm and quickly jogging off into the darkness.

Walking back towards my house, I opened the door and

locked it behind me, leaning against the door to catch my breath.

I considered following them, but I did not know if I would find myself in an ambush. One thing was for certain, someone in the city wanted me dead.

Chapter 12

WEEK TEN

Walking down the corridor in the palace, searching for Acqueline, I wanted to tell her what had happened at my house last night. I needed to warn her of the danger. For reasons I did not know, someone had tried to have me killed and I was worried for the royal family, especially the queen.

I heard footsteps quickly approaching me, then around the corner came Phoenyx, the princess's Guan. He stopped in front of me, startled, and looked at me curiously.

"You are Nyx, right?" I asked him, and watched as his eyes widened in surprise

"Yes," he replied nervously. "Forgive me for asking, but how do you know my nickname?" he whispered. I looked around to make sure that nobody was near us. Phoenyx watched me as he realised I was checking that nobody else was around.

"Let's just say we have a friend in common." I said, quietly smiling at him.

"You know Erik?" he asked. Quickly realising that I did, he continued. "I knew he had been sent to the Breeding House, and I had heard through the princess's gossiping that you had been sent there."

"He saved me you know," he added in a saddened tone. Thinking of Erik's scars, I imagined that he had saved a lot of people.

"What did he do?" I asked, questioning if I even wanted to hear a story that involved Erik's punishment.

"There was a slave in our group that would pick on others, he beat me regularly," he said, looking glum at the memory. "The guards never did anything; they simply didn't care as long as we could work. On one particularly bad day, the big slave grabbed me by the throat. Erik pulled him off and punched him in the face," he said, smiling at the memory.

"After that, our master decided we were more trouble than we were worth, so she sold us. Erik went to The Breeding House and I…. I went somewhere else," he said, looking down at the floor.

"You were sold to the Pleasure House?" I asked him.

"Yes. I thought that things couldn't get any worse, until their best supporter made it clear she wanted me for herself, and they gave me to her. Now I wish I was back there," he said, closing his fist angrily.

We stood quietly for a moment.

"If there was something I could do to help your situation, I want you to know I would," I told him. He looked at me in surprise.

I started to walk away when he grabbed my arm.

"He's at the end of his life," Phoenyx said with a pause before adding, "I never got to tell him thank you for that day. Will you tell him for me?" He clearly cared for his friend as much as I knew Erik cared for him. Despite what they were, despite what they would go through, they still had bonds as strong as we elves did. I nodded to him.

"Of course." Then I walked away. Pushing back the emotions that were swirling around in my head about Erik's protective sacrifice. I continued on with the mission at hand. Finding Acqueline to inform her of the assassination attempt, was my priority right now.

~*~

I went to the Breeding House for another scheduled session. Collecting my items, I walked down the corridor towards room twenty-three. Just as I walked past another room, the door opened and out walked a tall woman, surprised at bumping into me.

"Apologies General, I didn't see you there," she said. In her haste and fluster, she had left the door to her room open and inside I saw a young man. He was sitting on the bed crying, he also looked beaten and bruised. The elf woman noticed me looking at the slave with confusion.

"Sometimes they can be a little reluctant and need a bit of motivation," she said with a snigger, then closed the door and locked it. Giving me another smile and salute, she walked back to the reception desk. Surely all elves were not like this; cruel and unkind to all humans? I thought about Princess Callidice and this woman, thought about the scars on Erik's back, and felt sick.

I continued on to Erik's room. Walking in I saw him rush to put his hands behind his back. When he saw it was just me, he pulled out the book and continued to read.

He almost seemed too engrossed to pay any attention to me. I smiled as I locked the door, placed the items on the table and walked over to the bed. He scooted his large body to make room for me near where he sat, then looked up smiling at me, only to frown when he saw my expression.

"What's wrong?" he asked, putting down the book. I was thinking about my people and how cruel we could really be. Humans are our servants and have to know their place, but there is a difference between discipline and abuse.

"You look lost in some serious thoughts there," he continued.

"Do elves really treat all humans so poorly?" I turned to face him, I felt confused. I had spent my whole life fighting for good, killing the rebels before they got close to the city, and after being off duty for a few months, they break into our city and free some slaves, ones that no doubt would have gone through some kind of torment and abuse from their masters. Were we the real enemy?

Erik looked at me with concern in his eyes at seeing my internal struggle. He placed his hand under my chin, lifting my face to look at him.

"Not all elves," he said to me. I stood, startling Erik as I moved away from him abruptly. I walked over to the table, emptied the contents out the gap in the brickwork and picked up the key.

"I saw your friend again today, he asked me to pass on a message to say thank you for what you had done for him." Erik looked at me, then his eyes drifted to the floor as he nodded. He knew his friend was saying his thanks while he could.

"I have to leave early tonight," I said, walking towards the door. Erik sat up on his knees.

"Please don't, stay with me," he pleaded. I looked at him and he looked sad, obviously not wanting me to go. A strange feeling washed over me, like I felt comforted in his need for my company.

"Fine, I will stay for one story."

Looking down at his book, he shuffled back in his position and patted the bed for me to come sit next to him.

He went to hold my hand and I winced. That is when he noticed the bruise and torn skin on my knuckles.

"Truda, what happened?" he asked, full of concern.

"Nothing," I replied, folding my arms to hide my hands.

"That doesn't look like nothing," he said while frowning at me. I sighed and looked up at him.

"I was jumped last night by three elves, they tried to kill me," I told him. He sat back on his knees and grabbed my hands from under my arms to study them better, then he looked up at me.

"Are you okay?" he asked, while brushing his fingers over my hands lightly. I pulled my hands away from him again, feeling strange by his gentle touch.

"Erik, I am fine, these marks are from the damage I inflicted on them, they came out a lot worse, trust me," I said as I huffed, annoyed at the look of worry over his face.

"Do you know who it was?" he asked me.

"Not yet, but I will," I said under my breath. Then I looked back up at him. "Come on, I would rather you were reading than worrying." Erik nodded and smiled. Still looking concerned, he came back down to sit next to me and opened the book.

We took turns reading to each other. Erik's reading was coming along quickly and although his reading was still slow, he did not struggle with every other word as he had last week. In the end, I did not just stay for one story, enjoying the soothing sound of Erik's voice, I stayed for three.

~*~

I was on my way to the last place I thought I would go, the Mages Temple. They had a great library which was open for anyone who sought knowledge, and I certainly had some questions I wanted answers to, as I knew little about the history of our people, and even less about what started the rebellion. My mother and the queen had only told me bits and pieces, which I had been satisfied with, until now.

Spending time with Erik had made me feel differently towards him. I did not see him as a slave anymore. I saw him as a person with his own thoughts and feelings, I considered him my friend.

Then I thought of Castor who was so much more comfortable around me now. I was speaking to him more nicely, I even said thank you when he gave me some breakfast this morning. Then I thought of Tobias and the relationship we had. I had never been cruel and treated him fairly, and now wondered if he did see me as much more than his master, so much that he died for me.

Tobias, I realised, had planted the seed, Castor was watering it, and Erik was the sunshine that gave it life.

I needed to get to the root of the problem. I knew that not all elves treated slaves this way, but we did not exactly stop all the exploitation and cruelty that went on in the city.

I walked through the large temple doors and headed for

the library; it was not guarded since knowledge of our people was available to all who lived in the city. Perhaps this was one of the reasons why I never questioned our way of life or the truth behind the rebellion. Why would they fill us with lies, if we could so easily unravel them?

I was grateful that it was not guarded as I was hoping I could get in and out without being seen. Right at the entrance were three pedestals that each had a copy of the index. Stepping towards one, I looked through the pages until I found reference to the subject I was interested in, making a mental note of the stack number and making my way to that section in the library. There I collected a few books and went to sit in a nearby small seating area and began to read.

The first part of my research took me to the histories of our people. It said how over a thousand years ago we were also once human, but weaker and smaller and dominated by men. The world was harsh and uncivilised, people starved, and wars reigned, men fought over lands, food, and over the possession of women. Thousands of people died while men ruled, killing and raping as they saw fit. They were primitive and destructive people with no discipline or moral compass.

Until something changed. A small group of women had discovered that they had the skill of magic, they were able to tap into an energy flow that gave them the ability to manipulate nature. It was written that some were so strong that they could control the elements and even change the weather.

This was the beginning of our race. Over the years, the magic had evolved us into something more than human; we were larger, stronger, faster, most of us were born warriors. Some of us inherited a concentrated amount of magic flow, although through the generations their power was limited, not having the ability to control the elements as the original mages had, but able to imbue weapons and armour with special abilities, as well as make potions and ointments with extraordinary properties. The human men became our Guans.

I thought about what the world must have been like then, full of primitive beings. The beginnings of our people had changed everything, they had saved it. But this did not stop me from wondering if we should be reminded more of our origins. After all, the way we were now treating the Guans did not seem much better than those savages?

After taking in my fill of the history, feeling enlightened but not really learning anything informative, I returned the books back to the shelf and continued on to the next section of the library, one that I was much more interested in.

Except, when I reached my destination, the shelf that held the records for battles during the rebellion, were missing. That was strange. I could see where the books had been disturbed as the dust had not yet settled in their wake. We wrote down and recorded everything in our history, free for anyone to read. Why were these books missing? I looked through the other shelves, checking nearby stalls just in case the index had been wrong. I found nothing.

Hearing a rustling noise, I quickly glanced around me and it appeared I was alone, with no-one else present in the library with me. But I could not shake the feeling I was being watched. I checked back to the main walkway which was still empty.

Then, hearing a fluttering noise this time, I looked up and saw it. Freyja's raven Jetta was perched on the top of the stall, and it was staring at me. It had a small, jewelled metal chain around its neck with a ruby stone at the centre. When it saw me looking up, it squawked loudly and flew off.

~*~

Erik was reading to me, but I was not listening to the story; I was too distracted by what happened in the library. Why was Freyja's raven watching me? Had it seen the section of the library I was looking at? Did it see what I was trying to research? More importantly, why were all the books missing?

I wanted to go and talk to the queen and ask her directly, but I was worried about what suspicion that would bring me as I had never questioned these things before. I did not notice Erik had stopped reading at first, until it registered that I could no longer hear his voice. I turned towards him to find him staring at me.

"Sorry," I muttered as I climbed away from the bed and walked across the room.

"You don't want to be here?" Erik asked me, looking a little hurt.

"It is not that at all, I just have a lot on my mind," I told him, walking back towards the bed but not sitting. Erik put the book down and shuffled forward so that his legs were now hanging over the edge.

"You don't want to talk about it?" he said.

"I do not think it will make a difference," I told him honestly.

"Then it wouldn't hurt to tell me," he said with a smile, clearly just trying to make me feel better.

"I went to the Great Library inside the temple today, looking for some answers about our history," I told him.

"And did you find them?"

"I found lots of old texts about what the Kingdom of Nysa was like in the early years, most of which I already knew, but..." Erik looked at me, clearly eager for me to continue. "I also tried to find out more about the rebellion and how it started, and I could not find anything. The books were missing."

"I see," he said. "Maybe they contained something that they didn't want the public to know?" well, that I knew was obvious, but I had never known it to happen before, for a collection of books to go missing, but then again, the library was not exactly somewhere I frequently visited, so it may have happened.

"Why were you looking?" Erik asked me, his eyes full of

curiosity.

"I'm not entirely sure. I suppose I just wanted confirmation that my career, everything in my past that I have done, was in the name of justice." Erik stood. He walked over to me and took my hand.

"I won't pretend to know about the battles or the rebellion, all I know is that you're not evil, and have always acted with your good heart. If you've ever done anything wrong, it's because the world has deceived you."

I looked up into his eyes, it was the sweetest thing anyone had ever said to me. He really believed that despite who I was, despite what had happened to him, I was inherently good and nothing else mattered. I smiled at him, feeling my face blush slightly at the light touch of his hand.

"Let us continue reading that story." Still holding my hand, he smiled and led me over to the bed where we sat down together and took turns reading the chapters.

~*~

I had been summoned to the throne room by the queen. I had no idea what it was about and was shocked to find when I entered the room, that Princess Callidice was also there, sitting in her chair next to the queen. I knelt on one knee before Queen Cassandra and signalled the salute of respect.

"My Queen, you requested my presence," I said, now standing.

"Yes, I wanted to give you my condolences Truda, and apologise," she said to me sincerely. I was confused as to why she was sorry. I glanced at the princess who looked at me with annoyance.

"I am sorry to hear that you still have not successfully conceived a child, even more so because we had forced you into the programme bringing much more anguish and stress into a situation that I know you did not want to begin with." I nodded in response, thanking her silently for her words.

"It is not common, but for an elf your age, things like this do happen that not even magic can resolve," she said. At least I knew my plan had worked, they obviously did not suspect anything out of the ordinary, believing I had been unable to conceive naturally because of my age.

"With this in mind, we would like to offer you back your responsibilities as general," the queen said to me.

At this I paused and looked at her in surprise.

"We are allowing you to terminate your time in the programme. You can relieve your captain and resume your normal duties."

If I had heard these words weeks ago, I would have been thrilled, and even though I knew I only had a few sessions left, the thought of not seeing Erik brought me pain inside.

"If you do not mind my queen, I only have one week left and would like to continue my sessions." At this, both the queen and the princess looked shocked, so I quickly added,

"I admit that if I had been told this many weeks ago, I would have gladly taken the opportunity you have presented to me, but now I would like to continue my last few sessions in the hope that I may yet be successful." The queen's eyes softened.

"Of course, Truda, I understand. Very well, we will leave you to complete the programme fully, and I wish you luck in conceiving a child."

As I nodded and turned to leave, I saw the princess's face, her eyes almost squinting while thoughts swam around her mind and it was clear then that the queen believed me, but the princess did not.

Chapter 13

WEEK ELEVEN

I was meeting Acqueline at the stables. I had walked with Castor this morning and watched him as he was now looking after my horse, petting him and grooming with a brush. They had obviously bonded I thought with a smile. When I saw Acqueline walk in, I stood and met her halfway, leaving Castor with Thio.

"Morning Tru. I see you've introduced your new Guan to Thio," she said, pointing towards them.

"You know I always like to make sure he gets the best care," I said with a shrug.

"Shall we go for a walk along the wall?" she asked me, to which I nodded, then looked back.

"Castor, when you are done here, return home and finish

your morning chores." He nodded at me with a slight smile before turning his attention back to my horse.

"Well, you certainly have that one well trained already," said Acqueline with a laugh.

"So, have you had Freyja followed?" I asked Acqueline as we walked along together.

"Yes, and her activities have been mostly boring, except one night my guard reported that Freyja visited the Breeding House."

"What did she do there?" my interest now peeked, wondering if Freyja was the one getting the information to the queen about my visits.

"Well, that's the odd part. Apparently, after being in the building for a few minutes, she walked out and searched the back ally, looking up at the wall and scanning the ground."

Why would Freyja be doing that? Then it hit me. She was looking for traces of the potion. She knew that I was not taking them, but how? Was she also behind the attack? The assailants did look surprised when I had easily thwarted their assault.

"Tru, what's going on?" Acqueline asked me.

"I think Freyja planned the attack on my life." I said to her.

"What, why?" she said in shock.

"I do not know yet, but keep having her followed, and let me know if you find out anything else," I said to her. Acqueline nodded and we continued walking along the wall.

"What do you know of the rebellion?" I asked

"The same as you," she told me. "That a group of women tried to overthrow Queen Cassandra's mother, a fight had broken out in the city and after stealing some slaves they escaped. Why do you ask?"

She turned to me, looking inquisitively.

"Have you ever read facts from the books in the great library about it?" I asked her.

"Well, no, I have only heard stories, but it's well known. Why do you ask Tru?" I paused for a second, wanting to be careful with my words but also knowing I could trust Acqueline.

"Because I visited the library in the Mages Temple to read for myself and all the books regarding the rebellion were missing."

"Maybe they didn't write it down, not wanting to give credence to the bad part of our history," she said, obviously trying to think of other logical explanations as to why the books were missing.

"They were listed in the index, but when I searched in that area of the library, they were nowhere to be found." I could see in her face she found that hard to believe, which confirmed my theory that books simply did not just go missing from the library, they were taken on purpose, hidden or destroyed so that nobody could read them.

"Why would they be missing?" she asked.

"I do not know, the only conclusion I have come to is that someone is trying to hide something."

~*~

"Have you heard any strange noises outside this past week? I asked Erik, peering through the gap in the window, examining the stone around the edges of the wall with my finger to find any traces of the discarded red liquid.

"What kind of noises?" he replied.

"Any noises, people scuffling, talking, anything?"

"Umm no, nothing out of the ordinary, why do you ask?" he looked at me puzzled as he observed my erratic behaviour.

"Because I am being watched, and I think it is connected to the assassination attempt the other night."

"Wait what? Truda, explain." Erik walked over to me and placed his hand on my arm, pulling me away from my examinations. I paused for a moment and sighed. Being in close proximity to Erik certainly offered some kind of calming effect that I could not explain, and in that moment, I was grateful for it.

"I think one of the elders may be poisoning my breeding potions, perhaps something with weakening properties."

"I don't understand, why would they do that?" he asked.

"Because they know I would not be easily defeated, and obviously thought it better to increase their chances of success."

"No Truda, that's not what I meant." I looked at him

confused. "Why would an elder try to have you killed, why go through the effort of poisoning your potion?" he added.

"This particular elder is not my biggest supporter."

"I'm sure you have the ability to upset a lot of people Truda, but that doesn't exactly explain why she would want you dead."

I gave him a quick glare.

Although, Erik was right. Why would Freyja go to all this trouble, it made no sense? I had my suspicions that she had been heavily involved in the decision to send me to the breeding programme in the first place, something she must have engineered with the sole purpose of having an opportunity to poison me, then arranging the assassination attempt, which of course failed because I was not drinking Freyja's tampered potions. But this did not explain why she would want me dead in the first place, it would not benefit her in any way.

"What are you going to do?" Erik asked, taking a few steps back to give me space.

"Honestly, I do not know." Of course, my initial reaction was to go to the queen, but she would need evidence of my claims and I currently had none. If I had friends on the inside of the Mages Temple, I could have asked them to examine one of the potions, but I did not due to my automatic dislike of them. The only person I could really trust was Acqueline. Perhaps I could sneak her one of the potions to have it analysed by someone she trusted.

"I need to go check outside," I said to Erik, heading towards the door.

"For what?"

"I need to know if Freyja found any evidence of the potions I have been discarding through the window." I started to open the door, but it abruptly closed. Turning, I saw Erik leaning on the door with one hand, stopping me from pulling it open.

"You won't find anything, I made sure no-one would," he told me, looking nervous. I moved away from the door and folded my arms, looking at him.

"What do you mean Erik? What did you do?" my voice was low and angry at the thought of Erik meddling.

"I have been using some of the bathing water to wash down the wall after you leave."

"Why would you do that?" I asked him, not feeling so angry anymore.

"Because I didn't want you to get caught. I didn't want to stop seeing you," he whispered, keeping his head down, too embarrassed to look at me, perhaps more worried that I would be angry. It made me smile. He had taken a risk, but it was warming to know that he was protecting me.

"Thank you," I told him. He looked up and smiled in relief.

"You are not mad?"

"No Erik, I am not mad. I know you only did what you did to protect our secret friendship, and I appreciate that." He half smiled in response, making me question if that was the reason, or was he just protecting himself?

"However, you will not need to do that anymore, it is clear I need to find a different way. I cannot risk using the same method," I told him, my voice assertive, hoping he understood I was instructing him not to interfere further.

~*~

At home, I sat on my long-cushioned chair in front of the fire, Erik's book in my hand. We had finished reading all the short stories it contained and he returned it to me, not wanting it to be discovered after, well, after he was gone. Next week would be my last week in the breeding programme.

My last week with Erik.

I did not want my time with him to be over, I felt closer to him than I had to anyone. Growing up, many looked up to me or wanted to spar with me, but no-one really knew me as anything more than a great warrior. Acqueline was the only person I could truly call a friend, but I would never feel as relaxed in her presence, not in the same way I did with Erik. Now, in this house, I had never felt so alone in my entire life.

My mind raced through complicated and impossible scenario's. Perhaps I could just take Erik to be my personal Guan, like Princess Callidice had taken Phoenyx. But to what avail, it would be frowned upon if I asked, and would never be granted anyway as Erik was at the end of his life. Not to mention if I did that, and in some bizarre reality my request was granted, what would happen to Castor? No elf had the need for two Guans, and I worried that the boy may end up in the hands of someone cruel.

The truth was, nothing could be done, and it was better if I just pushed these confusing and unwanted thoughts out of my mind. Guans died, it happened every day. My feelings now were clearly from the result of my own actions. I had become attached and would just have to let go.

Just then Castor walked in with a plate of fruit. I smiled as he bounced over to me and placed the food on the table next to where I sat.

"Thank you, Castor."

"Did you need anything else? If not, I was going to go to the market to get some fresh bread." His voice was high pitched, like that of a small elf girl, making me smile.

"Thank you, that will be all." He smiled and turned to leave. I glanced down at the book in my hands, about to put it on the table and replace it with food, when I paused.

"Actually, Castor wait!" I called, causing him to come back into the room, looking slightly stunned.

"Here, I have a gift for you," I said, extending the book to him, waving it in the air to urge him to take it.

"For me?" he replied as he stepped forward and took it from my hand.

"It has some pictures in it, but I will teach you to read the words." His eyes lit up as he opened the book and started gazing at the pictures, getting lost in the detail of the drawings of the heroes and monsters.

"Go and enjoy it, take the afternoon off. I can go to the market," I told him. Castor's beaming eyes looked up from the pages towards me.

"Thank you General, thank you so much." His eyes filled, rimmed with tears as he closed the book and hugged it in his arms, like it was the most precious thing in the kingdom. I nodded and watched him skip out of the room. Going to the market would give me the perfect opportunity to look for a small glass bottle, particularly one that mimicked the shape and size of the breeding potion vial.

~*~

Leaving my home, I felt in the best mood I had for a long time. Giving Castor the book as a gift this morning opened my eyes to how wonderful an act of kindness could feel.

Ahead I saw the stalls and headed in the direction of the freshly baked food, but as I walked by, another stall caught my eye. The large wooden table was full of glass vials in all different shapes and sizes. As I scanned across the table, I found exactly what I was looking for; a small glass bottle with a cork top. Exactly the same style used for the breeding potions.

"General Truda, it's a pleasure to see you," said the elf behind the table while saluting.

"I will take one of each size," I instructed, not bothering

with pleasantries.

"Of course, I will arrange them to be sent to your house this afternoon," she replied. "May I ask what you are using them for?" In truth, I only needed one, the others were useless, but necessary to cover up my future intentional use with the bottle.

"Decorational purposes," I replied curtly.

"Apologies General, I didn't mean to offend, ignore this silly elf's curiosity," she said politely. I turned, continuing towards the fresh food section of the market.

It was not long before my arms were full of bread and fruits, ready to be taken home. How did little Castor manage to do this by himself? By the time I reached home and walked in the kitchen, I grinned as my table was full of glass bottles, in all different shapes and sizes. Castor appeared from his room, helping me put away the food items. As soon as my hands were free, I walked over to the table and picked up the tiny glass bottle I needed and left the room.

~*~

Walking into the Breeding House with the empty bottle carefully hidden within my clothes, I collected my items and walked to Erik's room. I laughed when I walked in and caught him looking through one of the windows. He jumped back when he heard me enter.

"Sorry I am late. I gave Castor the afternoon off and had some things to do at home," I told him, realising he must have been looking out the window to check if I was still coming.

"You gave Castor the afternoon off?" he said, walking over to the bed and sitting down.

"Yes, and I gave him your book. I will teach him how to read it."

"You will?" he asked me, looking surprised.

"I see no harm in teaching a young boy how to read a children's book, Erik."

"I'm not judging. I think it's great you are going to teach him how to read, you will just need to be careful," he said, sounding serious.

"I am not going to get caught reading a book with Castor in my own home, Erik," I said, feeling frustrated. He was dampening my good mood.

"I didn't mean be careful regarding just yourself. Castor will be persecuted by elves and other slaves if they find out he can read. You will have to teach him to conceal the skill."

Of course, how could I have been so stupid. Feeling good about my gift, I had momentarily forgotten the potential consequences of my actions, after all why would a Guan need to read? It certainly was not something our people would encourage, and if slaves could be equally as cruel as Erik had told me, Castor would be picked on for being treated better by his master out of jealousy.

I sat glumly on the bed, instantly feeling regretful and naïve. I had wanted to do something nice for Castor, but it just so happened that the laws of my society would never allow it, just as they would never allow me to keep Erik, or save him from his scheduled death.

After spending a few hours with Erik, I left the room locking it behind me, an action that seemed to take me longer to complete each time I was to do it. Before I reached Peril, I concealed the full red vial within my clothing, ready to return the key and my spare empty bottle. At least now I could discard of the potion in my own home, safely away from elders' eyes, leaving me with a perfectly empty bottle to return with next time.

Chapter 14

THE FINAL WEEK

Preparations for the event at the coliseum were well underway, with people running to and fro to set up the large arena. It was early morning, and I was helping the twins through their own preparations in the Training House.

Acqueline soon joined to help with training. We were watching them throw knives at some targets when a familiar and unwanted voice entered the room.

"Ah, my least favourite place," remarked Princess Callidice as she entered the Training House with Phoenyx walking closely behind her. She had a collar on him and was leading him like a dog through the open court, walking towards us and the twins.

"And what brings the princess here, after refusing to attend any more of my training sessions?" said Acqueline, bitterly.

"If you must know, I am here to help with preparations for tomorrow's event. I'm helping to get everything in place," she said proudly.

"Which reminds me General Truda, isn't it your last session in the Breeding House tonight?" she asked me with a wicked grin on her face.

"Yes, and what of it?" I replied sharply.

"Oh, I just wanted to check that I wasn't interrupting your sessions by having your slave help with a little pre-entertainment." I saw Phoenyx look up from behind the princess, then he looked towards me with worry all over his face.

"What kind of pre-entertainment?" asked Shanor, hearing the conversation regarding tomorrow's events.

"I have arranged a slave death match with the two biggest Guans I could find, that included General Truda's breeding slave and another."

Princess Callidice beamed with excitement as she looked to me, clearly hoping to see some kind of reaction. I realised this was my fault, I had obviously given something away in the throne room when I turned down the opportunity to exit the breeding programme early.

"I think that is a fantastic idea," I said to her, showing no emotion whatsoever. Phoenyx looked at me, shocked.

"You do?" said the princess in surprise.

"Of course. The slave is to be terminated anyway, so why not make good use out of him first. Besides, he is quite large, it should be very entertaining," I finished.

The princess looked furious. She had clearly come here intending to catch me off guard, to invoke a reaction out of me. However she had made it obvious and I was able hide my concern knowing that it would anger her. With that, she turned and stormed out, pulling Phoenyx's leash harshly so it pulled at his neck while he tried to keep up. I tried to remain calm throughout the day, desperately waiting for the evening to come.

~*~

"Tell me it is not true," I said as soon as I walked through the door of room number twenty-three. When I saw him look at me sadly then drop his gaze to the floor, I knew it was.

"It's not how I thought I would go, but I knew this day was coming. I suppose it doesn't really matter how it ends," he said, still looking at the floor.

"It matters to me!" I shouted, startling him. "Do you think I want to stand there tomorrow and watch you fight for your life in the arena?" I snapped. He looked at me and sighed.

"You won't have to," was all he said. I walked over to the bed and sat next to him.

"You are not going to fight, are you?" I asked him.

"No," he said, looking away from me again.

"So, you are giving up!"

"There's no point Truda, I've made up my mind. I would rather go quickly and get it over with." I turned away from him, crossing my arms. I knew it was pointless being angry, there was no reason for Erik to fight. Even if he did win, he would only be killed later for being at the end of his life, they were just using him as a last form of entertainment. Still, I was angry he did not want to fight, did not care enough to live, to even try.

I felt the bed move and as I looked towards Erik to see what he was doing, he slowly cupped my chin with both hands and moved in to kiss me. Hands shaking, his lips touched mine and he closed his eyes, pausing as if waiting for me to push him away.

At first, I was in shock, telling myself that I needed to do just that, but I knew this would be our last moment together, the last time I would be this close to him, the last time I would be able to feel his lips on mine. So, I kissed him back. It was slow and gentle and we pro-longed it for as long as possible, as though we were using our lips to say the goodbye that we could not say in words.

When the kiss ended, we both slowly moved back to lay on the bed together. We faced each other, his hand holding mine. We silently looked at each other, and there were no words. There was nothing I could say that would describe in that moment how I felt, gazing deeply into those crystal blue eyes for what was to be the last time. In that moment, I wished I could freeze time, to allow my eyes to study every angle of his face, every mark that scarred his skin, so I could burn the memory of him in my mind forever.

However, after what felt like a short amount of time, I knew I had lingered too long, and it was time to leave. Though I did not want to, I slowly rose from the bed. Erik sat up with me and released his hold on my hand. I instantly felt cold without the warmth of his fingers. I stood up and walked over to the table, collecting my items, and walked towards the door, pausing just before opening it.

"I am thankful for our time together. I understand your choice not to fight, just know that I will be with you tomorrow when you take your final breath," I said, looking at him. "I will miss you," I whispered just before I turned the lock and left without waiting for him to respond.

I locked the door behind me and stood by it for a moment, turning around to look at door number twenty-three. My hand reached up and touched the wood just as I felt a single tear fall down my cheek.

I wiped it away and turned down the corridor, handed in my items and left the building, never again to return to the Breeding House.

~*~

It was the morning of the twins' initiation into the royal

guard at the great Coliseum and I met with Acqueline. As we walked together, she was buzzed with excitement, looking forward to seeing the twins' hard training from the last few weeks pay off in the trials.

I tried to listen and keep a smile on my face, but it was hard. All I could think about was the pre-entertainment that involved Erik giving his life so that my people would get riled up and excited for the next part of the event.

I felt angry. Despite all the research I had done in the library, in this moment I knew we were no different than the primitive people that were here before us. We abused and murdered humans for our own benefit and pleasure, hiding behind our civilised culture to claim we were better than they were.

When we reached the Coliseum, I paused before entering, and pulled Acqueline off to the side, out of sight, next to a shaded wall. I handed her the breeding potion I had kept from my last session.

"Tru, why are you giving me this? Is this a breeding potion?" I nodded, silently answering her question.

"Do you have contacts in the Mages Temple you trust?" I asked quietly, looking around to check no-one was listening.

"Yes."

"I need you to have them analyse this, I think they will find weakening properties," I told her.

"You think this is linked to the assassination attempt?"

"Can you get this done discreetly? I do not want anyone else on the council to know."

"Of course Tru, I'll let you know as soon as I get results," she replied, safely tucking away the little vial under her armour chest plate. She nodded before I continued on and followed close behind me.

We took the side stairs to get to the private balcony where I could see the queen sitting in her seat. She was talking to her daughter Princess Callidice, who sat in the chair beside her. Kneeling on the floor beside the princess's chair was Phoenyx, with his collar and leash still around his neck. He looked as sad as I felt. For a moment I envied him being able to show that emotion while I had spent all morning trying to keep it concealed.

Acqueline and I took our places on either side of the royal family, hers was next to the princess, and I was next to the queen.

Opposite us we could see the bench filling up with people from the city and after a few moments all the seats were full. You could hear the echoing sounds of the crowd's voices as they talked and shouted amongst each other. The queen stood, walking to the edge of the balcony and raised both her arms. The crowd instantly went silent waiting for their great queen to address them.

"Elves of Kven, I welcome you to a most glorious day, where the strength of two special warriors will be tested before you to

show they are worthy of becoming part of my Royal Guard."
The crowd cheered at hearing this, clearly very excited for the
entertainment they were about to witness.

"But first, my daughter Princess Callidice has arranged a
special pre-entertainment show for us, a fight to the death!"
she shouted. With that, the crowd went wild, standing and
cheering in excitement. I looked down as the gates opened
and the first figure walked into the open arena.

It was Erik. He had been given some basic armour, just
covering his forearms and his shoulders, his chest remained
bare apart from a belt strap that ran across his shoulder. He
wore leather trousers and carried a sword and shield. His
hair was tied back.

He slowly walked out into the centre of the space, head
down, ignoring the crowd. I was afraid he would search for
me and was thankful when he did not.

Just then, another slave entered the arena. He was also
quite large, with much darker skin and the same style in
armour, holding a shield and sword. As he approached Erik, I
could see they were roughly the same height, although Erik's
shoulders were certainly wider.

It would have been a close match if Erik had intended to
fight. I wanted to close my eyes, not wanting to see his death,
but I knew I could not do that to him. I told him I respected
his decision and would be a witness to his end. I looked at
the two of them, the other slave circling Erik, I could see his

mouth moving, he was saying something to him.

Whatever it was, it was making Erik angry as suddenly his stance changed. He was gripping the sword and shield more tightly and separating his legs to stand as if ready to attack. I almost gasped as I saw the opponent charge at Erik, swinging his sword as though to slice off his head. Erik used his shield to block the attack and countered by swinging his sword at his opponents' leg, catching him in the thigh.

Puffs of sand billowed around their feet as they circled each other like wild bulls. Charging, their swords clanged again and again, their muscles glistening with sweat as they strained against each other's weight. Erik's opponent moved quickly, dodging his attacks and for the first time, I felt real fear as I saw the other man's sword slice into Erik's back as he passed him, blood emerging from the shallow wound. Erik regained his balance, and despite his injury, stood to face his opponent again.

My hands balled into fists as I watched their swords clash, my heart racing the entire time, unable to tear my eyes away. It was a close fight, the two of them quite evenly matched. However, Erik soon got the upper hand when his opponent stumbled while avoiding an attack, and Erik took the opportunity to run the sword straight through his chest.

I felt a huge wave of relief flow over me as I watched his opponent feebly grab at the sword sticking out of his chest, grasping his last breath before falling to the floor dead.

Despite the crowd cheering much louder than before, Erik did not even look at them, he just dropped his shield and walked out of the arena through the gate.

It was in that moment I knew I could not let Erik die. I had to find a way to break him free and get him away from this place.

~*~

The rest of the celebration was as expected. The twins overcame every challenge and were awarded at the end with a final ceremony to congratulate them and promote them officially to the royal guard. I had spent the entire time thinking about how I was going to help Erik. Hoping my absent-minded behaviour had not been noticed, I congratulated the twins and swiftly headed home.

It was now the middle of the night and I was preparing for something I never thought I would do; I was going to break into the slave prison and rescue Erik. I knew which building they were keeping him in, although not the exact location within it. I was going to have to be stealthy and quiet.

I covered my body head to toe in black leather trousers and an armless top that had a hood, common armour I had acquired from the Training House. A black face mask covered most of my features. Instead of my usual large sword, I strapped two small daggers to either side of my leg and wrapped my hair up into a tight bun.

I looked out of my window down at the streets. It was silent, and I could not see a single soul around; it was now or never. I crept down my stairs, not wanting to alert Castor to my movements, and I walked through my front door, slowly closing it so as not to make a sound.

Once outside, I snuck down the side of my house, choosing to use the smaller alleyways between the buildings to make my way to the prison rather than using the main streets. Using the darkness and shadows to my advantage, I stepped quickly but lightly to remain unnoticed.

The prison was located next to the Coliseum and had an entrance access through the battle arena. I chose to use this entrance to sneak in, knowing that the prison entrance was more likely to be guarded.

I climbed over the wall, placing my feet in the recesses of the stone. When I reached the top, I slowly let my body hang and then dropped to the floor in a crouch. The wall was not very high, and I was more worried that my landing would make a loud noise.

I remained crouched for a moment, listening around me. Then, feeling it was safe to do so, I quietly ran alongside the wall. I reached the black gate entrance that Erik had used earlier today to enter the arena.

I opened the gate and slipped through, sneaking down the corridor. When I reached the prison, I saw a torch from a guard walking up and down, keys jingling at her side. Creeping slowly, I walked up behind her and wrapped my arm around her throat, squeezing to cut off her air supply. She tried to struggle, but I had the element of surprise and she had reacted too late. I felt her limbs start to sag as she fell unconscious. Placing her gently on the floor, I picked up the torch and placed it in a holder on the wall. Then, bending down, I searched her body in the flickering light. Finding the keys, I took them from her belt and walked hastily to the first cell.

I unlocked the lock on the metal bars and pulled it open. Walking inside I saw a slave, it was not Erik. Before I turned to leave, I spoke in a husky tone to mask my voice.

"The black gate is open, leave now if you want to escape."

Then I turned and continued down the corridor. I did the same to every cell, hurrying as I went, knowing that the commotion of dispersing slaves running from each cell towards the battle arena would soon alert the guards.

After unlocking half a dozen or so other cells, I found him sat on the floor. Looking up, he was clearly shocked and confused, not knowing who I was or what was going on, he stood up. I heard loud noises coming from the corridor, the guards had clearly been alerted due to the prisoner's escape. I rushed over to Erik and pushed him into the corner, out of view from the cell entrance, pressing my body tightly up against his so he would not move. I heard the guards shouting and ordering each other and sighed with relief when they ran past his cell heading straight for the coliseum battle grounds.

That is when he realised who I was.

"Truda?" he whispered in a surprised tone.

"Shh." I said to him, holding a single finger over my mask.

"Follow me and keep quiet," I said, creeping back to the cell entrance. I carefully looked around the corner to check the corridor was clear, then began walking in the opposite direction from where I had come. My hope was that all the guards were now busy rounding up the slaves that had run through the coliseum.

As we continued on, Erik walked close behind me. We reached the prison door, and much to my delight, it was now unguarded as I had hoped. Quickly leaving the building, I guided Erik through the city. Luckily, the commotion seemed to be focused around the Coliseum and once we sneaked out of there unseen, it was easy to navigate through the alleyways until we reached my home. Opening the door quietly, I nodded for Erik to go in first, then after doing a final check to make sure no one had seen us enter, I walked in, closing and locking the door behind me.

Chapter 15

THE ESCAPE PLAN

"Truda, what…" Erik started saying.

"Shh," I hissed, worried he would wake Castor.

"Follow me," I said to him as I walked up the stairs towards my bed-chamber. When we were inside, and I was content that we had not caused a disturbance, I released a long-held breath, pulled down my hood and removed my face mask. I looked at Erik, who was watching me carefully, waiting for my explanation.

"I don't understand, why would you risk yourself to save me?" he asked quietly, still clearly confused by the whole ordeal.

"I could not let you die. After witnessing your brush with death earlier today, I knew I had to get you out of there," I said, rushing out my words while still trying to keep my voice low.

"They'll kill you if they find out what you have done," he said in an angry tone. "You should've just left me to die."

"If you wanted to die, you had your chance earlier today Erik, but as I recall you still decided to fight for your life, so do not be angry at me for wanting to do the same," I snapped back at him.

"I didn't fight for myself," he said, looking down to the floor.

"Then why did you fight?" I asked, angrily crossing my arms. I did not expect him to be thankful, but I also did not expect him to be mad at me for doing what I felt was right.

"I fought for the others," he said to me. "The slave they put me against, I knew him. He enjoyed hurting and dominating other slaves, beating them and stealing their food."

"So, you decided to finish the job out of revenge?" I barked in frustration. He looked at me, hurt by my words.

"No. He was boasting to me about what he would be able to do to the others once he was rid of me. I wanted him dead so that he couldn't hurt anyone else anymore."

Now I understood. Erik was the protector of slaves, always willing to put his life on the line to save others. We stood for a few minutes, not knowing what to say to each other.

"I am going to have a bath," I told him as I removed my gloves and released my long hair from its bun so it fell across my shoulders, instantly feeling the relief as it unravelled from the tight grips. I needed to get out of this room and have time alone to think. Then, without looking at him, I left the room, closing the door gently behind me.

After spending a good half an hour in the bathroom, soaking in a bath and cleaning my hair, I thought about what Erik told me. He had not wanted to be saved, he had not fought to live, he had fought to protect the lives of others. Erik and I were more than just a species apart, we were opposites. I had acted selfishly. I was not thinking about what was best for my people, I was not protecting our kingdom, I had just committed treason. I had risked my position for an ungrateful Guan, who was now likely sulking in my bed-chamber, while I sat in the bathtub, washing my body twice, trying to decide what my next move would be.

Because, grateful or not, I was seeing my plan through. I was going to save Erik and get him out of the city, somehow. I dried myself and put on my crop cotton top and trousers, throwing my stealth gear in the corner. Looking at the black leather I knew I would have to hide these from view, it had been easy to acquire the common armour from the Training House but would be too risky to return it from where it came.

When I returned to the room, Erik was lying on the floor next to the bed, he had removed one of my pillows to rest under his head.

"You are injured, you should sleep on the bed," I told him, thinking of the cut that still ran down his back from his fight with the other slave.

"I've slept on worse," he mumbled.

"Fine," I said, walking around the other side of the bed and laying down. He was clearly still angry at me for saving his life. After a few moments, Erik broke the silence.

"What are we going to do now?" he asked. That was a good question. I needed to get him out of the city but I had no idea where he could go.

"I have a plan," I stated.

~*~

My statement last night was not true. I had no plan. At least, not yet. I could not exactly keep him hidden in my bed-chamber forever. Light broke through my room as I laid wide awake staring up at the ceiling, listening to Erik's breathing on the floor next to me as he slept.

He was obviously exhausted from the events of yesterday, and I wanted to let him rest for as long as possible. I was thinking about my next move. I needed to keep Erik hidden here for a few days. If I requested to leave the city now, it would raise suspicion. Waiting would give me the valuable time I needed to formulate my plan, I needed a safe location.

I reacted too late when Castor suddenly walked in the room, dropping the plate of fruit he had in his hands when he saw Erik's large body next to the bed. Erik woke, jerking up at the noise. Castor stared at us both in shock and started to turn to leave.

"Castor wait," I told him. He did as I asked and slowly turned around to face me.

"I'm sorry, I'll clean this up," he said, looking down to the floor at the mess he made.

"It is alright Castor, leave it for a moment, you can come in," I said more softly so that he knew not to be afraid.

"Is he one of the escaped slaves?" he said as he entered the room slowly, still keeping a safe distance from me.

"Yes, this is Erik." I told him. "You do not need to be afraid; he will not hurt you."

"I think he's more afraid of you," said Erik. I glared at him as I got off the bed to walk over to Castor.

"I need you to keep this a secret. No one can know he is here, do you understand?" I asked him, keeping my tone gentle.

"Yes," said Castor, glancing at Erik.

"Clean up the mess and fetch us some fresh fruit," I kindly instructed. He nodded and then hesitated as he approached the bed-chamber door.

"How did you know about the escaped slaves?" Erik asked him. Castor looked at him, frozen in place.

"What is it Castor?" I asked him.

"A guard came for you urgently this morning. She mentioned about the escaped slaves and told me to inform you that you have been summoned urgently to the palace," he told me.

"Thank you, I will leave shortly. Get some fruit for Erik and yourself," Castor looked over to Erik who smiled at him. Castor smiled back and nodded. I waited until he had picked up the mess off the floor and left the room.

"You need to send me back so there is no evidence that it was you," Erik said as he stood.

"No, I do not, you will stay here hidden until I return from the palace," I said to him as I walked over to get some clean clothes out of the chest.

"Truda, this is ridiculous, you're going to get caught," he said in a panicked tone.

"Calm yourself Erik, there is no way they know it was me. I will be able to use the situation to my advantage."

"Really? Then why are you being summoned to the palace," he said with a sarcastic tone mixed with what I detected was a little fear. I turned to look at him, he stood in the middle of my room with his arms crossed.

"Because, I am the General of Kven, and they are now going to be looking to me for answers, and that Erik, is what I am counting on," I said with a grin.

~*~

The council meeting was what I expected it to be, lots of angry voices shouting at each other. I sat with my arms crossed in my chair, letting the scene unfold.

"How could this happen?" said the queen in anguish. Her

daughter had decided not to turn up for this meeting, it must have been too early for her.

"It was obviously the rebels again," said Peril.

"How did they get through undetected? I thought we were on high alert after the last time!" exclaimed Acqueline.

"We need to find out how this could have happened," added the queen.

"And who's incompetence we can blame," spat Freyja, immediately glancing at me. This was it, the moment I had been waiting for.

"That is enough!" I shouted as I stood. The room went quiet and everyone's eyes were on me. "Apologies my Queen, but I think you will agree that this squabbling is not solving anything. Now that I have finished in the breeding programme, I am officially taking back the full extent of my duties. I will get to the bottom of what happened last night, starting by interrogating the prisoners that failed to escape." My eyes were fierce as I held my head up high. I wanted everyone to know that I was in charge of this situation.

"Very well Truda, we give you full responsibility in finding out what happened," said the queen.

As I turned from my chair, I signalled the salute towards the queen and then looked around the table as one by one, they nodded their heads and saluted the signal recognising my rank and authority. As I left the throne room, Acqueline was fast on my heels.

"Tru, wait!" she called. I stopped and looked to her.

"Let me help with your investigation."

"If the queen grants it, then I could use the help from someone I trust," I agreed. Feeling like this was the natural response to have, if I denied her help and demanded on acting alone, it would seem out of character for a situation such as this, and I needed the council's trust. Besides, Acqueline would be the last person to believe that I had committed the treacherous act. A moment of guilt flooded through me at the thought of having to lie to my friend, but I knew I could not risk telling her know the truth, not yet.

"What would you like me to do?" she asked, ready to take my orders.

"Go to the prison, find out how many prisoners escaped and interrogate the ones that were re-captured, see what they can tell you about the people that helped them." She nodded that she understood.

It would be more useful to have someone else ask the questions, find out what they really knew, and also gave me the opportunity to do something else very important.

"What will you do?" she asked.

"I am going to question some houses. If it was the rebels, then someone must know something about the escape attempt," I said. With that, Acqueline walked back into the throne room, and I continued down the corridor. I had not completely lied to Acqueline, I planned on doing exactly that, except I was not planning on visiting multiple households, I was only going to one.

~*~

I rode Thio to the outer edges and stopped in front of the Farmhouse. I saw her immediately, wearing plain clothing similar to before, moving bags of flour from a cart into her house. When she saw me, she froze in fear. I dismounted my horse and approached her front door. Tying his reins to a wooden post, I walked closer to the woman.

"Can we talk inside for a moment?" she nodded quickly and put down the bag of flour. Rubbing her hands clean, she walked into the house as I followed closely behind her. I closed the door and stood by it, blocking her exit, which she noticed, looking at me with concern. When I had come here before with the twins, I thought she was quite young, but now, standing closer to her, I noticed things I had not before. There were subtle signs of wrinkles by her grey eyes and aged dimple lines on the edges of her cheeks. Her strawberry hair was tied in a long side plait that hung over her shoulder.

"Have you heard about the prisoners that escaped last night?" I asked her.

"Yes, but I don't know any details, just what I heard at the market this morning," she rushed to answer.

"I would be concerned if you did know more about it," I said, smiling to myself, which she obviously took as a threat as she began to walk backwards, her hands raised.

"Please General, I promise I don't know anything."

"What is your name?" I asked her.

"Kayla," she responded.

"Well Kayla, I need your help," I said to her, trying to think carefully about my next words as I did not know yet if this woman could be trusted.

"With what?" she asked me.

"I need to know if you know the location of the rebel base and how I can find it?" I said to her quietly.

"Please, I already told you and the warriors before, I don't know anything." She was crying now, clearly afraid for her life after what had happened on our last visit.

"Kayla, I promise you I am not here to hurt you. I have a friend who needs help, they cannot stay in the city and I need to take them somewhere safe."

Now she looked confused.

"Who would you know that wouldn't be safe in the city, and how do I know this is not a trap to get the answers you were seeking all along?" I saw her face as she instantly regretted her words. My instincts were right, she knew something.

"Kayla, I need you to trust me," I said. She stood, staring at me worriedly, obviously stopping herself from speaking and giving anything away. The only way to gain her trust now was to tell her the truth.

"The friend I speak of, they are not an elf, they are…were a breeding Guan and I need to get him out of the city." I heard her gasp as I spoke the words. I could feel the panic rise in me. This situation was about to go one of two ways. The first was that she would believe me and give me the information I came here seeking. The second would result in her death, as I could not afford for her to run off and tell someone what I had just said.

After a long pause, she spoke.

"It was you? you released the slaves?"

"I broke out one Guan and used the others as a distraction to get him to safety," I told her honestly.

"Why?" she asked me. That was a complicated question, one I did not have time for right now.

"Can you help me or not?" I demanded.

"I don't know where the rebel base is," she told me. Just as I was about to think I had wasted my journey, she said, "but I can help you get out of the city through a secret passageway, and send you off in the right direction." My eyes lit up and I smiled.

"Will you mark it on the map for me?" I asked. She hesitated for a moment and then shook her head.

"No, but if you bring your freed Guan to me, I will show you where to go on your map then." She wanted evidence that I was really the one who had broken out the slaves. It was smart, not compromising what she really knew without knowing if I was telling the truth.

"I will return in two nights time," I said to her. "If you mention this to anyone, there will be consequences."

"I won't speak of this to anyone," she promised, looking nervous at my mild threat. I left her house and mounted my horse. Kayla stood in the doorway.

"I wish you luck," she said with a hopeful smile, clearly still not completely confident that I was telling the truth but wanting to trust me.

"Thank you, we might just need it," I replied. As she signalled the salute, I pulled on Thio's reins and galloped back into the centre of the city.

~*~

When I returned to the city, I met up with Acqueline at the prison.

"What did you find out?" I asked her.

"Well, I am not sure you will believe this, but according to the prisoners, they were helped by one elf," she told me. I tried to act as surprised as I could.

"Just one? They must be lying!" I said to her.

"I thought so too at first, but they all said the same, and that's not even the best part. They described to me what the elf looked like," she said. I felt a slight panic rise in me. Had they been able to describe enough detail to my friend so that she knew it was me?

"What did they say?" I asked.

"They described what she was wearing, and Tru, it was city armour, this was an inside job."

"What!" I snapped, holding back my relief and thankful that clearly, they had not given her information that was too detailed.

"I must report this to the queen immediately, thank you Acqueline." She nodded towards me and signalled the salute of respect as I turned to walk away.

"Tru, wait. There is one more thing," she added. I kept my distance but looked back to her so she could continue.

"All the prisoners were caught and returned to their cells except one, and he was the slave you were partnered with at the Breeding House."

At this not-so-shocking news, I tried to look as angry as possible before turning away again and heading towards the throne room. I walked straight past the guards, trying to keep my appearance by looking outraged, knowing this would help me for what I had to do next. The queen was sitting in her chair talking to Princess Callidice who was sat beside her. Behind her chair stood Phoenyx who, this time, did not appear to be wearing his leash and collar.

"My Queen, I have just learnt the most disturbing news," I shouted across the throne room. When I got close enough, I saluted the signal of respect.

"What have you uncovered General Truda?" she said to me, clearly startled by my obvious anger. I told her what

Acqueline had learnt from the prisoners, that all evidence was pointing to an inside job. I also told her that all the slaves had been re-captured, all but the Guan I was partnered with at the Breeding House.

"What will you do?" she asked me.

"I plan to have the city searched while I scout outside the city for the escaped Guan," I told her.

"I do not think you should go alone Truda, take a small group of warriors with you."

"That will not be wise, as I do not know who can be trusted. Either this was an inside job, or the rebels had help from someone in the city. Besides, I will take personal pleasure in bringing back the slave for punishment or kill him if he resists." I said with a wicked grin.

"Then I wish you happy hunting Truda," said the queen. I saluted and glanced over to the princess, wondering why she had been so quiet. She was staring at me, a puzzled expression on her face, as though she was trying to penetrate my mind with her thoughts. Behind her I saw Phoenyx who was also looking at me with concern and fear in his eyes. Just as I turned, I smiled toward him, making the princess even more confused as she thought I had smiled at her.

Chapter 16

SECRET DOORS

When I returned to my house, I walked straight upstairs to my bed-chamber. In my room I saw Castor sitting on the bed talking to Erik, Castor's eyes beamed up at Erik with whatever he was telling him, they were both smiling. At seeing me enter, they both stopped talking and Castor shot up off the bed standing with his hands in front of him.

"Go run a bath Castor," I instructed politely. He nodded quickly and left the room, closing the door behind him.

"Where have you been? You've been gone all day," Erik asked standing up.

"Did I not tell you I am the General? My days are usually busy," I stated abruptly.

"I was worried about you," he said in a much softer voice.

"Well, you did not need to worry. Today went better than I could have possibly hoped," I replied, facing away from him and walking over towards my chest of clothing.

"Truda, I wanted to apologise for last night, and I want you to know I do appreciate what you're doing for me." Hearing that, I turned to look at him. "I was only angry because of the risks you are taking; I don't want anything bad to happen to you." He took a step in my direction, walking closer to me. Just then, I heard the running water stop.

"When was the last time you had a bath?" I asked him, grinning.

He looked embarrassed and leaned down as though to smell himself, which only made me laugh.

"Go, the bath is for you, use whatever soaps and oils you like."

"Thank you," he said, walking from the bedroom to the bathroom. I walked over to my chest of clothing and pulled out some clean cotton, taking my time as thoughts of the day clouded my mind. I could only hope that Kayla was telling me the truth and that she would be able to guide me and Erik safely out of the city.

Removing my leather and armour, I replaced them with the soft clean fabric. Once dressed, I walked over to my bed-chamber door to go downstairs, only to walk into a large body standing in my doorway, wearing nothing but a towel around his waist. Droplets of water ran down his muscular torso. The heat from his body radiated over me and his chest heaved with quickening breaths. I looked up. There was longing in his eyes.

I thought back to the kiss we shared only a few days ago, the kiss I never should have allowed, thinking it was going to be the last time, as I thought we were saying goodbye to each other. Erik searched my eyes as I looked up to him and then slowly bent down, hovering his lips just above mine. Panicking, I stepped back and straightened my body to compose myself.

"Now that Castor knows you are here, you can sleep in the guest bed-chamber across the hall," I said.

His gaze travelled down my slightly revealing cotton nightwear, with clear hunger in his eyes. I coughed to break him out of his trance, folding my arms, which worked as he nodded and started to turn from me.

"I will have Castor fetch you some of Tobias's old clothes," I told him as he walked silently down the hallway. Tobias's clothes would be a tight fit, but it would be better than Erik walking around my home half naked all the time.

~*~

Later that night I watched him. I had tried to sleep, only managing to doze off for a few hours, but it was no use, all I could think about was the man sleeping in the next room. I had gotten up and crept out of my room into his. Now, sat in a chair at the opposite side of the room, he was frowning, and I wondered what he was dreaming about.

He was moaning quietly, and his hands were clenched. It was obviously a bad dream, and I hoped he was not thinking about me. Suddenly, as if his dream had frightened him, he woke and sat up, running his hands through his hair. I tried to remain still and soundless, but it was no use as he looked around the room and saw me.

We just looked at each other for a moment, then I got up to leave the room. As I reached for the door, I felt him grab my arm from behind me. I froze, afraid to turn and look at him.

He stepped closer, pressing his chest against my back and slowly wrapped an arm around my waist. My breathing started to quicken as his other hand stroked up my arm, up to my shoulder and moved my hair away. He bent down and kissed my neck. I closed my eyes as I felt his soft lips slowly kiss and nip at my skin, as he whispered in my ear.

"No-ones watching us now, we can be together if you want to." Is that what he thought? That I had broken him out of the prison so I could use him the way other elves did? I thought of Phoenyx and the other slaves at the Breeding House and felt angry. Clenching my fists, I turned and pushed Erik away from me.

"No!" I shouted at him. Then I turned and left his room.

~*~

The next morning, I sat at my kitchen table. Castor was chopping various fruits and slicing bread on the counter next to me. I was looking at my map of the Kingdom of Nysa, trying to figure out the best route once out of the city. Of course, that would depend on where we were going. We would need to leave in the middle of the night, it would give us our best chance at not getting seen, travelling through the darkness of the night to get out of the city's view. Taking horses would have been better, but since I had told the queen I would scout on my own, I knew it would raise suspicions to take two. Besides, we were going to be a lot harder to spot on foot, so I would use that to my advantage.

I heard Erik approach from behind me, and gasped as I looked at him. I thought that him wearing Tobias's clothes to cover up his nakedness was going to help, but I was wrong because Tobias's clothes clung to every muscle on his body. They were very different in size, and the sleeves on his arms looked like they were about to tear due to the strain on the fabric.

"Morning," he said to me with a smile, obviously liking the way I was currently gawking at him. I frowned angrily at myself for being caught looking once again, returning my concentration back to the map.

"What are you doing?" he asked, taking a seat next to me. It also did not help that he smelled amazing, and a mix of his natural musky smell now accented with my fruity oils and soap.

"I am deciding on the best route to take once we are out of the city," I told him, not looking in his direction.

"Do you know where we're going?" he asked, pointing towards my notes and markings on the map.

"Not yet, but I will," I said.

"Where are you thinking?" he asked me.

"Somewhere that will hopefully lead us to a safer place," I said, slowly feeling frustrated at his constant questions and close proximity. Not wanting to tell Erik more than that for now, he knew I was taking enough risks getting him out of the city. I was putting myself in greater danger trying to find the rebel base, if it even really did exist.

"Castor, I need you to go and take this message to the palace tomorrow morning," I said as I passed him a scroll I had written earlier.

"What does it say?" Erik asked. Why was he so full of questions this morning?

"What does it matter what it says?" I snapped.

"Truda, there is something you're not telling me," he replied more sternly.

"Erik, there are a lot of things I do not tell you because you simply do not need to know. I will be gone for most of the day," I replied curtly. Then I rolled up my map and stepped away from the table, leaving both Castor and Erik looking at me bewildered as I walked out of the kitchen.

~*~

I left to go meet with Imelda, to give her instruction on

213

searching the city. I walked into the Training House and saw her. As we spoke, I immediately began to get distracted with thoughts of Erik, tuning out the sound that belonged to Imelda's voice as I pondered over my thoughts. I did not mean to get so angry with Erik but being close to him in my home was becoming difficult, and after last night, I felt like I was losing my mind around him.

Things had definitely changed between us, and he clearly wanted to take it to the next step, a line which I knew could not be crossed. I had changed everything when I broke him out of that prison. I had changed the terms between us. I admit that there was something more than the friendship we had developed during our time at the Breeding House, and I was clearly drawn to him.

I could not help but think about his half naked body from last night. I was attracted to him and I felt wrong because of it. Elves did not have relationships with Guans and they certainly would not find them attractive, or did they?

The princess had obviously taken a personal liking to Phoenyx, taking him from the Pleasure House to keep for herself, and I knew the things that went on in there. The things they did there were not out of necessity like the breeding programme, they indulged themselves doing all manner of things with slaves that I really did not want to think about right now.

The underlining fact was that I was an elf, and he was a

Guan, there could be no more to it than that. Things would be better when I got Erik out of the city to safety, wherever that may be. Then I could return, and my life would go back to normal.

"General?" asked Imelda. Shaking my head briefly, I looked at her. She looked confused and annoyed that I had not been paying attention, but I could not help it, her drib voice was boring and allowed for distracting thoughts to enter my mind.

"Please, continue," I said, lightly rubbing the side of my temple with two fingers, as if massaging a headache that wanted to emerge.

We discussed rotations of guards throughout the city. I told her that I wanted patrols walking the streets and extra guards posted at the main gates, the prison and the east wall that was still under repair. I made sure that all of our warriors were spread out in all areas of the city except one, near the farmhouse. I could only hope that Kayla was telling me the truth and knew a safe way out of the city.

~*~

"It is time," I told Erik. We were in light tanned hide clothing with hooded cloth cloaks. Erik had a sack on his back that was holding our provisions, I had my sword and daggers. Putting on my face mask, I slowly opened the front door to check it was clear.

I looked back to Castor, who nodded his head. Earlier,

when not in ear shot of Erik, I told Castor that once he had delivered the note to the palace informing them I had left during the night, to stay in the house out of sight until I returned, which I told him should not be more than a few days. Castor said goodbye to Erik, they had obviously become friends in the short time they had spent together.

"Follow me and stay close," I told Erik, then ducked out of the house, waiting for him to pass me before I closed the door. I walked quietly down the side of my house using the back roads to hide us from view. Kayla's farmhouse was situated close to the edge of the wall on the outskirts of the city. Knowing that if we followed the wall slowly and quietly, we would remain hidden in the shadows and be able to reach the farmhouse unseen.

When we reached our destination, I tapped quietly on Kayla's front door. As soon as it opened, Erik and I quickly slipped through.

"So, you were telling the truth," Kayla exclaimed.

After nodding, I grabbed her arm gently and led her to the table. Looking back, I told Erik to keep watch out of the window, then whispered to Kayla.

"Will you mark on my map where the rebel base is?" Rolling the map out on her dining table she walked over to me and looked at the map. After closing her eyes for a moment, obviously second guessing what she was about to do, she looked back at the map and pointed to a pass in the far desert cliffs. I immediately used a bit of charcoal to mark where her finger was.

"And this will lead me to the rebel base?" I asked her.

"No, it will lead you to a guide who will show you the rest of the way," she said quietly.

"Thank you, Kayla," I said, placing my hand on her shoulder hoping I looked sincere. "I will keep this between us, no one will know what you have told me today," I said to her. "Now, can you tell me this safe way out of the city you mentioned?" I said a little louder now, letting her know that it was okay for Erik to hear this part of the conversation.

"Follow me," said Kayla, looking at both me and Erik. We followed her into her living room. In the centre was a large rug, she quickly got on her hands and knees and rolled the carpet away, revealing a hidden door. "This will lead you to a tunnel that takes you right into the lower foundations of the wall. There you will find a secret door that will lead you outside," she said, looking between the both of us.

"Thank you, Kayla. I am grateful for your help." With that, she nodded and saluted towards me. Then, reaching for a bit of rope tucked into a recess in the trap door, she pulled it, revealing the ladder that would take us down into the tunnel.

I nodded for Erik to go down first, then quickly followed him. As soon as I was below ground, I looked up to Kayla who smiled at me with hope. As she closed the trap door and I heard her unroll the rug back into place.

~*~

We walked down the tunnel for a few minutes until we reached the other end and saw the door. The tunnel had been dank and dark, but luckily, I had thought to bring a torch which I had lit to help guide us through. I tried the door and grunted in frustration when I found it was locked.

"I need the bag," I said quietly. Erik removed it from his back, gently dropping it by my feet. After looking inside for a few moments, I found what I was looking for; tools to help me pick the lock. After kneeling down by the door and working on the lock for a few moments, I heard the click and smiled at Erik. Then, giving him back the bag, I raised my hood and opened the door to the beautiful green that surrounded the city.

"I don't think our tan clothing is going to camouflage with the grass," said Erik.

"No, the darkness will do that, our tan clothes will camouflage us when the sun rises over the desert," I replied, turning to walk out the door. Erik grabbed my arm, holding me back.

"Truda, we don't have to do this, you could just take me back," he told me. I glared at him then, feeling my anger building up. I closed the door.

"Is that what you want Erik?" I snapped. "You have said it enough times now. First when you said you would not fight in the Coliseum, then when you were angry at me for rescuing you from the prison, and now here, by the door to your freedom." I crossed my arms in a poor attempt to contain my frustration.

Erik looked back at me angrily, dropping the bag to the floor.

"Do you even care what I want?"

"This is pointless, and we do not have time to waste," I mumbled as I began to turn back towards the door to ignore him. Erik rushed at me, quickly pinning me against the wall. It was the wrong move to make, as I pushed him harshly back and, grabbing my dagger, I held it up to his throat.

We were both clearly angry and breathing heavily, but after staring into his crystal blue eyes, I felt my anger lessen. As I sighed, I took the knife away from his throat and put it back in its sheath strapped to my thigh. Then I took a step back and looked at him.

"Okay Erik, the decision is yours. Either you can let me lead you out of the city, or you can ask me to take you back and hand you over. I leave it to you to choose," I said, crossing my arms again. This is what it needed to come down to. I could not force him to leave the city with me, he had to want to. After a few moments of silence, he picked up the bag, and threw it back over his shoulder.

"Let's leave the city." I smiled and opened the door to the outside.

Chapter 17

A REBELLIOUS STORY

By the time we reached the desert, the sun was making its appearance. Like a giant glowing ball, its edges wavering from the heat, it slowly rose over the barren landscape. We had walked across the grassland hastily all through the night and had not spoken to each other for hours. I wanted to think that was because we were too busy focusing on the journey, but I knew it was because of the tension between us.

We could no longer see the shape of the city behind us, meaning we had already covered a great distance, and this would be a good time to rest. I slowed my pace, heading toward a small group of long cacti.

"We shall rest here for a few hours," I told Erik. He looked exhausted, breathing heavily as he had obviously struggled keeping up with my constant quickened pace.

"You should sleep, the sun is likely to be harsh and we will cover greater distance later in the day when it is cooler." I Looked up to the sun, already feeling its warmth, it was going to be a hot day.

"You need your rest also," replied Erik as he sat on the floor beside me.

"I will be fine. I am only stopping to allow you to catch your breath, it will be a lot harder to get to where we are going if I have to carry you," I snarked at him. Erik sighed and laid back into the sand, using his cloak hood to cover his eyes from the sun.

"How much further?" he said to me without lifting his hood to look at me as he spoke.

"Another day, perhaps two," I said, not wanting to give away more than that.

"Now sleep," I commanded.

I thought at first, he might be stubborn and try to stay awake, or ask me more questions, but it was not long until his breathing became rhythmic, and I knew he was asleep. I sat close beside him, listening to the sounds he made as he slept, watching his broad chest rise and fall. I stayed awake, keeping watch, all the while resisting the urge to touch him.

Soon, hours had passed, and the sun's heat had been at its worst. Luckily we were shielded from the harsher sun rays by the large cactus shadows. I tapped Erik to wake him. At first, he did not move, so I hit him harder in the arm, which did the trick, as I saw him jolt awake and sit up straight.

"We need to move," I told him.

Standing, I grabbed the bag, tossing it over my shoulder. Erik stood slowly, attempting to wipe the sand that had found a home in the creases of his clothing, and after squinting up at the sun, he stepped to follow me.

~*~

It was getting dark by the time we reached the desert edge, and ahead of us were the sand dunes. I stopped and rolled out my map, leaning against a nearby rock, trying to determine how far away we were from the pass that Kayla had shown me.

Erik leaned on his knees catching his breath.

"How much further?" he asked me again.

"You do realise you sound like an impatient child," I retorted without looking up from my map.

"Well, you haven't exactly said much to me since we left the city," he said to me. I sighed in frustration as I rolled up my map and put it back onto the bag.

"Not too far now," I said, walking past him.

"Truda, stop. Did I say something wrong?"

I turned to look at him, his face was creased from concern.

"Erik I…" However, I stopped when I saw some stones roll down the surface of a craggy rock face, as though they had just been disturbed. I looked back to Erik, holding my finger to my lips. I grabbed my sword handle, pulling it from my back, and walked forward slowly. I heard a scuffling noise ahead and saw a few more rocks roll in front of me.

Then I saw it. Just as I turned around the corner between the giant sand rocks, in the middle of our path sat a little white fox. Not just any white fox, it was the one I had seen in my dream weeks ago. At first, as I approached, it just sat there. Then, as I stepped closer, it started to back away. I stepped slowly, putting my sword behind my back and crouched, out-stretching my hand.

"Truda, what are you doing?" Erik called to me, but I ignored him.

The fox, peering at my out-stretched hand, stepped towards me slowly as it sniffed my fingertips, its whiskers tickling my thumb. Then, out of nowhere, it started circling and bouncing in excitement. I stood quickly and watched its curious behaviour. It continued to look at me, bouncing around then started to run off looking behind. It would step towards me and then run off again.

"I think it wants us to follow it," I said.

"Truda, it's just an animal."

"Actually, I think this is our guide," I said, not particularly to Erik but just speaking the words out loud. I began to follow the little fox with Erik walking closely behind me. The fox looked back every now and again to check we were following.

Then it picked up pace and took off in a little run. I sped

up my steps, but it was not long until it was out of our sight. I stopped, waiting for it to come back, but it did not re-appear.

"Truda?" Erik called.

"Not now Erik, let me think."

"Truda!" He shouted louder.

"What!" I snapped as I looked back at him. He was not looking towards me but was looking above him. I followed his gaze and saw them. At least a dozen elves had surrounded us on the rock edge holding bows with arrows pointed at us. Half of them stayed in position while the other half climbed down to approach us. Erik edged closer to me as I reached for my sword.

"Lower your weapon and get on your knees," shouted an elf woman who was walking towards us.

"Not likely," I replied to her as I gripped my sword tighter.

"Truda don't, there are too many of them," Erik said.

"He's right General," shouted another elf from above. "Come quietly and we won't kill you or your friend." I looked at the women. I was weary from the journey but was sure I could at least take a few of them out. But then what? They would overpower me and likely kill us both.

Looking at Erik, I nodded as I slowly crouched to the floor and dropped my sword on the ground in front of me. The elf closest to me walked forward slowly, still with her bow aimed ready, and kicked the sword away from me.

"A friend sent a message raven, warning us of your arrival," she grinned. Kayla had betrayed me. She had not helped me at all, instead she had led me and Erik into an ambush.

The elf stepped closer, and, releasing her grip on her bow, she quickly thrust the wood toward my face. I felt a sharp pain in my head.

"Truda!" Erik screaming my name was the last thing I heard before I fell back, and everything went black.

~*~

I could hear voices nearby, they were angry and raised, shouting at each other. One I recognised to be Erik, but the other I did not know.

"Do you even know who she is?" said the voice.

"Of course I know, she saved me," replied Erik.

"No, you were obviously tricked, she is our enemy," insisted the deep voiced female.

My head was pounding, and my forehead felt damp. I squinted my eyes open and at first only saw darkness, then, as I felt the warmth on my face from my own breath, I realised I had some kind of hood over my head. I was sat on the floor, but my arms were trapped behind me, my hands tied together, bound by rope, around what felt like a wooden beam. I could just make out a light ahead of me through the hood. From what I could make out, it looked like I was inside some kind of tent, and I could see a line of light between the entrance of the canvas.

Just then, the fabric parted revealing the daylight as a figure walked through. They walked directly in front of me and pulled the hood from my face.

"General Truda, we meet again," she said.

I looked up at her, my eyes still squinting from the pain in my head. She was wearing brown leather clothes, with gold armour plates over her chest, shoulders and shins. Her skin was dark, her golden braided hair in a ponytail. I recognised her but did not know her name.

"Who are you?" I said, my voice croaky as my throat was dry.

"My name is Maiya, a leader of what you know as the rebels. I must congratulate you General, for getting so close to finding our location, it's a shame you won't be able to tell anyone about it," she sneered folding her arms.

"That is not why I'm here," I coughed.

"Then why are you here?" she said, pursing her lips and squinting her eyes.

"Let me see her," I heard Erik shout from outside the tent. Maiya glanced towards the entrance and grunted in frustration.

"It seems that your Guan is quite attached," she said, looking back at me.

"He is not my Guan," I spat, then coughed again.

"Hmm," was her only reply, then she turned back towards the entrance of the tent.

226

"If I let you in, will you keep quiet?" she asked. I did not hear a response but a few minutes later, Erik came inside the tent and rushed over to me.

"Truda, are you alright?" he asked as he dropped to his knees in front of me. I started to nod, but my head pounded in pain from my movements.

"Where are we?" I asked him quietly.

"We are in the rebel base."

~*~

I must have fallen asleep again as I woke with my head resting on Erik's shoulder. Thankful that when I moved my head it was no longer pounding, I Looked up to see Maiya staring at me curiously.

"She's awake," she shouted towards the tent entrance. I felt Erik move against me as he turned his head to look at my face.

"Are you okay?" he whispered.

"You obviously have that one well trained, he refuses to leave your side," Maiya sneered at us. This time I heard Erik growl in response to her words and before I could say anything, the tent opened and a man walked through. He was older, his hair turning grey, wrinkles on his face. I had never seen a human this aged before. He was tall and quite well built. Despite his ageing skin, his muscles were still defined, his large hands full of scars and callous rough skin, similar to Erik's.

"Maiya, will you give us a minute?" he said, glancing at

her briefly before returning his eyes to me and Erik.

"I don't think that is wise," she replied to him while frowning toward me.

"I will be fine Maiya, just wait outside," he said to her again. She huffed, keeping her arms crossed, and then walked out of the tent. The man stepped closer to us and then crouched to the floor so he could meet me at eye level.

"I'm Cobal, it's a pleasure to finally meet you General Truda." He nodded his head respectfully.

"Let her go," said Erik.

"Is what he claims true?" he asked, while glancing from Erik and looking back to me.

"Is what true?" I replied.

"Erik told us that you saved him, hid him in your home and then helped him escape the city?" Cobal asked. I nodded, confirming Erik's story.

"Tell me General Truda, why would you do that?" he asked, looking at me curiously. I did not know what to say, it was not a question that could easily be answered in one sentence.

"How about I tell you both a story," he said, positioning himself more comfortably on the ground.

"Twenty years ago, I was a Guan in the city of Kven. Specifically, I was a breeding slave, used a number of times by your kind to help the elf and Guan population. One day I was paired with a beautiful elf called Lilith. She was different, and I was drawn to her immediately. She was kind and gentle, a

228

healer amongst your people. I loved her from the moment I met her, and after spending a few weeks with me, she returned my love. It wasn't long before she found out she was pregnant and we spent the next few months apart, although we never forgot each other. After giving birth, she convinced the queen to let her re-enter the breeding programme to be with me again."

Erik shifted beside me and I felt his hand lightly stroke my arm.

"What happened?" he asked Cobal.

"We were discovered, and she was killed," Cobal said while looking to the ground. "I was scheduled for death a few days later. I wanted them to kill me instantly, but I wasn't important enough to be executed straight away. They chose to let me suffer, to rot in my grief."

"Until I came and saved his ass," said Maiya as she returned back into the tent. Cobal looked behind him towards Maiya and smiled, then looked back to us. He did not miss the fact that Erik had shuffled closer to me and purposely brushed his fingers across my arm.

"Bring some water and food," shouted Cobal to someone outside the tent.

Chapter 18

THE UNKNOWN

Erik and I were alone, my hands still tied behind my back. Next to him was a bowl of water and he was using a damp cloth to gently clean the cut on my forehead.

"How do you feel?" he asked, dampening the cloth in the water again. He gently dabbed my face, wiping the blood and carefully moving the hair that had stuck there, tucking the strands behind my pointed ears.

"Like my head had a fight with a boulder and I lost," I said. Erik laughed lightly.

"You tell jokes now?" he asked me. I looked up at him.

"Did you not hear Cobal's story? It seems my whole life has been a joke," I said to him. It made perfect sense why the books had been hidden or stolen from the great library.

Who would want our people to know this truth about how the rebellion war started? We killed one of our own for caring about a Guan. Maybe the old Truda; before I had lost Tobias or before I met Erik, would have agreed with the previous queen's decision to have her killed. Love between Guans and elves was forbidden, we all knew it, but now, looking at Erik, I could not understand why. Men were no longer the barbaric, murderous creatures of this world like our histories told us; we were.

"I understand," Erik said, still gently wiping water across my face.

"How could you possibly understand, you do not have blood on your hands," I told him.

"No, but now I know this has happened before, that what I feel is not… wrong," he said, pausing his movements as he spoke, looking deeply into my eyes.

"What do you mean?" I asked him. Before Erik could speak, we heard talking outside the tent, three voices, two I recognised as Maiya and Cobal and a third I had not heard before. Erik and I paused; our gaze focused on the entrance of the tent as we attempted to hear the quiet conversation.

"This is dangerous," said Maiya, "even if what the Guan said is true, how do we know she hasn't used him to find us?"

"I don't think that's why she helped him, I think she brought him here to keep him safe," said Cobal.

"You're thinking foolishly Cobal, don't look to them and

compare it to what you had," spat Maiya. The third voice whispered, and I could not make out what they said, the voice sounded soft and light, like that of a child.

"Well, I hope you both know what you're doing," said Maiya with a frustrated sigh. She walked into the tent with Cobal close behind her.

"Release her," said Cobal, looking to Maiya who approached and crouched down to untie my arms. I looked up to Cobal and nodded, hoping to let him know that I was thankful. Then a flash of white caught my eye by the tent entrance, the tail of a white fox!

~*~

After Maiya had reluctantly released me from my bonds, Erik held my arm tightly, helping me steady as I rose to my feet. I motioned to push him away, showing that I was able to stand without assistance, but my head was still pounding. Feeling dizzy, I felt my body crumple, only to be caught in Erik's arms. He held me, putting my arm around his shoulder to help me walk.

"I've got you," he whispered in my ear. Cobal and Maiya led us out of the tent. I waited to see which land we were in, only to discover we were not even on land.

We were on a platform in a giant tree, inside a huge forest. As I looked around, I could see other trees with large platforms on them, planks and rope bridges connecting them. I was in the rebel base and it was huge, hidden at great height amongst these giant trees.

It was dark, with only a small number of lit lanterns to help Maiya lead us to our destination. The walkways were narrow, making us continue crossing the bridges in single file, to reach the next connecting platform. Erik walked closely behind me, holding the rope edge as we crossed another bridge. I looked down to see how high up we actually were, and felt my legs shake as I could not see the bottom. I did not know I could be nervous of heights, but then I had never before stood on a surface that creaked and wobbled with every step I took. Feeling suddenly dizzy again, I froze and slumped slightly, only to be once again propped up by Erik's large arms.

We continued on, Erik using one hand to balance himself while the other was wrapped under my armpits and across the front of my chest, making me feel more secure as I used both of my hands to help steady me.

They had untied my hands, but I was not free, they had not given me back my weapons or armour.

Maiya led us to an empty run-down shack on the outer edges of the camp, situated on a platform that was furthest away from the others. Parts of the roof were missing from the rackety looking hut, with a door loosely hanging from its hinges.

"Only the best accommodation for the famous General Truda," Maiya sniggered, before walking away, still laughing at her own joke.

My presence was known throughout the base, and I was hated, eyes glaring, following my every movement. As did Erik, not wanting to leave my side, clearly afraid that something might happen if he did. As we entered the hut, the first thing I noticed was the smell, a waft of rotten fruit and damp wood hit my nostrils. There was a hole in between the ceiling planks, allowing a small beam of moonlight into the shack. It had very little in the way of furniture with only a small table, a single chair, and one small cot bed.

"At least this is nicer than the Breeding House," Erik chirped, trying to lighten the reality of our situation. I think if I had the choice, I would have chosen the accommodations at the Breeding House over this small depressing excuse of a home, if you could even call it that. However, I would not wish for the world, that Erik be back in the Breeding House as a slave, so at least in that sense, Erik was right, this was better.

"I need some rest," I told him, ignoring the mess and smell, as I walked over to the cot and laid down, facing the wall, not looking at Erik. For a moment I heard him shuffling around, moving things, then I fell asleep.

~*~

In the coming days, Erik started leaving the hut for short periods of time, wandering the camp and meeting the people. Clearly enjoying his new sense of freedom being able to come and go whenever he wanted. My leather and armoured clothing had been replaced by loose dresses and thin footwear; I had never felt so naked around people. It appeared Erik and I had swapped places, now I was the prisoner. He returned inside the hut with a bowl of warm soup, passing it to me.

"I've spoken to Cobal, he said you are free to walk around the camp and nearby forest as long as you don't wander too far," Erik told me. I looked away from him, ignoring his attempt at passing me some food.

"I do not need you to be my ambassador," I snapped. It was evening and I was lying in the cot. During the nights, Erik would sleep on the floor, and I would always wait until I could hear his breathing slow, telling me that he was no longer awake, before residing to sleep myself.

Erik came and sat next to me.

"Truda?" he asked me.

"What?"

"Why didn't you tell me you were bringing me to the rebel base?"

"If I had told you that I was bringing you to my enemy, would you have come?" I asked him, still looking at the ceiling in the hut. He was quiet for a moment, which gave me my answer; of course he would not have.

"Do you still think of them as your enemy?" he asked. I thought about this for a moment. A lifelong career of hunting down the rebels and killing them all, for what? For wanting to free people like Castor, Tobias and Erik out of slavery, how could I hate them?

"No, but that does not mean they do not see me as theirs."

"Well, you haven't exactly made any effort to get to know them since we have been here," Erik replied, placing the soup down on the table beside me.

"What would you have me do?" I said to him.

"You need to show them you are not," was all he said. Of course, why did I not think of that? I could walk around the camp waving a white flag and everyone here would know I was their friend. I did not say that to Erik of course, but chose instead to lie down and roll away from him. He did not understand this world, nor had he seen the things I had done. The rebels had good reason to hate and fear me, I had hunted and killed many of them over the years.

I felt the cot shift as Erik got on it beside me. I turned to face him. He was looking at me worried, almost like he could hear my thoughts, the internal battle that I was now having with myself. He lifted his hand and stroked my cheek with his knuckles. I closed my eyes and rolled into him, letting his arm come around my shoulders as I now placed my head on his chest. I knew it was wrong, that I was sending him the wrong signals but, in this moment, I needed the comfort he could provide.

"There is more to Cobal's story, do you want to hear it?" he said to me quietly. Without looking up, I nodded against him. Regardless of the story, I just wanted to hear his soothing voice. Erik lightly stroked my arm as he continued to tell me more about Cobal and Maiya's history. It turned out that Lilith was well loved and had many friends including Maiya, who was her best friend. Erik suspected that Maiya had been in love with her. After Lilith's death, Maiya and a small group of others had attacked the palace, escaped the city and freed a number of slaves. They had started the rebellion and had spent the last twenty years fighting for freedom and justice, in memory of Lilith.

It was a beautiful story, that through no fault of Erik, only brought me more pain. I felt ashamed of my conquest to rid the rebels from the kingdom, with wishes of my name going down in history as being its saviour. A saviour of what? Cruelty? Murder? Slavery? That ambition had long gone, dissipating the moment I discovered the truth that the city had tried so hard to cover up.

~*~

The next morning, I awakened to the sound of chirping birds. Looking around, I realised I was alone in the hut, Erik must have left to mingle with the camp and do his part to help out. I thought about what he told me last night, before I had shamelessly spent the night sleeping in his arms. He was right, I had not made any effort with the people. I needed to get back to the city, but 'General Truda' was too big a threat

237

to the rebellion and there was no way I was getting out of here in one piece if I did not gain their trust.

I got up, dressing myself in the thin and poorly stitched garments they left me, which consisted of a beige cotton dress and matching slippers with leather soles. I walked to the door, opened it, and leaned forward to look outside before taking my first steps. It did not seem like many people were about, which suited me just fine. I decided to go and look for Erik to join him in whatever activity he may be doing that seemed to earn the rebel's approval.

Leaving the hut, I walked towards the first rope bridge that would take me across to the next platform. I did not know where I was going, the camp was huge, with so many bridges that connected various platforms and rope ladders that led down to the forest floor.

Pausing at the first bridge, I had hoped that the daylight would make me less nervous about crossing, but that was not the case after I looked down and was able to see how high up we actually were. The trunks on the trees were far beyond the width that I had seen a tree grow before. Although the platforms seemed to be positioned high up the tree, as I looked up, I could see the trunk continued on much higher, and I had to crane my neck to see its top. Where the rope bridges looked flimsy, the platforms looked much more secure as I could see layers of rope and steel fixings hammered into the meat of the trunk. Looking around, I counted twelve platforms, and suspected that I would find more once I reached the other edge of the base, making me wonder at the true numbers of the rebellion.

Taking a slow step forward, I placed my foot on the first plank of the bridge, holding on tightly to the rope edge, the only barrier preventing me from falling to the ground.

Once I reached the other side, I wandered around searching for Erik, feeling more confident with each bridge I crossed, getting used to the noises and movements it made. I was not brave enough to actually speak to any of the elves or many humans that I passed, mostly because they did not exactly appear to be friendly with their glares of hate.

"You look lost General; is there somewhere we can help you get to?" spoke an unfriendly female voice. I turned and saw two warrior elves glaring at me. They both wore leather armour that looked old and worn, and both were armed with weapons. The first elf was tall and lean, with long brown hair plaited into two tails that fell on each shoulder, daggers were on her waist band. The other was much shorter, even Acqueline's petite height would be considered tall next to this elf. She was also very broad, large muscles visible through her armless top. She had no hair on her head and was smirking at me menacingly while playing with the blade of her axe. Immediately sensing danger, I held my head up high and turned to face them, hoping to seem confident and not intimidated.

"Yes actually, I am looking for Erik, can you point me in

the right direction?" I asked them.

"Oh, dear Shea, it appears the General is looking for her Guan," spoke one of the elves. She stepped forward and I saw her hand grip tightly onto the axe handle.

"Perhaps you should explain to her Igit, that the rebellion doesn't keep Guans," said the other elf, now reaching for her daggers.

"Erik is not my Guan, and if I was to stand before you, holding my sword, you would not so recklessly attempt to threaten me," I said sternly.

"You don't scare us General Truda, and you don't belong here," said the one called Shea, holding one dagger in each hand.

"Well, do not worry, I have no intention of staying here for long."

"You're not going anywhere," said Igit through gritted teeth.

"So, now you want me to stay?"

"That's not what I meant," Igit smirked, then, dropping her grin, she suddenly charged towards me. I jumped back to avoid her swing but did not react fast enough before she quickly twisted her body and kicked me hard in the chest. Losing my balance, I fell back and hit my head hard against the wood on the platform. My eyes suddenly filled with little specks of white light as my head pounded and I cried in pain. Igit climbed on top of me, holding her axe to my throat.

"Get off her!" I heard Erik cry as he ran to us and pushed Igits' body off me.

"You won't hurt her, I will make sure Maiya and Cobal hear about this," Erik said as the elves turned and backed away from us. Once they were out of sight, Erik helped me slowly stand.

"Are you hurt?" he asked, while carefully inspecting me for any new injuries.

"I'm fine, I just need to get back to the hut and rest." I lied to him, trying not to show how painful the thumping in my head felt.

"Maybe I should take you to the camp healer," he said.

"No, Erik please, I am fine, will you just help me back to the hut?" I looked up at his face, my eyes watering from the pain in my head. Seeing my expression, he closed his eyes and sighed. Then, opening them again, he nodded and wrapped his arm around mine to help keep me steady as we made our way back.

Chapter 19

THE WHITE FOX

Erik had integrated into the rebel camp well and was liked by many. He spent a lot of time with the others, especially Cobal and Maiya. After my incident with Igit and Shea, I had not left the hut, feeling totally out of place. In the city I was respected and feared, here I was hated and not one person would salute the signal of respect. Not that anyone did here. In the rebel base, everyone was treated like equals, except for Maiya and Cobal of course, who were looked up to and admired by all of the people. I had not spoken to anyone, except for my first day here when Cobal told us his story.

I filled the days that followed by moping around in the hut, barely eating or sleeping, only looking forward to the end of the day when Erik would return and tell me things he had learned from speaking with the people.

It was the next morning and I was moving fruit and nuts around on a plate, making odd shapes and patterns. Erik entered and looked at me, folding his arms across his chest.

"You're coming with me today," he told me, standing firmly in place.

"I am not going anywhere," I replied, looking back down towards my plate of uneaten food.

"Yes, you are," he stated, walking over towards me on the cot. I ignored him, picking up a nut and putting it in my mouth. Erik grabbed my arm and pulled me up from the cot.

"What do you think you are doing?" I shouted at him, pulling my arm away from his grip.

"We're going to go for a walk," he said, reaching out to grab my arm again.

"Erik, I swear if you so much as try to grab me, I promise you will regret it," I threatened, through gritted teeth. He paused, then smiled.

"Oh good, you're still in there then, I thought your injury might have caused some permanent brain damage."

"What!" I shouted back at him.

"I thought for a moment that this mopey, sad creature was the new you," he teased, still smiling. I looked at him puzzled. Did he have a death wish today or something? The more he spoke in that mocking manner, the more I felt my anger build up inside me.

"Erik, whatever you are doing I suggest you stop because I am not in the mood," I said, walking back to the cot to sit again.

"Then come take a walk with me and I promise to stop." I looked up at him. He stood close now, with his arms crossed again, a strong determined look on his face, making it clear to me that he was not going to be satisfied until I ventured out of the hut.

"Fine, but a short walk," I said as I walked past him toward the entrance, pausing at the door. Erik walked up behind me, his hand stroking down my arm until his fingers laced in mine to hold my hand.

"Come on, I want to show you something," he said as he pulled my hand, leading me out of the hut. It was a bright and warm day. I could see movement from people nearby and immediately felt myself stiffen. Whether Erik sensed it or not, I was grateful when he led me in the opposite direction of the people. We walked along the platforms and rope bridges until it seemed we had reached the edge of the camp.

"I spoke to Maiya and Cobal, they assured me that the people have been spoken to and no harm will come to you again," Erik told me. I did not reply but I nodded. Thinking about the lack of impact those words would have had on the camp's inhabitants. I was not afraid, but I was also confident that my safety was not of paramount importance to the rebellion.

Briefly Erik squeezed my hand and looked back with a smile, before turning his attention to our destination. Ahead of us through the trees, I saw the largest and most beautiful waterfall and I stopped to look at its magnificence. Erik was still holding my hand and I felt his thumb lightly brush across my knuckles.

"It is beautiful," I whispered.

"You remind me of the waterfall," said Erik, who had stepped closer next to me. I looked up at him confused. He looked back towards the water as he spoke.

"Strong and unstoppable, but also graceful and pure." I laughed. I could not help it. I felt stupid and nervous. He was trying to be sweet and it sounded ridiculous. Shaking my head, I began to turn away.

"Why do you have to do that? Can you not see I am trying to tell you something!" Erik shouted. I dropped his hand and stepped away from him.

"I know what you want to tell me Erik, but you will not," I said to him sternly.

"I will if you would just give me the chance," he said, stepping toward me again.

"And I will not give you that chance Erik, because whatever you think, it is not going to happen." He looked at me shocked and I knew now was my chance to clear the air and set aside the tension that had built between us. "I admit we are friends, and I care about your wellbeing, enough to break you out of the city and find a safer place for you, but that is all, do you understand?" and as I looked at his shocked expression, I finished with the final blow. "There is nothing more between us Erik, I do not feel that way towards you," I said loudly.

He looked angry, glaring at me. I waited for him to shout back, to tell me I was wrong and that there was something more between us, but instead he turned and stormed off, leaving me alone on the platform staring at the waterfall.

~*~

I walked through the base, ignoring the looks of worry and hate, until I found a face I recognised, Maiya. She was sitting in front of what I guessed was her hut, sharpening a blade with a flat stone.

"I need to talk to you," I said to her as I got close. She looked up at me briefly and then looked back down at her blade as though to ignore me. "I need you to let me leave," I said, then felt extremely angry as I saw her head snap back as she laughed so loudly that I was positive the whole camp could hear.

"Yeah, that's not going to happen," she finally said, chuckling.

"The city believes that I was out hunting for the escaped slave. When I return, I will just tell them that I killed him, and left his body to rot in the desert. I will not tell them anything of this place," I said to her, trying to sound sincere, which was extremely difficult considering how angry I felt.

"The answer is no General," she said sternly, saying the word 'General' in a mocking tone, reminding me that my title meant nothing in this place.

"Then what can I do to gain your trust, there must be something useful I could do to help?" I said to her, keeping my voice calm despite my ever-rising frustration at being reduced to almost begging. She stood and walked over to me, her sword still in her hand.

"You want to help?" she asked. She bent down, picked up an empty basket and shoved it into my stomach.

"We could use more fruit and vegetables from the ground," she finished with a menacing grin, then sat back down. I turned and walked away, finding a rope ladder on one of the platforms that would take me to the forest floor. As I slowly climbed down, the basket handle resting on my forearm, I looked up to see I was being watched. On all the sides of the surrounding platforms, warriors stood watching me, clearly Maiya was not taking any chances.

When I reached the ground, I winced as I stood on a sharp stone, the sharp edge piercing through the thin hide sole on my slipper. How far did they think I could get with barely any clothes, no weapons and poorly crafted footwear!

I sighed and walked forward, stepping along a softer patch of ground. I bent down beside some wild mushrooms and started picking them, placing them in the basket. This was ridiculous, I was not gaining the rebel's trust by harvesting mushrooms, I was being mocked. The great General Truda, being reduced to foraging for food. As I looked up, I gasped, the white fox was sat right in front of me.

"Not you again. Every time I see you something bad happens."

"Maybe you're the one that brings trouble with you," said a soft but high-pitched voice. I looked at the fox in confusion.

"Did you just... speak to me?" I spoke slowly to it. Then I heard a squeak of laughter come from my left. Turning, I saw her. A cloaked figure stepping out from behind a tree and dropping down her hood.

She was a beautiful petite elf in a shimmering green and silver silk dress. She was quite short and her hair was platinum blonde and long, flowing past her slim waist. She walked over to me very slowly and carefully. As she got closer, I could see her facial features, her small, young face with rosy lips and plump cheeks. She had a small button nose, and on her eyelids was a soft pink shimmer paint. As she looked up, I saw her eyes and gasped; they were cloudy white.

I looked at myself then. I was wearing a sage green cotton dress with my hair down loose, a basket full of mushrooms on my arm, just like in the dream that I had the morning Tobias had died.

"How is this possible?" I whispered to myself. How had I seen this happen? The fox, my clothes, the figure with the white eyes? The little white fox rubbed up against my leg making me jump.

"That's Yuki," she said, moving to stand close to me.

"Who are you?" I asked.

"Oh yes, I'm sorry. My name is Fortuna," she smiled as she spoke, but her eyes did not look up to me. Looking at the white in them I realised, she must be blind.

"I saw you. I mean, I have seen you before," I said, still confused and shocked as I looked at her.

"In a dream."

"How did you know that?" I asked.

"Because it was my dream, although sometimes without meaning to, I share them."

"I do not understand."

"I'm sorry Tru, I guess I was so excited to see you, I'm not really explaining myself very well," she giggled lightly.

"Come, walk with me. Yuki, will you show me the way?" she said sweetly to the fox, who now bounced up and down again and walked slowly in front of Fortuna. I watched as she stepped around the trees and over the roots on the ground. How could she do that if she was blind?

"Yuki is my eyes, he allows me to see the forest through him," Fortuna said, answering my unspoken question. I had seen it done before, mages could give animals bracelets or a necklace so they could see what they saw. It was how I imagined Freyja had spied on me in the library, using her raven.

"You are a mage?" I asked, following Fortuna and Yuki as they led me through the forest.

"Yes, I suppose you could call me that," said Fortuna. After a few minutes of walking, we stopped by a stream. Fortuna sat down on a tree stump and started laughing as Yuki jumped straight into the stream, rolling around and splashing in the water. I sat down opposite Fortuna, watching her curiously. Even though I did not know her, she seemed so familiar. Although I could not explain it, I felt that she was a soft and gentle elf that meant me no harm. I was drawn to her and trusted her immediately.

"I told them to release you, that you would help us," she said, still smiling at Yuki who was now trying to catch a fish.

"I am not here to help the rebellion," I said to her.

"But of course you are Tru, why else would you come here?"

"I came here to help my friend, to save him from his fate and find somewhere safe for him," I told her. Her smile faded for a moment, my answer had obviously disappointed her and I almost felt sorry that I had not said what she wanted to hear.

"Well anyhow," she said, smiling as she looked up to the sky, "you're here now and that's what matters." I smiled, not really knowing what to say.

"Are those mushrooms I smell?" she said suddenly with great excitement. I looked down at my basket and back to Fortuna.

"Uh, yes."

"Brilliant, I make the most amazing mushroom soup. Come, I will show you how to make it," she said as she stood and waved me to follow her and Yuki back to camp.

Chapter 20

PROVING MYSELF

Spending time with Fortuna had soon become the highlight of my days here and I noticed that the more I did, the less nervous everyone else was around me. Fortuna was well loved and respected, and although not a leader or even as she liked to tell me, a true mage, even Cobal and Maiya would often consult with her.

I had not seen much of Erik, who was clearly avoiding me after our argument. When I went in search of Fortuna that morning, I had seen him briefly. He had been on a bridge talking to Maiya when he saw me, and I could see the pain in his eyes, which soon turned to anger as he turned and walked away. He had not come back to the hut in the evenings, and I had not dared to ask where he had been sleeping.

Instead, I distracted myself in Fortuna's presence. She was like no elf I had ever met. She talked to the animals and whispered to the trees, most of the time we walked on the ground of the forest, collecting fruit and mushrooms. During one of our walks, we stopped to sit by the stream eating berries, while Yuki played in the water.

"How did you two meet?" I asked Fortuna.

"Oh, that's one of my favourite stories," she replied chirpily. "You see, poor little Yuki here was the runt of the litter, we found each other wandering the desert, half starved," Fortuna told me.

"We?" I asked.

"Well, I suppose you could say I was the runt of the litter too, leaving the city when I was very small, until I found Yuki and we both found our way here."

"You used to live in the city?" I asked her.

"Uh yeah, but I was rejected from the Mages Temple because I was blind. I was very little, I don't remember much."

"Fortuna, that is awful and not what I would say is a happy start in life," I remarked.

"My life started here, in these woods. At first it was just me and Yuki, then I found the rebels and helped them build a home here," she told me. I watched as Fortuna bent down and picked up a dried dead leaf, its corners brown and crooked.

As she held it in the palm of her hand, it unfolded, the brown dried tips turning back into green. She whispered something to it and then blew it from her hand, letting the now green leaf get carried away in the wind. Laughing, she started making little fish shapes in the water, and we both laughed hysterically as Yuki pounced, trying to catch them. I watched, in awe of her abilities.

Fortuna was the most magically gifted elf I had met. She did not need to enchant items or potions like Freyja, who had used an enchanted necklace to be able to see through her raven's eyes. Fortuna had a direct link to magic, here she used it to help the forest. I suspected she was the reason the trees grew so tall.

We heard movement behind us, and as I looked, I saw Cobal approach. He nodded and smiled towards Fortuna and Yuki, who had now stopped playing in the water and was stretched out on the bank, drying his fur in the sun.

"I hope you don't mind, but I was hoping to talk with you General Truda," Cobal said. I smiled and nodded, pointing to a trunk of a fallen tree for him to sit. He sat down and looked to me.

"I hear you want to leave," he said to me. Fortuna's head dropped as though she was saddened by his words.

"It is more of a need rather than a want," I said in reply.

"I am sure you can understand that we have more than a few concerns regarding letting you go," said Cobal.

"Actually, letting me go would be in your best interest," I replied.

"Really, how so?" Cobal asked.

"The city knows I left in search of the escaped Guan. If I do not return, they will suspect something happened to me and may even come looking."

"Okay, so we let you leave, then what happens?" Cobal asked.

"I return to the city and put a stop to the search for the rebel base, start making a difference from the inside. It will not be easy, but I have people who are loyal and trust me, including the queen," I told him.

"And you think that will work?" he asked.

"To be honest, I do not know. What I do know is that I am of more use to you in the city, than if I stay here."

Cobal looked over to Fortuna, raising one eyebrow as if to ask her a question without forming the words. She replied with a simple smile and a short burst of nods.

"I appreciate your honesty General Truda, I would like to trust you. I understand you have responsibilities in the city, and it warms me that you want to help in your own way," he said to me.

"Then you will let me leave?" I asked him.

"How about we make a deal."

"What kind of deal?" I asked sceptically.

"Maiya needs to get back into the city for supplies, how about she escorts you?" It made sense. Cobal wanted to trust me but knew what he was risking. Maiya escorting me would be reassurance and I needed to gain his trust.

"Alright, I have a few conditions," I said to him.

"What conditions?"

"That Maiya take my house Guan Castor while I sneak into the palace alone to free another Guan called Phoenyx. They will both return to the rebel base with Maiya," I said to him.

"I see no problem in that," Cobal replied.

"Just one more thing," I stated.

"What is that?"

"Erik does not come with us, and no one tells him that I am not returning," I finished.

~*~

I was in my hut making my preparations. Maiya and I were to leave in the morning to head for the city. I was startled when Erik stormed through the door, slamming it behind him. He looked furious.

"I want to come tomorrow," he burst out.

"It is not my decision," I told him.

"You're lying, you told them not to let me come," he said as he walked over to me.

"I just got you out of the city Erik, I do not want you back there," I said. Erik grabbed my arm, making me stop and turn to face him.

"You're not coming back, are you?" he asked me, with shock in his eyes.

"It was always my intention to go back to the city once I knew you were safe." I told him.

"Stay, stay with me," he said, almost pleading.

"I cannot, I have to go back. I belong in the city." I told him, feeling sad and confused at the thought of leaving and never seeing him again.

"Then just stay with me tonight," he said softly, walking closer. I did not reply, I just looked up into his eyes as he gently stroked my cheek with the back of his knuckles. Cupping my face with both of his hands, he bent down and kissed me. I did not move away, Not wanting to break the contact. I closed my eyes as Erik passionately kissed me, stepping forward to push his body against mine. I did not realise we had been moving backwards until my back hit the wall.

He stopped, his breathing heavy. With his hands still cupping my face he paused, looking into my eyes. He was waiting for me to push him away, to tell him no, like I had many times before. Except this time, I could not deny what I felt anymore. I wanted him, wanted to be close to him, to feel his hands on every inch of my body and most of all, I wanted him to kiss me.

I reached up, using my hand to pull his head back down to me so I could kiss him again. Our kiss became urgent as our lips barely separated to let us catch our breath.

His hands slowly caressed down my sides. I felt a heat igniting everywhere his hands touched and it was lighting a fire inside me. When he reached the hem of my dress, he lifted it, slowly grazing the outside of my thighs as he lifted it up above my hip, past my waist, forcing me to raise my arms as the dress went up and over my head.

Dropping my dress to the floor, he stepped back and looked at me, gazing up and down my body. I thought I would feel embarrassed seeing him looking at me naked but the look of desire on his face only made me want him more. I stepped towards him and he kissed me again, my hands desperately tugging at his top as my finger reached underneath to touch his skin. He moved his hands from me, giving me better access, allowing me to pull his top over his head.

He was so beautiful, his sun kissed skin, I could not help myself as I let my hands stroke over his chest, down his abs, until I reached the top of his cotton pants. His head rose away from my lips as he shuddered from my touch. I stepped forward and started kissing across his chest, taking in his musky smell as my face and lips travelled across his body.

I stopped when I reached his brand on his right peck, the brand that he had earned when he was placed in the breeding programme, number twenty-three. I lifted my fingers to touch it, my fingers gently tracing the indents on his skin.

Erik had frozen and was looking down at me as I touched the scar. I looked up at him and placed my lips on his brand to gently kiss it. Suddenly, Erik lifted me and wrapped my legs around his waist, kissing me passionately as he walked me over towards the cot, gently placing me down and crushing me with his weight.

We were kissing and exploring each other until Erik broke the kiss from my lips and began kissing my neck. Moving down, he then kissed my breasts, using his tongue to suck and stroke my nipples. I cried out with pleasure and let my hands grip his shoulders.

Erik continued to move down my body, tasting every inch of me with his tongue. When he reached the bottom of my stomach, he let his hands slide down further until he was holding both of my legs by the thighs, he pulled them apart as his face came level with my most sensitive part. Keeping his hands gripped on my thighs, he started running his tongue along my skin. I writhed under his grip, losing myself to the feel of his touch. I gasped as I felt him taste my centre, using his tongue to reach the bud within the flower folds as he sucked and licked. I grabbed his hair with my hands as I arched my back and moaned with pleasure. I felt like my whole body was on fire as this heat built up inside me and my body began to shake.

I cried out loudly with pleasure and pulled at Erik's hair, demanding him to come up and kiss me. When our lips touched, I moaned into his mouth as I tasted what he had just done to me on his tongue. Whilst our lips were still connected, I moved out from underneath him and used my hands to push him back to lie on the bed, then I straddled him so that my centre could now feel his bulge under his cotton pants.

I could feel he was hard as I slowly started rubbing myself against him. Erik moved his hands down, pulling at the tie on the top of his pants and then, lifting his chest slightly, he reached down and pulled his cotton barrier down and off his legs.

He was naked, lying under my body. I broke the kiss for a moment and stared into his eyes. Both panting, I felt the head of his shaft touch the very wet and ready part of me. Here I hovered, whilst looking deep into Erik's eyes, amazed at how natural this all felt. He was the key and I was the lock; we were meant to be together. Then, not able to hold back any longer, I lowered my body slowly onto him. He was large and thick and ready for me. Erik moaned as he filled me and grabbed my face to kiss him again.

We began to move, rocking slowly at first, allowing my tight body to become used to his size as he touched parts of me I did not even know I could get pleasure from.

I felt so good, like every inch of me was on fire only because it was connected to his. As the pleasure built between us, we picked up speed, working a perfect rhythm together as we let our need for each other build. Suddenly, I felt my body heating up again and shaking. I felt myself tense and tighten at my core, and as I did, Erik growled and picked up speed beneath me. I screamed in pleasure as I reached my peak. Erik also cried out in pleasure with me, as he reached his.

I collapsed onto his chest, my eyes closed and breathing heavily from what we had just done. He stroked my hair and kissed the top of my head. We both laid silently, listening to each other's heavy breathing, and he wrapped his arms around me, lightly stroking my back. I could hear his breathing slow as he began to drift to sleep, but not before whispering words that would make my heart ache.

"Truda, please don't leave me."

I did not reply, not wanting to wake him from the sleep he was drifting into. Besides, there was nothing I could say, no promise I could keep. I had to let him go, give him up for the greater good of my people and his. Instead, I pulled my body in closer, wrapping my arm around his chest tightly, and like this we remained as I fell asleep.

~*~

I woke, still naked in Erik's arms. He was fast asleep, and I smiled up at him. In this moment I wished I could stay, to be held in his strong arms forever. I should not have let last night happen, but I could not stop it, I wanted it as much as he had. Perhaps I was hoping it would free us both from this unspoken need for each other, but after what I had experienced with him, I now knew it would never be enough.

If I stayed, I would want to be with him.

But I knew I could not, I had to go back to the city, back to the queen and make changes from the inside. I did not know how, and would probably be killed for trying, but if I could get Queen Cassandra to understand, perhaps I could make a difference and Erik would remain safe with the rebels.

Quietly I rose from the cot and walked over to my dress on the floor, pulling it over my head. I snuck out of the hut, only to bump into Maiya who had obviously come to get me. She looked me up and down noticing my dress loosely hanging from my shoulder and messy hair.

"Wow, you are really playing both sides aren't you," she said. Ignoring her, I walked past and headed towards Cobal's hut. As much as I would have liked to tell Maiya to mind her own business, I did not want to create a commotion that would wake Erik. I did not want to say goodbye, afraid that if he asked again, I might never leave. When we reached Cobal, he walked over to Maiya and whispered something in her ear, then after a moment he pulled her into a hug, they were clearly close friends and had been through a lot together. After saying goodbye to Maiya, Cobal walked over to me.

"Thank you General Truda for your help. I wish you a safe return to the city." Then he reached behind him and one of the other warriors gave him a pile of leather clothing and weapons. I recognised them as mine. Turning back towards me, he passed them to me.

"Keep him safe Cobal, that is all I ask. I will do what I can inside the city," I said as I took back my armour and weapons. He nodded, understanding what I was asking of him.

After I dressed, instantly feeling more like myself, we climbed down the ladder and started walking through the forest. Just before we reached the forest edge that touched the start of the mountains, I saw Fortuna and Yuki. She walked towards us, Yuki bouncing ahead in front of her. She stopped before me and pulled me into a hug, Yuki was rubbing up against my leg.

"Good luck and see you soon," Fortuna whispered in my ear.

"Fortuna, I am not coming back," I whispered back to her.

"We'll see," she said to me, laughing. I suppose being blind meant she was allowed to make such jokes. As Maiya and I walked away, I turned to see Fortuna still smiling and waving at us as we left. Maiya led me through the trees until we reached a cave entrance, then she stopped and turned to face me holding out a single piece of leather.

"Put this on," she instructed.

"A blindfold, really Maiya? I said to her bitterly.

"That's right General, the only way I am going to take you through the catacomb maze is if you put on this blindfold," she told me with a confident smile. With a sigh, I grabbed the leather from her hand and placed it over my eyes. I felt Maiya's hands as she must have stepped behind me to make sure the blindfold was secure and knotted tightly. Once she was satisfied, she grabbed my wrist and pulled me through the cave tunnels.

Chapter 21

RETURNING HOME

We passed the sand mountains and crossed the desert in record time, arriving at the edge of the grasslands. We chose there as a good place to rest and regain our strength, knowing it would be best to cross the grasslands nearer the end of the day so that it would be night when we reached the wall.

I looked up at the warm sun and thought of Erik, wondering what he would think when he woke up to find me gone. Would he be angry with me? Would he shout at Cobal for letting me leave without saying goodbye? Would he miss me?

I knew what my answer would be. Erik had become my sun, the light that cleared my mind and brought warmth to my face. I saw what a life with him could be like and it would have been beautiful, full of love, but I knew it was not to be, could never be. It was just something I was going to have to live with, or not, depending on how my return to the city went. Just then, the light was blocked from view as Maiya stood directly in front of me. Extending out her arm, she passed me a hide canteen.

"You should drink," she barked.

"You still do not trust me, do you?" I said, taking the water from her.

"No, I don't, but you seem to have everyone else fooled," she replied, crossing her arms as she stood in front of me. I removed the cork and tilted my head to drink the water, keeping my eye on Maiya the entire time. Once finished, I handed it back to her. "I don't want to be in the city longer than I have to be, so we will split up to fetch these Guans, the ones you decided deserve rescuing."

"I am surprised you still call them Guans, I thought the whole point of the rebellion was to free them from slavery?" I asked. Maiya did not reply, instead grunting in amusement.

"If you hate them so much, why do you help them?"

"I don't hate Guans," she spat.

"Well, you do not exactly glow with loving support for them either."

"Not all of us have a personal Guan to glow with General," she smirked.

"Fine, forget I asked," I said, turning away from her, angry that she had used my feelings towards Erik against me.

"If you really want to know the truth, I do it for her, for Lilith. If the laws of our people were different, she would still be alive."

"You loved her," I said, feeling sympathy as she gave me a glimpse of the heart hidden inside the bitter exterior.

"Of course I loved her, she was my best friend." But I could see it in her eyes, Lilith meant more to her than that, she had felt the very same thing I felt for Erik.

"If only I could have saved her children," Maiya sighed.

"Children? I thought she had only given birth once," I questioned.

"She did, she had twins." My thoughts instantly became overwhelmed with images of the only twins I knew in the city. What were the chances? Were Shanor and Shanon Cobal's children? They were the right age, it all fit in well with the timeline of when the rebellion started. We had been told that their mother died during childbirth, but perhaps this was a lie to cover up what really happened. Kicking the sand from the bottom of her boots, Maiya broke me from my thoughts.

"I would advise that you don't tell your friends in the city about the location of the rebel base. Once they hear you have seen it, all they will care about is getting the co-ordinates of its location from you, no matter the cost," she said, turning away from me.

"I can promise you Maiya, that no matter what happens to me, I will not give up the location of the rebel base," I told her.

"Good, and just so you know, if you betray us General, I will make sure that Erik dies a slow and painful death." She looked at my shocked expression and grinned. Then, she walked away.

~*~

We reached the door to the tunnel that ran under the wall to Kayla's house. I opened the door and after peering down to check it was clear, Maiya walked through with me close behind her.

When we reached the ladder, Maiya climbed up and tapped lightly on the trapdoor. We heard some scuffling noises from above and then the door lifted.

"Maiya!" Kayla said as she helped her climb up the ladder and into her farmhouse. I followed just behind her, shocking Kayla as I came into her view.

"General Truda?" she said. I paused and glared at Kayla, her face showed the surprise I expected at seeing me alive. Just as I'm sure my glare told Kayla, that I had not forgotten that she had led me into an ambush.

"Did you receive my message?" Maiya asked Kayla.

"Yes, I have your supplies in the kitchen. I will go and get them," she replied, glancing her worried face over to Maiya and then looking back at me.

"Not yet, we are taking a little trip into town first," she said. Kayla looked confusingly between us again. "It's okay

Kayla, General Truda is going to help me free some slaves, we will return before dusk," Maiya told her. Ignoring Kayla, I walked past her and glanced back to Maiya, nodding towards the door. Once we were outside, I put on my mask and turned to give Maiya my instruction.

"Remember where I told you, do you know how to get there?" I asked her.

"You know I used to live here, right?" she retorted.

"Okay fine, just go. I will meet you back here," I snapped back.

"Don't forget what I said General, if you betray us, he dies," She glared at me before pulling the cloak hood over her head and disappearing into the shadows. I had sent Maiya to my home to find Castor while I made my way into the palace to find Phoenyx.

I jogged forward, sticking to the shadows and alleyways of the buildings so that I would not be seen. At first, I contemplated just casually walking, conveying a less suspicious approach. But I changed my mind when I remembered that I had been gone for weeks, and I did not have time for someone to stop me and question my absence. My return would soon be announced, once I presented myself to the queen in the morning. It took me much longer than I hoped to reach the palace, as more guards than usual appeared to be patrolling the city. I chose the smaller side entrance rather than the main door, which was, to my surprise, heavily guarded. Luckily, I knew the palace better than most and was able to slip down the corridor unseen. Heading towards the throne room, I needed to get into the royal chambers to find Phoenyx as quickly as possible.

As I turned the corner, I was startled when something grabbed me from behind, wrestling me to the floor.

"Well, what do we have here?" she said, whilst pinning me to the ground. I recognised her voice instantly, I refrained from struggling.

"Acqueline?" my muffled voice said from my position on the floor.

"Tru?" she replied, jumping off me, letting me off the floor. I turned and looked at her shocked face.

"Where have you been? We thought something bad happened to you," she said, her eyes tearing, relieved to see me alive.

"I'm fine Acqueline," I said, reaching out to her and touching her shoulder.

"What happened? You've been gone for weeks," she said.

"It is a long story and I promise to fill you in but right now I need to get to the princess's chamber," I said in a whispered rush.

"Why, she's not there," said Acqueline looking at me, a tear now running down her face, making me think the worst. Something bad had clearly happened while I was away.

"Acqueline, what is going on?" I asked her.

"She's dead Tru," she whispered as another tear followed.

"Who? the princess?"

"No Tru, the queen."

~*~

Acqueline rushed to tell me everything, how the queen had suspiciously fallen ill a few days after I left and was found dead in her chamber a week later. The council wasted no time in announcing the princess as the new queen. She told me the city had been on high alert for days now and that Freyja had told the council that I must have been caught by the rebels and killed. Imelda had been promoted to General.

I told Acqueline the partial truth, that I had helped Erik escape and led him to safety. I wanted to tell her that I had found the secret base and that we had been lied to about the rebellion, but I knew I had to keep my promise to Maiya. I had shocked Acqueline enough by telling her it was me that broke into the prison that night, and judging by her current facial expression, I did not think she could take much more of the truth.

"Is Phoenyx still the princess... I mean the queen's Guan?" I asked. She looked at me in confusion.

"Is that why you're here Tru, to free another slave?" she asked me angrily.

"Acqueline, I wish I could explain," I started to say.

"Don't bother," she spat. "Yes, he is still her Guan, he will

270

be in the queen's chambers with her."

"Come with me?" I asked her. I did not know why thoughts of including Acqueline in my plan had crossed my mind, but it pained me for her to think of me as a passing enemy.

"I have responsibilities Tru, I can't just leave, you felt the same way once." I looked at her, my dear friend. We had been through so much together and it saddened me to think how she must see me now. I wanted to say something to make her feel better, to tell her that I was still the same Tru, but the words did not come, I did not know what to say.

"Just go, I won't tell anyone I saw you." She turned away from me as she spoke, and before her face was out of my view, I saw another tear roll down her cheek.

I wanted to stop her, to tell her I was sorry, but I did not have time. I had to find Phoenyx and get him to Maiya so that they could get out of the city safely before morning. I would come back tomorrow and tell Acqueline everything, and if she chose to arrest me, then so be it.

Reaching the throne room, I was pleased to find that no one was guarding the door as I snuck in. Once through however, I was faced with two guards in the middle of the throne room. It did not take them long to recognise who I was.

"General Truda, what are you doing here?" asked the first.

"I'm just checking after the queen's safety," I said. I walked up to them slowly, and they looked at me cautiously as though they did not entirely believe my words.

As soon as I was close enough, I punched the first one hard in the jaw, knocking her unconscious with one blow. The second charged me but I swiftly round house kicked her in the face, knocking her to the ground. She stumbled to her feet and pulled out her sword. Afraid that it would not be long until she called for help, I wasted no time.

I lunged forward, not even bothering to unsheathe my sword, dodging her swing and twisting my body swiftly to reverse into her as I grabbed and twisted her wrist, making her drop her weapon. Then, bending over, holding her arm, I launched her body over my shoulder, slamming it into the ground. Satisfied that they would be out cold for at least a few minutes, I rushed past the throne chair towards the queen's entrance. I opened the door and ran up the spiral stairs. I had been here a few times before, so I knew which way to head.

Once I reached the top, I ran down the corridor that would lead me to the stairs to the queen's tower. I stopped suddenly when I saw Phoenyx walking towards me. As he saw it was me, his eyes opened wide with disbelief.

"General Truda?" he asked.

"Remember when I said that if there was something I could do to help you, I would?" I said, catching my breath.

"Yes," he said curiously.

"Then consider me breaking you out of the city something I can do to help," I said as I grabbed his arm, gesturing him to follow.

~*~

We ran together out of the palace and towards the farmhouse. I hoped that we had not been too long and that Maiya was waiting for us. It was lucky timing when I approached the farmhouse and saw her running towards us with little Castor behind her.

"General Truda!" he exclaimed and smiled when he saw me, only to be smacked lightly across the back of his head by Maiya who had clearly told him to keep quiet.

"Castor, it is good to see you," I said, frowning at Maiya for hitting him as she walked past us.

"What is happening, where are we going?" he asked me.

"I am setting you free Castor. You are no longer my Guan and I want you to leave the city with Maiya and Phoenyx."

"What about you?" Castor asked me.

"I am going to stay here and try to convince Queen Callidice to free other Guans, just like you," I told him sweetly.

"She won't let you do that," interrupted Phoenyx, making both of us look over to him.

"What do you mean?" I asked him.

"She won't give up control over the Guan's, she loves the power it brings her too much."

"So, you should come with us General Truda," said Castor.

"We don't have time for this, I need to get the supplies and get them out of here," Maiya said to me. I nodded and motioned for Phoenyx to follow us into the farmhouse. Perhaps Castor and Phoenyx were right, what good could I do now that Queen Callidice was sitting on the throne? I needed time to think, but first I needed to get them safely out of the city. I opened the door and walked inside, only to be hit with sheer panic at what I saw.

The twins!

Shanor and Shanon were inside the farmhouse. Shanon had Kayla by the throat with a knife. When they saw me, they gasped in shock.

"General Truda? How could you, how could you betray us?" Shanor shouted.

"The queen and Freyja were right, you were the enemy all along," said Shanon.

"No! That is not true." I shouted back to them. "We were lied to, you were lied to, the rebellion is not what we think it is." They looked at me, both angry, clearly not believing a single word I was saying.

"You both need to trust me, because I know the truth of your parents." I said to them.

"What?" Shanor asked, and I saw her face soften slightly.

"Don't listen Shanor, it's a trick," spat Shanon.

"It is not a trick. Your mother did not die in childbirth like we were told," I said, holding my hands up as a sign of surrender to let them know I did not mean them any harm.

"Please, come with me and hear the truth," I said to them.

"No Truda," said Maiya

"They deserve to know," I said looking back at her. Besides, what other option did we have? I was not about to let Maiya attack the twins, my only hope was that I could convince them to come with us. I looked back at the twins, who both were looking at each other, confused.

"Please, you know I will not let any harm come to you," I said to them.

They looked at me for a long moment, then Shanon lowered her daggered hand, letting Kayla move away from her grip.

"Okay," said Shanon, reaching over to hold her sister's hand.

"We will come with you," said Shanor, continuing her sister's sentence.

"Kayla, would you mind," I asked her. She nodded. After glancing wearily at the twins, she walked over to her living room, rolling the large rug out of the way, revealing the secret hatch that would lead us outside the walls.

"I knew it," said Shanon, sheathing her knife.

"They can't come with us," said Maiya, now standing on top of the hatch door preventing Kayla from opening it.

"Maiya, I have known the twins their whole life, they can be trusted," I said, looking back at Shanor and Shanon, prompting them to agree with me.

"They leave their weapons here," said Maiya.

"And how do we know that we can trust you?" spat Shanon.

"You do not need to trust her, you only need to trust me," I replied, raising my voice. We all stood in silence for a moment, Maiya clearly against the twins coming. I understood why, it was risky, taking them to the rebel camp, but I knew that once they heard Cobal's story they would see the truth like I had, that the rebels were never our enemy and we had been lied to. I walked over towards the twins, resting a hand on each of their shoulders.

"Please, you need to hear the truth, and it is not my place to tell you," I said to them quietly. They looked at each other and then back to me. Nodding, they started to remove their weapons, placing them on the table one at a time. Once they were done, I looked over at Maiya and tilted my head, raising an eyebrow.

"Looks like I am coming back with you," I remarked.

"Fine, let's go," she huffed, opening the hatch and swiftly disappearing down the shaft.

I looked behind me, gesturing for Castor and Pheonyx to follow behind us. Both looked cautiously between me and the twins before stepping down through the hatch, using the ladder to reach the ground safely. Once we had all climbed down, Maiya walked past us to look back up at the hatch entrance.

"Thanks Kayla, I will send word soon," and then I heard the hatch door close. Maiya took the lead, glancing back at the twins every now and again to watch them. Every time her gaze met mine, she gave me a furious look. We walked silently down the passage. Reaching the door, we stepped through and set off at a jog across the grasslands to reach toward the desert. It was still dark, but I knew the sun would be rising in a few hours. After a little while, I saw Castor was struggling to keep up.

"We need to rest a moment," I called out to Maiya. She slowed and looked back to me and saw me glance towards Castor.

"We need to reach the desert before the sun rises, we have to keep up the pace," she said before turning back picking up her pace again.

"I've got it," said Phoenyx as he dropped one of the bags of supplies and turned to pick up Castor, swinging him on his back, holding his legs in each arm. I stepped over and picked up the bag he dropped, as we continued to jog next to each other behind the twins and Maiya.

"Thank you," I said to Phoenyx and smiled at Castor, who was falling asleep through exhaustion.

"Is Erik where we are going?" Phoenyx asked me.

"Yes, and I am sure he will be pleased to see you," I said, smiling at him. I hoped that by freeing Phoenyx and sending him back to the rebel base with Erik, that he would forgive me for leaving him. I had not intended on returning but after hearing of the queen's death and coming face to face with the twins, I knew that Maiya would have never allowed them to travel without me.

The twins needed to hear the truth, but I knew my actions were partly for selfish reasons. I had felt so estranged from the city for weeks now, seeing things differently, hearing the rebel's story, the truth of what really happened and how the war had started. I did not want to feel alone anymore, I needed others to know.

I did not know how Erik would react when I returned, but I was hoping that bringing Phoenyx back would soften the anger he had no doubt felt after I left. I was nervous to see him again, not knowing what I would say to him, what was going to happen between us.

When we reached the desert, Maiya chose a spot amongst the tall cacti for us to rest. She stepped away from the group sitting alone, I took this opportunity to walk over and talk to her. As I approached, she looked up at me with fury sparkling in her eyes, she hated me.

"I don't want to talk to you," she said looking away.

"Look, I know your angry but…" I started saying.

"Angry?" she spat, standing so we were eye level, her face inches from mine.

"I am furious. Do you have any idea what danger you are putting us in?" she said through gritted teeth.

"What would you have had me do? They needed to come back with us," I held my ground.

"Us? There is no us General Truda, you don't belong with us. I still consider you my enemy, you have no voice in our matters," she spat back angrily.

"Then why did you allow them to come?" I asked, folding my arms and keeping my feet planted where I stood. She could be angry at me all she wanted, but I had taken charge of the situation because I knew what was right. Maiya glared at me, and I saw her clench her hands into fists.

"I allowed it only for Cobal, because I know if he were here, he would have made that same decision, but it doesn't mean it was the right thing to do for my people," she said, shaking from anger.

"That is where you are wrong, those twins are your best chance. If they learn the truth, it will change them, spark change for the future. Your methods of attacking the city and freeing the slaves only makes them hate you more," I said.

I felt it before I saw it. Maiya punched her clenched fist directly into my face, catching me off guard and making me stumble back.

"You don't know of what you speak!" she shouted. Shanor and Shanon ran to my side, holding up their fists ready to fight back in response. I held up my hand and shook my head. I started to walk away, back towards Phoenyx and Castor who were watching wide eyed, the twins followed closely behind me.

"You should have stayed in the city General," Maiya yelled after me. I stopped and turned to her.

"Perhaps I should have, or perhaps you need me more than

279

you realise," I replied. Maiya did not respond but watched as I continued to step backwards away from her. "By the way, you have a sloppy right hook," I finished with a grin, then turned and sat next to Phoenyx and Castor.

Chapter 22

A FAMILY REUNITED

When we reached the edge of the desert, we stopped looking towards the great sandstone cliffs. Maiya walked over to one of the supply bags and pulled out some hide. Using her knife, she cut the material into strips and walked over to Phoenyx.

"Use these to cover the twin's eyes," she told him. Phoenyx looked at her in surprise then looked over to me. This made Maiya angry again.

"She's not in charge here Guan, now use those strips and cover their eyes!" she shouted. Phoenyx stood still, not knowing what to do. I walked over to him, putting my hand on his shoulder.

"It is fine Phoenyx, do as she says," I looked over to the

twins, nodding once to let them know they could trust me. Phoenyx walked over to the twins and blindfolded them one at a time, the twins did not argue or fight, trusting that I would not let them come into harm's way. I looked over at Maiya who was still glaring at me.

"Just consider yourself lucky that I didn't instruct him to do the same to you," she spat.

I refrained from responding. Maiya was on edge, we were getting close to the base and I did not want to do anything at this point that could jeopardise the twins' chance of coming with us. I walked over to Castor who had been unusually quiet for the past few hours.

"Are you okay Castor?" I whispered.

"I guess so, I'm just a bit confused," he said looking up at me, but not holding eye contact for long.

"You do not need to worry, we are taking you to a safe place," I said to him gently.

"Will Erik be there?" he asked me.

"Yes, we are taking you to the same safe place I took him," I replied. This seemed to put Castor at ease as his shoulders relaxed and he smiled at me.

We continued walking on. I held Shanor's hand to lead her through the pass, and she held Shanon's. As we turned the corner, I saw a familiar white creature sitting in the centre of our path, and when it saw us, it jumped up to attention and walked towards us. It walked past Maiya and brushed against my leg, making me smile.

"Hi Yuki," I said, smiling down at my little friend. Then Yuki looked behind me and stopped. He stared over towards Phoenyx who looked at the fox with curiosity. Then, suddenly, it bolted towards him, jumping around him with excitement.

We watched in amazement as Yuki circled around him, rubbing against his legs and rolling over onto his back, making a little yelp noise. Phoenyx laughed and bent down slowly to the fox stroking its tummy and patting its head.

"Well, hi there, who is this cute little creature?" he said to the fox. Maiya sighed in frustration and walked over towards them.

"Yuki, where is Fortuna?" she asked him.

Yuki rolled back onto his belly to stand and then looked to Maiya before running back the way he came through the cliff path. We all followed behind. I looked back at Phoenyx who was watching the fox with a smile. As we walked, Yuki looked back to check we were behind him. Every now and again he would get excited and run over to Phoenyx playfully before running back ahead of us down the path.

"It looks like you have made a friend," I said to Phoenyx with a smile.

"It would appear so," he said with a light laugh.

Maiya was not amused by Yuki's behaviour one bit, shouting at him a few times to just pay attention to where he was going. At the end of the cliff pass we saw the cave entrance. Maiya did not hesitate and walked straight through, navigating her way through the correct tunnels that I now knew would lead us back out into the forest. It still amazed me that anyone could find their way through this maze of a cave.

We walked out and straight into the heart of the forest, continuing on until we reached the edge of the rebel base, there I saw Fortuna standing and waving happily. Yuki ran on ahead and started jumping and bounding around Fortuna as we approached. She bent down to pick him up in her arms, giggling when Yuki started licking her face.

When we reached them, she let Yuki jump out of her arms. I walked over to her and she hugged me instantly.

"I said I would see you soon, didn't I?" she whispered in my ear. Then I felt her body freeze. I pulled back and looked at her shocked face. When I looked down, Yuki was also frozen in place, his gaze staring at Phoenyx, which was odd considering how friendly the fox had been with him mere moments ago. When I looked over to Phoenyx, he was also frozen with shock on his face, staring straight back towards Fortuna.

"This is Phoenyx, Erik's friend," I said, taking a few steps back, deciding to break the awkwardness with some introductions.

"This is Castor my house Guan, and this is Shanor and Shanon," I said as I removed the twins' blindfolds. They looked around in amazement at their surroundings, standing close to each other for comfort.

"It is nice to meet you all," Fortuna said, looking sadly away from Phoenyx.

"Come Tru, there is someone who needs to see you," she, said holding my hand and leading me away from the group. Phoenyx stared at us both as we left.

"Is Erik okay?" I whispered when we were out of earshot from the others.

"No, but he will be now," she said with a smile, glancing quickly over her shoulder. I heard Maiya behind me giving instructions to the group as they followed closely behind her. When we reached the first platform ladder, Fortuna turned to me.

"He is with Cobal. Go, I will catch-up with you later," she said with a smile, then walked off through the forest with Yuki walking just ahead of her. Strange, maybe Fortuna felt odd around the newcomers. She always behaved curiously around people, preferring to spend her time walking bare foot in the forest alone, but she was always friendly. I shrugged as I watched Fortuna and Yuki disappear from my view, and I turned to begin my climb up the rope ladder.

~*~

We all climbed to the top of the ladder onto the platform. Maiya gave instruction for the twins to be taken to the holding tent and kept quiet. Shanor looked over to me with a worried face.

"It is okay, go with them. I will come find you soon," I directed them. They nodded and turned, following an elf over a bridge connecting to another platform. Maiya looked over at me, Castor and Phoenyx.

"You three, follow me," she said. We walked over to Cobal's hut and as we got closer, I felt butterflies in my stomach. Nerves overtook me as I anticipated what I would face when entering.

Maiya walked in first, followed by Phoenyx and Castor. I stepped through last behind Phoenyx, leaving the door open. I saw Cobal as he walked towards Maiya, putting his hand on her shoulder with a smile. She smiled back, obviously pleased to see him.

Then, glancing around discreetly, I saw Erik. He was sitting on the floor in the corner of the hut, a book in his hand, reading the pages, and he looked sad. When he looked up and saw Castor and Phoenyx, his face lit up.

"Nyx!" he called happily, getting up to walk over towards us. I remained hidden, standing at the edge of the hut trying to use Phoenyx's large body mass to hide me out of sight. Erik grabbed Phoenyx by the arm and pulled him in for a hug, patting his back as he laughed.

Looking over Phoenyx's shoulder his laugh stopped abruptly as he saw me. My heart was pounding, and my stomach was twisting in knots looking at him. Why was I so nervous?

He stepped back, still smiling from seeing Phoenyx, but his eyes fixated on me. He did not hold an angry expression, nor did he look happy with the sight of me, but he could not tear his eyes away and neither could I.

"Hi Erik," said Castor cheerfully. Erik looked away from me for a moment and looked down at the young boy.

"It's good to see you again Castor," he said to him, ruffling his hair with his hands making Castor giggle.

"Cobal, I need to speak to you urgently," said Maiya.

"Of course, Maiya, come sit," replied Cobal, who was smiling at seeing Erik reunited with his friends.

"General Truda has put us in great danger," she loudly stated.

My eyes shot up at her, but before I could speak, I was distracted by the look Erik was now giving me, his expression full of concern.

With that, I could not take it, seeing him look at me like that, so I just walked out, leaving Cobal's hut and heading back to what used to be mine, hoping I could still use it as a place to rest and hide. At first, I expected Erik to chase after me, demand what I had done, but he did not.

He obviously wanted to listen to Maiya's account of things. I knew she was angry, but I did not expect her to immediately put the blame on me for bringing the twins back. I was only doing what I thought was right and my only hope was that the others would see that.

I reached the hut and walked through, closing the door behind me. I was shocked as I looked around the room, it was a mess, with things thrown around everywhere including a broken table and what used to be ceramic pots and bowls, now smashed all over the floor.

I stepped over the mess and walked towards the cot in the corner, the only thing in the room that still appeared to be intact. I laid down, putting my head on a cushion. I slid my hand underneath it, getting more comfortable. I felt a lump of fabric and pulling it out, I saw it was my dress. The dress that I had worn the night before I left. The dress that Erik had taken off me when I spent the night in his arms.

I threw it on the floor with the rest of the mess and turned towards the wall, not wanting to think or look at anything. I closed my eyes in the hope that I could get some sleep.

I must have fallen asleep as I then felt a light tap on my shoulder. At first, I remained still, not wanting him to know I was awake. I did not know if I could face him yet, did not know what I would say. When I felt the light tap again, I rolled over, only to see it was not Erik, but young Castor looking down at me.

"Sorry to wake you General Truda, but Cobal sent me to come get you," he said, with a troubled look on his face.

"It is fine Castor," I replied as I sat up and stepped off the cot. We walked out of the hut and headed back towards Cobal's.

"I need to ask you something," Castor said with his fingers twitching in his hands.

"Of course, Castor, ask me anything," I said to him.

"Cobal says I can stay with him, says he's getting too old and could use some help with things, but I told him I would have to ask you," he said, still looking nervous. I stopped walking and put my hand on Castor's little shoulder.

"Castor, you are a free young man now, you can do what you would like to do," I said softly with a smile.

"Then I can stay and help Cobal?" he beamed.

"If that is what you want, then yes," I nodded. Castor stepped forward and hugged me. I did not know what to do at first, momentarily stunned by his actions, but then I leaned down and wrapped my arms around him.

"Thank you Castor, for all you did for me. I enjoyed having you in my company," I said to him. After a moment, Castor let me go. Smiling at me, we continued walking towards Cobal's hut.

~*~

Just before we reached the door, Maiya and Cobal stepped out, followed by Erik and Phoenyx. I looked at Erik, searching his eyes for something, anything. He met my eyes briefly before looking away, whispering something into Phoenyx's ear, before they both walked off.

"General Truda, thank you for coming. I was hoping you

wouldn't mind coming with me to meet the twins. From what Maiya tells me, they trust you and your presence will put them at ease," Cobal said to me.

"Of course," I said walking beside him, ignoring the pain I felt from Erik's absent-minded glance.

"Maiya, you stay here with Castor," Cobal said, looking back at Maiya, who had crossed her arms and was glaring at me, making me wonder if she even had a different facial expression or if this is how her features naturally sat.

"Good idea Cobal. Maiya's presence will definitely have the opposite effect to mine with the twins," I said to Cobal, glaring back at her. She could be angry at me all she wanted but she did not intimidate me. Cobal looked between us and laughed as he stepped away, I followed behind him, leaving Castor and Maiya by his hut.

"I don't think I have seen Maiya rattled by someone that bad for a very long time," Cobal laughed.

"Really, now that surprises me with her charming personality," I said, which made Cobal laugh even harder.

"I take it as a good sign. I have seen her like this before, she will come around," he said to me.

"Why would you say that?" I asked him.

"Because that's how she used to act around me when we first left the city, and now look at us." He chuckled. "Maiya is a very guarded person and it takes a long time for the trust to build, but once you have that, you won't know a more loyal friend."

It must have been hard for them in the beginning, different from Erik and I who had found each other, feelings slowly developing into whatever it was that we now shared. However, Cobal and Maiya's only connection was the love that they both shared for another, they had been brought together with grief and anger. I could not imagine how hard that must have been for them both to go through.

When we reached the holding tent, I saw Shanon and Shanor tied to the same post that I had once been.

"Is this necessary?" I asked, looking over to Cobal before walking over and removing the bonds that tied them. Cobal did not speak at first but when he saw the twins, he looked at them in shock and dropped to his knees.

"You're both so beautiful, so much like her," he whispered.

"Like who?" said Shanor, looking at him curiously.

"And who are you?" snapped Shanon.

"This is Cobal, he is the leader of the rebel's, and part of the reason the rebellion started in the first place," I told them, trying to calm the twins after Cobal's immediate change in demeaner.

"Truda, we don't understand, what is going on?" said Shanor, looking confused.

"Cobal has an important story to tell you both. It will be hard to hear, but you must listen, you deserve to know the truth." I told them, finally taking a step back and nodding to Cobal that it was his turn to talk. The twins glanced from me to him and waited for him to speak. Still sat on his knees, unblinking as he gazed at the twins in front of him, he slowly swallowed so he could speak.

"For years I've cried over the fading memory of her, forgetting the shape of her eyes and the curve of her lips, but you... you have both inherited the most beautiful features of a face I had long forgotten." Cobal whimpered, wiping away the water that had welled in his eyes.

"Who are you talking about?" snapped Shanon.

"A long time ago, before you were born, I lived in the city. I was a breeder, that was how I met her, your mother."

I stood back and let Cobal tell his story, watching the twins and their reactions to his words. Shanor burst into tears the moment she heard about her mother's death. Shanon looked furious and confused, her eyes darting in different directions as she digested what Cobal told them. He held back until the very end of his story, before he told them the one thing I knew would shock them to their core.

"I am... your father," said Cobal, stuttering on his words. Both the twins gasped in shock.

"I loved your mother so much, there was no one else like her, she was strong, beautiful and kind. When she died, I wanted to die with her, then Maiya came and saved me. We retreated here to this forest, vowing to save as many as we could, starting what you both grew up to know as the rebellion," he finished saying.

"And now you both know the truth," I said, stepping towards them. They both looked at me, clearly stunned by the whole situation, looking back to Cobal. Shanor was the first to speak.

"Why didn't you take us with you?" she said, tears rolling down her face. Cobal leaned forward and touched her hand.

"You have no idea how much I wanted to sweet girl, but you were taken and hidden from us. By the time we discovered where you were, I thought it was too late, that it would be too dangerous for you," he said. "I was worried that they would hurt you, just to keep you from me. I thought about you both every day and dreamt about when I could meet you."

Shanor suddenly leapt forward into Cobal's arms, tears running freely down her face. The whole situation had shaken her, and she could not hide the pain in her eyes. Cobal cradled her in his arms like a smaller child and stroked her hair. He looked over at Shanon who looked confused watching her sister, he outstretched his hand to her.

Shanon flinched and shuffled back.

"I need time," was all she said, to which Cobal closed his eyes and nodded in understanding.

Feeling like I had fulfilled my purpose, I walked towards the tent's exit, they needed some time alone to really talk things through.

"I will be in my hut if you need me," I said to Cobal as I left.

Chapter 23

FACING MY FEAR

It was dark outside, and I was lying on the cot in my hut staring at the ceiling. I thought about getting up to clean the mess around me, but I could not. I figured the mess was a result of Erik's anger. I had not spoken to him since my return, he was clearly avoiding me.

I wanted him to take his anger out on me, to shout anything to help me move past the pit I had in my stomach. But maybe I had hurt him so much that he no longer wanted anything to do with me.

I felt drained. I had not eaten anything in days and had barely drank water. I wanted to sleep, to sink into darkness and let my mind rest for a while, but a whirlwind of questions plagued me. Not just about Erik, but about the queen's death, bringing the twins here, and watching them being reunited with their father.

What did the future hold for us? Were we now part of the rebellion? Could I completely turn my back on my responsibilities in the city, or rather Imelda's responsibilities, now that she was General?

The one person I wanted to speak with had been gone all day. Fortuna had not come back to base, but instead had spent the day walking through the trees, remaining on the ground.

If she was not back by tomorrow, I would go and seek her out. She somehow knew I would return to the rebel base, so maybe she could help me figure out what to do next.

I had not realised I had fallen asleep until I felt the cot move. I was half dazed and could not open my eyes. I was lying on my side facing the wall, but I knew it was Erik, I could smell his scent.

At first, he sat still on the edge. I felt his hand stroke slowly down my arm, and when he reached my hand, he held it and I interlaced my fingers with his. I heard him sigh, then, still holding my hand he shifted himself to lie down beside me.

With my back resting against his chest, I snuggled in closer to him and pulled our hands closer to my chest to wrap his arm around me. He held me close and nestled his head in the crook of my neck. I heard his breathing change as he drifted off to sleep. Feeling secure in his arms, I smiled and let myself do the same.

~*~

I must have rolled over during the night because when I opened my eyes, I saw crystal blue eyes looking back at me.

"Hi," I whispered, feeling suddenly shy and unsure of what reaction I might get.

"Hi," he replied back. He did not smile, in fact he also looked nervous. We both gazed at each other, obviously not knowing how to begin. His eyes searched my face, and he raised his hand to stroke my cheek. I felt my face go warm from both his touch and my embarrassment. He lifted his head from the cushion and leaned over to me, my heart racing as he stopped just before touching my lips, hesitating to get closer.

I leaned forward and kissed him, just once at first, then, as I moved my head back, I felt Erik grab the back of my head and he pushed his lips against mine, with more urgency this time.

My hands cupped his face and before I even realised what I was doing, my body moved on top of him, straddling him. We were both fully dressed but that did not stop us from rubbing our bodies against each other. I felt him harden underneath my most sensitive part, and I could not help but let myself move over him. Erik held my shoulders, then pushed me away slightly so I could no longer kiss him.

"Truda wait," he said breathlessly. I looked down at him breathing heavily, still sat on top of him but no longer moving.

"I think we should talk," he said.

"Okay," I said as I slowly moved off him and sat back on the bed.

He moved from me, sitting on the cot on the opposite side, looking at me. Silence filled the room as both of us struggled with what to say to each other. As I looked around the room, I decided to speak first.

"Did you do this?" I asked.

"Yes," he mumbled.

"You were angry?" I asked quietly.

"Yes," he sighed. After a long while of more silence, just looking at each other, I spoke again.

"Sorry," I whispered.

"You weren't coming back," he said to me. It was not a question, just a statement, but I answered it anyway.

"No, I was not."

"Was it the twins that changed your mind?"

"Partly yes, but I had other reasons."

"Such as?" he asked. I knew what he wanted to hear. He wanted me to tell him that I had come back for him, but he did not know me well enough. I had missed him, yes. I was nervous about how it would be when we saw each other again, but I would be lying if I said I had come back for him.

The truth was that if the queen still lived and we had not been ambushed by the twins, I would probably be in the city right now. He would not have known how much I cared about him. Or how much I would have yearned for his company, to be held in his arms once again. I would have kept the rebel base a secret to protect him, to keep him safe. When I did not reply, I saw the sad look on his face, my lack of words hurting him.

"I am sorry," I apologised again, not knowing what else to say.

"It's okay Truda, I understand," he said after a little while and stood from the cot.

"I'm going to get us some food," he said with a sad tone as he left, leaving me alone in the mess I had quite literally created. I decided to get up, I needed some fresh air and, more importantly, I wanted to clear my mind and speak with Fortuna.

~*~

Walking out, I climbed down the nearest rope ladder to the forest floor, to find it was covered in a grey mist. A fog covered the entire vastness of green making visibility difficult in all directions. Luckily, I knew where I was heading, and it did not take me long to find Fortuna, knowing that she was likely by her favourite spot.

She was with Yuki, playing in the stream. Fortuna had lifted her long silk dress as she stood in the shallows while making little water fish for Yuki to chase.

"Hi Tru," she said drearily, with neither her nor Yuki looking at me.

"No offence, but for a blind elf, you're pretty perceptive," I said.

"I have ears you know, and you're not exactly a quiet stepper," she smiled. So much for my stealth training, I thought to myself. She then tip-toed out of the water, walking to meet me by the tree stumps.

"How did you know I was going to come back?" I asked her.

"In truth, I see things sometimes and I saw parts of your future," she replied.

"Like in your dream when you saw me in the forest picking mushrooms?"

"Yeah, something like that. I get visions, mostly when I sleep, but sometimes when I am awake, it's a sequence of pictures. Other times I get to step into my dream, and walk through like it's real, like the day we first met."

"Can you tell me what is in my future?" I asked.

"That's not how my visions work. Sometimes it's hard to tell if they are of the present, past or the future, all I can say is that I am sure you will find your answers in this forest," she said cryptically. Yes, but answers to what? To which of the dozens of questions I currently had swimming around in my head, where was my place in all this?

"Can I ask you another question, it is more personal? I asked.

"Do you see me in the future... with anyone?" I asked, thinking about Erik and what future was in store for us.

"You need to be more specific there Tru. When you say with anyone, who do you mean?" she asked.

"As in, with a special someone, together, happy," I said to her, feeling a little embarrassed for asking. Out of all the uncertainties in my life that I needed answers, why was this one so paramount in my trail of thoughts?

"You're talking about Erik of course," she said.

"Yes," I said, thinking how obvious my question must have been.

"You know the heart is a complicated thing, always seems to want to fight with our mind, arguing over what we want and what we think is right," she said with a sigh. Was she talking about me, or someone else?

"That is just another cryptic answer Fortuna."

"Sorry Tru, I know you came to me wanting answers but that's not my place. I'm only here to gently nudge and occasionally meddle," she said with a giggle.

"Then I guess I will just have to figure it all out on my own," I said, shifting uncomfortably on the log.

"The only real advice I can give you is to follow the path you think is right, not what the world wants you to believe is right," she said.

"Thank you Fortuna, you are a good friend," I said, smiling to her.

"You're welcome," she beamed.

"Are you coming back to the camp? I'm starving and need

to get some food," I asked her as I stood.

"Umm actually, I'm going to stay here a while longer," she said dismissively.

"Are you okay Fortuna? You have not been back to camp since I returned," I said, looking at her worriedly.

"Let's just say you're not the only one facing a battle between the heart and the head," she replied. Nodding, and walking away in confusion, I headed back to camp. One thing could be said for Fortuna, she really did love her riddles and putting your head in a spin more than it already was.

~*~

On my way back to my hut, I saw Cobal walking with the twins. Shanor was holding his hand, while Shanon remained a few steps behind them. I walked over to them and smiled as I heard Shanor talking with Cobal, asking him questions on how the tree platforms had been built.

"It is nice to see you outside of the tent," I said to them.

"I wanted to show the girls around, they're not my prisoners but very welcomed guests," Cobal said, smiling down at Shanor. I looked behind to Shanon who still did not look overly comfortable with the situation. I wanted to speak with them, explain my side of things, but I knew now was not the right time.

They had just learnt the truth of their parents and needed time to adjust, Shanor already looked happier for knowing the truth and I knew it would not be long before Shanon would come around.

"I was wondering if you would be up for a sparring session tomorrow, I could do with the workout," I said, looking to both twins. Both Shanon and Shanor looked at me with huge grins, clearly loving that idea.

"That is if you do not mind Cobal?" I said, looking over to him.

"Of course, I would love to see the girls in action. Maybe I could come and watch?" he replied. That is when I saw Shanon's smile drop, looking away from all three of us.

"Well, I will not hold you up, and will catch up with you later," I said, smiling at them, then I headed back to my hut. My stomach was growling, and I was starting to feel a bit queasy from the lack of food.

Luckily, when I stepped into my hut, I was pleasantly surprised to see a new table and two chairs had been brought in and the table was full of food, fruits, nuts, bread and soup. Erik smiled when I walked in and gasped at the food.

"Your stomach was making some funny noises last night, I figured you hadn't eaten much for a while," he said.

"You are not wrong, I am famished. Thank you," I said, walking over to sit in the chair beside him. We ate in silence and I consumed as much food as I could until my nausea turned to feeling slightly sick from how full I now felt.

"Feel better?" Erik asked.

"Actually, I think I have eaten too much," I replied to him, making him laugh.

"Then why don't we go for a walk?"

"That sounds like a great idea," I said as I slowly stood with him.

~*~

As we walked along the platforms, I was no longer nervous as I crossed the narrow bridges unaided. I could see the daylight fading, with more shadows being cast by the tree's surrounding us. We were walking side by side, close but not touching, we had not said much since we left the hut, making small talk about the food we had eaten. I wanted to be honest with him and tell him the truth, but it was hard for me, all I could think was what Fortuna had said to me earlier, about doing what I felt was right, not what the world was telling me was right.

"Erik, I want to apologise for this morning," I blurted out. He stopped and turned to me, his eyes meeting mine. I saw that same sadness there. "I let you think I do not care for you, and that is not true," I stated.

"What are you saying, you did come back for me?" he asked hopefully.

"I did not come back for you, but..." I started to say, and Erik shook his head.

"It's okay Truda, you don't have to explain," he said, as he

303

started to walk away from me.

"No wait, you do not understand," I said as I grabbed his arm, stopping him from leaving, though he did not turn to look at me.

"I brought you here to keep you safe, I left to protect you. You might not be the reason I came back, but you are the reason I came here in the first place." He looked at me, letting me look at him as I finished speaking. "Everything has changed, the queen is dead, and I am no longer General of Kven. I do not have the same responsibilities I had, nor do I have the same rules stopping me. Here the rules do not apply, and I can choose what I want, my future is up to me," I said, closing my eyes. Erik stepped towards me, lifting my chin to look at him.

"What do you want Truda?" he asked, looking nervously, searching my eyes for his answer.

"I want this, I want us… I want to be with you," I whispered to him. Erik exhaled with relief at my words and bent down to kiss me. I wrapped my arms around his neck and let myself get lost in this moment. For the first time, I felt free, like nothing else mattered but us, the connection we had, the rest of the world and its troubles falling away.

"Does that mean you're not leaving again?" he asked.

"Erik, you are the one thing in my life right now that makes sense. I do not know who I am anymore, but I know who you are, and there is no way I could leave you." I smiled up at him. That seemed to be the right answer as he pulled me in for a kiss again.

"I know who you are," he said. "You're the most beautiful creature whose lips I have ever tasted." I grimaced. I knew he was trying to be sweet, but when he said those words it only reminded me that I was not the only woman he had been with. I knew I should not have held it against him, it was before we had even met and he was only doing what he had to, just like I had, but it still reminded me that we had barriers that needed to be worked through. All I knew was that I wanted to.

"Did I say something wrong?" he asked, stroking the side of my face.

"Not on purpose, you just reminded me that, unlike me, you have been intimate with others," I said to him, feeling awful for saying the words but wanting to be honest with him.

"Anything that has happened in my past, doesn't compare to anything I have shared with you. I have never felt this way about anyone," he said to me, cupping my face.

"Me neither," I said honestly, looking up at him.

"Then nothing else matters," he said, planting a kiss on my lips. He held my hand and we continued to walk through the camp.

"Does it not bother you, that an elf back in the city is carrying your child?" I did not really want to ask, but it was bothering me, so I needed to get it off my chest.

"No, it doesn't. I don't see it as mine," he told me.

"But you helped create it," I said.

"I don't see it like that. When I think of making a child, of being a father, that happens when you create life with someone you love."

"Like Cobal and Lilith," I said.

"Exactly," he replied, squeezing my hand.

It may have seemed harsh, but that was the reality of our race. Lelane's child did not have any ties to Erik, as much as I did not have ties to the Guan that would have helped my mother create me. We continued to walk, holding hands and talking as we watched the last part of the daylight turn to night.

Chapter 24

MAGICAL MOMENTS

By the time we reached our hut it was night, and I was tired, but I knew I would not be able to sleep until I felt that closeness that Erik and I had shared the night before I left for the city.

Erik walked over and lit a candle, letting an orange glow fill the hut. I looked around and frowned at the broken mess on the floor and the leftover food on the table.

"You know, we should really clean this place up. I do not think I can sleep with all that food and mess around," I said.

"Who said anything about sleep?" he grinned. I felt my cheeks flush, which was ridiculous considering that is what I had been thinking about moments ago, but it made me nervous knowing he was thinking the same thing.

"Maybe just a quick tidy up?" I said with a sigh.

"Very well," Erik said with a chuckle, as he started picking up the leftover food and plates on the table. I walked over to the corner of the room that had a basket full of cloth and clean cotton fabrics.

I emptied the items onto a chair and then turned to start picking up some of the smaller pieces of broken furniture and ceramics and placing them in the basket.

When I stood back up and turned, Erik was watching me, he had cleared most of the table and the leftover food was gone.

"What?" I asked, as I put the basket back in the corner and walked to move some of the larger broken pieces of furniture. Erik walked over to me and took the broken chair leg out of my hands, discarding it into the basket, then cupping my face to look up at him.

"You are so beautiful that sometimes it's hard to believe you are real, that you're here with me," he said, kissing my forehead and then bending down to kiss my lips.

I reached my arms around his shoulders as I kissed him back urgently. He bent down to grab my thighs, lifting my legs to wrap around his waist. He walked with me over to the cot, placing me down gently and climbing on top of me. Our lovemaking was slow and gentle, using our hands and bodies to re-create the love that we had yet to confess in words to each other, until we were spent, and Erik's body remained on top of mine.

For a moment we stayed this way, our bodies connected as Erik planted gentle kisses on my lips, gazing into my eyes. Then he moved off me, collapsing to the side. I instantly missed the contact, which Erik must have sensed as he rolled my body towards him. I wrapped my leg over his and placed my head on his chest. He stroked my shoulder and tilted his head to kiss the top of mine.

"Erik? I have been wondering something," I said quietly to him.

"Hmm," he replied.

"Why was the cot the only furniture that remained in one piece?" I asked, thinking of how the hut had looked when I first walked in after my return.

"I couldn't destroy the place where we shared our special moment, after you left it was my only comfort, it still smelled of you," he kissed the top of my head again.

I understood what he meant; it was also probably the reason I had found my dress tucked under the cushions. He was mad at me for leaving and had clearly taken out his frustrations on the room, but he could not destroy something that reminded him of what we shared.

I pulled myself closer to him, so that my entire body was stretched along his, keeping my arm and leg wrapped around him, once again feeling secure in his arms as we fell asleep.

~*~

The next few days were a beautiful blur, taking our relationship to the next level as we connected emotionally and physically, especially physically, barely keeping our hands off each other as we spent hours discovering what our bodies craved, like a pair of wild animals in heat.

We also talked a lot. I told him about my life, but not the battles and the training, he had heard all that before.

I told him about my mother, the things Acqueline and I used to do to get into trouble as children. Erik told me more about himself too. He told me how he had started working in construction when he was very young, always being big and strong for his age. He told me more about his friends like Phoenyx.

Just as I had skipped all the talk of war and training, I had not missed the fact that Erik had skipped all the bad stories. Neither of us wanting to share any sad stories that would dampen our moods. I wished I could pretend that I believed in only the good stories, believe that Erik was raised kindly and had fond memories, but as Erik was currently lying on his stomach, while I stroked the scars on his back, I knew that was impossible. Seeing the damage that had been left there, was the only reminder I needed of the cruel world he lived in.

"You really remembered me from the day I stopped your punishment?" I asked.

"Not only did I remember you Truda, but I longed to know you whenever I saw you around the city," he said.

"Really? I suppose I can't say either way, I would have never noticed back then," I said.

"Until the day I met you," he said, reaching over to play with my hair.

"Oh yes, what a wonderful experience that must have been for you, meeting General Truda," I said with a mocking sound at my own title.

"Actually, it was really difficult. When you walked in the room, all I wanted was to talk to you, to look at you, but you had other things on your mind."

"That makes sense as to why I soon caught you looking at me," I said with a smile, still stroking my hand over his back.

"When did you first know?" he asked me, lifting up to lean on his elbow, looking at me.

"Know what?"

"That you had feelings for me," he asked. That was a hard question to answer. I was fairly certain that I was immediately attracted to him, remembering the times I could not stop looking at his body, but actually developing feelings?

"I think it happened gradually, but I suppose the day I actually knew, was the day I saw you fight in the arena," I told him. He smiled at my answer and leaned forward to kiss me again.

"How about you?" I asked.

"I had feelings for you before I even met you," he said.

"Erik, that is impossible. You did not even know me," I

said with a sigh, raising my eyebrows at him.

"I knew enough," he said, giving me a quick peck before climbing out of bed and picking up his clothes.

"Erik, it is late, where are you going?" I asked.

"I want to take you somewhere, will you come with me?"

"Where?" I asked, now sitting up and reaching for my clothes.

"Just for a quick walk, we won't be long I promise," he said, followed by a smile I could not resist. I sighed and got up from the bed, pulling on a dress over my shoulders and slipping on some hide flats on my feet. Erik held my hand and led me out of the hut.

It did not take me long to realise where he was taking me as we soon reached the waterfall. We both stood holding hands, looking over at its beauty, the sounds of the calming water rushing past the rocks to reach the bottom. Erik turned to look at me, raising my hand to his lips so he could kiss it.

"The day I realised I loved you, was the day you helped heal me after I had been whipped. You were so caring and kind, from that moment I knew there would be no one else," he told me. I held my breath as I looked up at him, for me it was a horrible memory, seeing him suffer from his injuries. I remembered how angry I felt towards whoever had inflicted the punishment, but for Erik it was the moment he let himself fall for me.

"You love me?" I asked, looking up at him.

"Yes Truda, I love you," he said, pulling me closer to him and lifting my chin so he could look directly in my eyes.

"And I love you," I said before reaching up to kiss him. He wrapped me in his arms, lifting me off the ground and twirling me in the air. When my feet landed again, I smiled and looked up at him, he had never looked so happy, his eyes wide, beaming down at me with the biggest grin, kissing me again before holding my hand to walk back to the hut with me.

"So, why did you choose here to tell me?" I asked, laughing lightly.

"From the first moment I saw the waterfall, I wanted to tell you here. I suppose I thought it would make it more special," he shrugged, now laughing with me. As I looked back to the waterfall, I knew he was right, we had made it special. Every time I would look at the cascading water, I would be reminded of this moment and that brought a smile to my face.

Our laughing stopped when we reached the bridge and I saw a frozen figure looking at both of us. It was Shanon and she looked angry. She glanced between Erik and I, looking at our entwined hands.

"Shanon?" I called to her, but she just looked at me in disgust and ran off. I looked behind me for a moment looking towards the waterfall and then back to where Shanon had stood. She had seen it all, seen the loving kisses and caresses Erik and I had shared. I had not been given the chance to explain our situation to them, and now I realised that Shanon must have been angry with me for not telling them the truth about Erik. I would have to go and see the twins in the morning to explain everything.

~*~

We woke to the sounds of hurried knocking. Erik quickly grabbed the cotton sheet and covered our naked bodies. I looked at him in confusion.

"Come in," I called.

In walked Castor, short of breath like he had just run here, his expression was panicked, something was wrong.

"Castor, what is wrong?" I asked, looking at him with concern.

"I'm sorry General Truda, Erik, but Cobal needs to see you right away," he said before nodding briefly and running out of the hut.

"What do you think is going on?" Erik asked me as we both sat up and reached for our clothes.

"I do not know, but it sounds urgent, we had better hurry." We both dressed quickly and left the hut, rushing to get to Cobal's hut. There were other warriors outside accompanied with a very angry looking Maiya. They were all in full armour like they had either just returned from a trip or were about to go on one. I looked back at Erik who also looked concerned at what we were seeing, we both stepped quickly inside the hut. Inside we saw Cobal, holding a very teary Shanor.

314

"What's going on Cobal?" Erik asked him.

"It's Shanon, she's gone," he said, looking back to both of us.

"What do you mean she is gone? Gone where?" I asked him. Shanor looked up, wiping the tears from her face.

"She came back late last night to our hut and told me she was leaving, she was so angry General Truda," whimpered Shanor, fresh tears streaming down her face.

"We have to go search for her," I said, directing my attention back to Cobal.

"We already tried. Maiya took a team and searched the woods, they lost her trail just outside the cave, we suspect she found her way through," Cobal replied.

"I don't understand why she would take off like that?" said Erik. I looked over at Erik and thought about what Shanon had seen last night. I had a pretty good idea what could have triggered her into leaving.

"Shanor, what did she say to you?" I asked her.

"She was so angry, raving and shouting about how we had been lied to, she said it was wrong for us to be here, that we should leave. I told her I didn't want to, that I wanted to stay here with Cobal, Maiya and you. Then she said that you had betrayed us, and no one here could be trusted," she looked back towards Cobal, who took her hand. "She gave me the choice, she said I had to choose between her or the rebels... When I told her again that I wanted to stay, she grabbed her things and just left!" she cried and Cobal wrapped his arm around her.

"It is a shock to us both," said Cobal. "I knew she was struggling here, finding it difficult to get close to me and my friends, but I don't know what caused her to finally come to this decision," he finished.

"I do," I said frowning.

Both Cobal and Shanor looked at me, puzzled, Shanor wiping her tears away to listen to me.

"What is it Truda?" Erik asked me, now walking closer and putting a hand on my shoulder.

"It was us Erik, me and you." I turned and looked towards Shanor.

"I wanted to tell you from the moment you both arrived here, but thought it was better to give you space with Cobal. I never got to tell you the reason I came here in the first place," I said, finishing the last part with a quiet sigh.

"What do you mean?" asked Shanor, looking briefly at Cobal who squeezed her hand gently before looking back to me.

"I broke the slaves out of the prison that night, I did it to free Erik. He was my breeding Guan and I fell in love with him. I hid him in my home until I found evidence of a possible location for the rebel base, then I helped him escape the city and we found our way here," I said to her. I waited for the anger, waited for more tears to fall, for her to scream and shout at me.

316

"I am sorry," I whispered, lowering my head in shame. This was all my fault, I should have told them both earlier, I had caused this. The twins were my responsibility. I had helped train them, built a bond with them. I brought them here to hear the truth about their parents, and then I abandoned them. I thought of only myself and my future, thinking that I could just go ahead and make decisions without consequences, that I could pursue a forbidden love because I was no longer confined to the rules of the city. I stepped away from Erik, wrapping my arms around myself.

"The reason Shanon left is because she saw me and Erik last night by the waterfall in a loving embrace. This is my fault," I finished. I was a fool, a selfish fool and I deserved whatever wrath was about to come my way. Shanor walked towards me and held my hand, making me look up at her.

"I understand," she said. I looked back at her in shock.

"You do?"

"You fell in love with your Guan, like my mother fell in love with hers," she said to me softly. "My sister struggled with the story of our parents, but I didn't. I accept that they loved each other and that we were the result of their love. To hear that you have gone through the same only makes me admire you more. I am only sorry that my sister couldn't see what I see," she said, looking sweetly between Erik and I.

I immediately pulled her in and wrapped my arms around her. I could not believe how strong and wise she was. She was still so young, but clearly understood more about the world than I did. She saw it through her heart and not with what her head had been filled with.

Chapter 25

PREPARATIONS

After a little while, Erik and I left Cobal's hut, giving Shanor some private time with her father to talk through her pain. A heavy downpour had started outside and Erik and I stood under the slant of the roof, huddled close together to get a bit of protection from the rain. Where was all this sudden horrid weather coming from?

Maiya passed us while we were standing by the hut and our eyes locked. She was staring at me furiously. Well, Shanor might not blame me for Shanon leaving, but Maiya clearly did, considering she had not wanted the twins brought back here in the first place. We stayed under the shelter of the hut until finally, the rain eased.

"Let's get out of the camp for a while," Erik whispered

to my ear.

"Shanor and Cobal may need us." I shook my head.

"We won't go far, perhaps just a short walk through the forest?" he suggested.

"Okay that sounds nice, and I know of just the perfect place," I relented, thinking of Fortuna and Yuki playing happily by the spot downstream.

As we walked through the forest, we soon saw a familiar face. As Phoenyx walked towards us, his head was down, and he was kicking the occasional rock and twig in frustration. He smiled in surprise when he saw us, then frowned when he saw our entwined hands. I instantly went to remove my hand from Erik's, but he tightened his grip, stopping me from letting go.

"Phoenyx, it is good to see you, how are you settling in?" I asked, ignoring Erik's strong hold on my hand.

"Hi General Truda, Erik," he replied, nodding towards both of us.

"Are you okay Nyx?" Erik asked. Phoenyx briefly looked behind him with a frown then looked back at us, quickly putting on a fake smile.

"I'm fine, I was just heading back to camp. They have me helping them build some new platforms and huts. Since numbers are growing, they need some more living space."

"That's great, we would be happy to help if you need extra pairs of hands?" Erik offered. I looked at him with a puzzled smirk. Did he not remember that I was a warrior elf and knew absolutely nothing about construction?

"That would be good, we could sure use the help," Phoenyx replied.

"Perfect, we will catch up with you later then," Erik said. Phoenyx nodded and half smiled as he threw a glance at our linked hands, and then walked past us, heading back to camp.

"Is he okay?" I asked Erik.

"I think he's just having a few adjustment issues," Erik replied. "It's good that he has been given the opportunity to do building work, he has a keen eye for design and will be a big help to the people here," he finished saying.

"Yes, and thanks for volunteering us to help with that by the way, you know I do not know anything about construction," I said, playfully nudging him.

"Well then I can teach you," Erik smirked, bending down to kiss me on the lips. I sighed and smiled back at him. I suppose it would not hurt to learn new things. I could not exactly expect Erik to spend all of his time with me in the hut, although that would have been nice.

When we reached the stream, I saw Fortuna. She was sitting on a tree stump looking towards the water. Her chin was rested on one palm of her hand, while her other hand was waving around slowly, the same action she made when she was making fish in the water.

Yuki was lying on the ground next to the water, his head

resting on his paws. He was watching the fish but not moving, his ears pinned close to his head. They both looked miserable.

"Hi Fortuna," I said as we walked close and sat opposite her on a fallen log.

"I would like to introduce you to someone, this is Erik," I said.

"We have already met Truda," Erik said, chuckling.

"Oh, sorry I did not realise," I said, feeling awkward.

"It's okay Tru, we spoke a few times when you were being held in the tent after you first arrived," she said to me.

Her tone was off. Fortuna was the happiest elf I had ever met, always beaming with positivity and smiles, but now she looked sad. Even Yuki did not bother to come and greet me like he normally would.

"What is wrong with Yuki?" I asked, looking at the fox who was staring away from Fortuna, focusing on the water.

"He's angry with me," Fortuna sighed.

"Angry, why?" I asked her.

"Let's just say we disagree on something and he's being stubborn about it. Oh, and I'm sorry about the weather too, my mood sometimes affects it," she said glumly. Looking up at the sky, I glanced at the grey clouds through the gaps of the tree's, it was still raining but much lighter than before. Did Fortuna really think that her mood effected the weather? I did not comment, instantly discarding the idea.

"Well, I suppose since you are here together, that means

you chose with your heart?" she asked cheerily, seeming a little more like herself.

"Yes, we both did," I said, smiling up at Erik who was still holding my hand, lightly brushing his thumb across my knuckles.

"Well, you made the choice. I had already made mine," Erik said to me, laughing lightly.

"This makes me happy. I am glad you took my advice Tru," Fortuna smiled. I did not exactly remember her giving me advice on telling Erik how I felt, I only remembered a cryptic message about my heart fighting my head, although I suppose she was hinting.

"Have you been to camp this morning?" I asked Fortuna.

"Maiya came to see me this morning. She told me that Shanon had left?"

"Yes, I think she saw me with Erik last night and was angry, not understanding the truth," I said in a sad tone.

"That's not your fault Tru, she had already made up her mind long before she saw you two together, Shanon was never on our side," she replied.

"How can you say that? You hardly knew her!" I snapped, not meaning to sound so angry, but I refused to see Shanon as anything but my student, my friend. How could Fortuna possibly know anything about what Shanon felt, or what she was thinking? Then it occurred to me.

"You saw this, you knew it was going to happen?"

"I wasn't sure, but I have seen things that make a whole lot more sense now that Shanon has left," she said. "And this is only the beginning," she finished.

~*~

Fortuna would not tell us what she meant, but I had the sudden urge to return to camp. We left Fortuna and Yuki by the stream and headed back towards Cobal's hut. When we stepped inside, I saw Cobal, Maiya and Shanor sitting around a small table talking.

"General Truda, I am glad you're here," said Cobal. I looked over at Maiya who had crossed her arms and was frowning at me, not hiding her disdain of my presence.

"We have sent a message to the city to try and warn Kayla, we're hoping she can get a message back to us soon," said Cobal.

"I have said this already Cobal, Kayla isn't going to get a message back to us because she is going to be dead!" Maiya shouted, standing abruptly from her chair, making Shanor jump.

"Not now Maiya," said Cobal, looking at her sternly.

"If not now, then when? You are deluding yourself Cobal, Shanon is going to go back to the city and will tell them everything. Kayla will be killed for treason and the queen will send her warriors to come and exterminate us," she fumed.

"You don't know that my sister will do that." Cried Shanor,

Cobal reached over and held Shanor's hand to try and comfort her.

"You're not helping the situation here Maiya," said Cobal, now looking angry at her for her outburst against his daughter.

"Not helping? All I have done is help. If you had just let me make all the decisions, we wouldn't be in this mess!" she shouted. "You should have just let me kill her the moment she arrived," she spat, now looking directly at me. This made Erik angry as he stepped forward in front of me.

"And I would have killed you for trying," he said.

"Don't test me Guan, best you stay out of things you don't understand," she said through gritted teeth.

"Enough!" I shouted, stepping forward in front of Erik and glancing at all of them.

"Maiya is right. If I had not come here, then none of this would have happened. The twins would never have known of this place and neither would anyone in the city. Kayla would be safe, everyone here would be safe," I said, keeping my voice raised. I looked over to Erik and sighed.

"But then Erik would be dead," I said quietly. My actions would have had consequences regardless of what choice I made, even if I knew what would happen if I freed Erik. Setting the current chain of events in motion, I could not tell them I would have acted differently because I would not have. I had reunited a family, rescued Phoenyx, freed Castor, and found love with Erik.

"So, we are all here in this situation because you fell in love with a Guan!" shouted Maiya, then she paused to suck in a breath, realising what she had just said. She knew as much as the rest of us did, that this rebellion started because an elf fell in love with a Guan.

Angry at her own words, Maiya kicked a chair across the room watching it break as it hit the wall, then she stormed past Erik and I out of the hut. Cobal stood and looked down to Shanor.

"I'll be back," he said, letting go of her hand gently and smiling at her. "She's just upset, I need to go talk to her," Cobal said to us as he walked past, and left the hut to find Maiya. I let go of Erik's hand and walked over to sit next to Shanor.

"Are you alright?" I asked as I leaned over and placed my hand on her shoulder.

"Do you think she will do it? Do you think she will tell the queen about our location?" she looked to me, tears forming in her eyes again.

"I think she will do what she was trained for, what she believes is right from the things she was taught," I told her.

"Then that means the people are not safe here, we're not safe here," she said. She was right, the rebels were no longer safe, Cobal and Maiya did not have enough elf warriors to be able to fight against the city's legions, their number of fighters were just too few. The queen would come for us, armed and ready. We would not be able to stop them.

As I looked at Erik, he looked between me and Shanor, sympathy in his eyes. He walked over and stood behind me, putting both his hands on my shoulders, and I leaned back resting my head against his stomach. I did not know what I would do without him, he had become my strength, and I knew it would break me if I lost him now.

Wait a minute, he is my strength. Erik is strong. A human yes, but strong enough to fight back. Thinking of our earlier conversation with his talks of teaching me a new skill, sparked an idea. I stood abruptly and turned to him.

"Erik, I need you to go and find Cobal and Maiya," I said to him, then I called to Castor who was sat just outside.

"Castor, I need you to go and find Fortuna. In fact, get Phoenyx too, bring them here as quickly as you can," I said to him. Watching, he nodded and then ran off out of the hut.

"Truda, what's going on?" Erik asked.

"I have an idea," I smiled.

~*~

I waited until everyone had returned to the hut, Cobal took a seat beside Shanor. Maiya; who did not make eye contact with me, walked and stood behind him. Erik and Fortuna sat next to Cobal, little Yuki curled in Fortuna's lap and Phoenyx stood by the door, looking confused as to why he was there.

"Okay General, why don't you tell us what this is all about," Maiya said, looking at me angrily with her arms crossed.

"We cannot beat the queen's warriors," I said, looking around the room. "You do not have enough skilled fighters to defend the camp, let alone to go out and meet your enemy in battle."

"Care to tell us anything we don't know?" Maiya spat.

"But you do have the numbers," I grinned. Everyone in the room looked up at me confused, except for Fortuna who was smiling. She had obviously seen this, and it only encouraged me to continue. "You have spent years, freeing Guan's from the city, and your camp is full of men who can help against our plight," I said.

"They are not warriors General Truda," Cobal protested.

"Not yet, but with some training and a good battle strategy, they could be." I looked at Erik who was now also smiling at me. He agreed with what I was saying, and it warmed my heart that he trusted and believed in me.

"This is ridiculous, your suggestion will only get them killed quicker," said Maiya. I was surprised when Phoenyx was the first to walk forward and speak up against Maiya's words.

"No, let us fight. We are not weak like you think we are. Some of us have more reasons than any of you to want to fight back," he said, throwing a glance at Fortuna when he spoke.

"I agree. Nyx and I have spent our lives building up our body strength. We can fight, all we lack is the skill," Erik said, smiling at me again.

"And we can teach them that, we have enough warriors

to help train the others," I said.

"We don't have enough armour!" shouted Maiya.

"We can make more," said Cobal, now clearly on board with the plan.

"Cobal, we don't even have enough weapons!" Maiya shouted again.

"Well actually, Fortuna can help with that," I commented.

"How?" Cobal asked.

"When I was in the city, my friend had a bow carved from wood and imbued with magic to produce arrows on command." I looked out towards the forest and pointed to the trees. "We have the wood," I said.

"And I have the magic," finished Fortuna, smiling with excitement.

"We can train the strongest of us to fight close combat in the front lines and distribute magical bows to those who can offer us support at a safe distance with ranged weaponry," I said, getting more excited as I looked at the faces around the room.

"This isn't going to work Cobal. Shanon will reach the city easily within the next day, they will assemble their warriors and prepare for battle immediately. We will have as little as three days, that isn't enough time to turn a bunch of men into warriors. We should just pack up and flee the base before they get here," she said.

"And where would you go Maiya? If you run now, you will

always be running. They will catch you eventually and kill us all one by one, crushing the rebellion forever and leaving the city to be controlled by slavery," said Erik.

"This is your chance to fight back, they won't be expecting it. Shanon will likely tell them that we have little in the way of warriors, they will underestimate us. We will have the element of surprise," I said to her, then looked at Cobal who nodded in agreement.

"We need you Maiya, you're one of our strongest," said Cobal.

"Fine, this is clearly what you all want. Of course I will fight, just remember that when you're all lying there on the ground bleeding out, about to take your last breath, this wasn't my idea," she said.

"Then let us get this plan in motion," I said, rubbing my hands together in anticipation.

Chapter 26

TRAINING

After we left the hut, Cobal wasted no time in gathering everyone in the camp and explaining the situation. I was encouraged by their reactions. A few looked scared and worried, but most stepped forward, ready to fight for their freedom and survival. I suppose it made sense; they must have known this day was coming.

Cobal took a group of the very young and old to make extra armour and shields, using foliage and bark from the forest as well as whatever suitable materials they could find in the camp.

Fortuna went to collect whatever strong bows she could find to work on her magic to give them the ability to produce arrows on command.

Shanor took a group of those capable, but not yet strong enough to fight in the front lines, to practise and teach them how to use a bow. For now, they were stuck using some makeshift arrows made of twigs and feathers until Fortuna could provide them with the magical ones.

Maiya and I, along with a few other warriors, gathered the strongest men, including Erik and Phoenyx. Most of them were big and muscled, although none could compete with Erik's impressive size.

"We should split them into smaller groups," I said to Maiya, looking at the dozens of men now standing before us, trying to think of the most efficient method of training them.

"What do you suggest?" she asked me, looking towards the men standing in front of us. After Cobal had told everyone our plan, I noticed a change in Maiya. She seemed more focused, rather than doubting or commenting on how we would fail. Perhaps now, looking at all of the potential in front of us, she could see the hope in my plan.

"Well, I would suggest we each take a smaller group and train them using our strengths," I said.

"I'm strongest with a sword, Shea over there is pretty lethal with a pair of daggers, the others range from Axe to Bow. What is your strength?" she asked me.

I did not know how to answer that question without making her angry. As much as I would have liked to boast about how good I was at everything, I knew that would threaten her, bringing out her anger, and right now, more than ever, I needed Maiya on my side.

"I would prefer to take as many as I can, one at a time for hand to hand combat, just to help give them some pointers on how to attack or defend if they find themselves without a weapon," I replied.

"Suits me," she shrugged.

Maiya instructed her warriors on what to do next, splitting the men into different groups, each elf taking a dozen men off into a different area of the forest. I watched as Erik was put into Maiya's group to practise with a sword, which pleased me. I had already observed him fight with a sword in the arena, and he had potential. I wished I could train him myself but knew it would be discouraging to the others if I gave him special treatment.

Instead, I walked over towards another familiar face, Phoenyx, who was placed in Igit's group. He was watching her swing her axe, demonstrating her skill to the group. Since the attack, I had only ever seen her at a distance, occasionally she glanced my way but never spoke to me. Erik informed me that her and Shea had been heavily scolded by Maiya and Cobal for what happened to me that day.

Igit passed a few of them some axe's and started showing them how to hold it, how to swing, and how to twist the wrist without allowing the weight to cause injury. I decided to watch for a moment, leaning against a nearby tree. Igit walked over to the tree next to her and swung her axe into it, I listened as she instructed.

"Holding the axe nearer the top gives you better control and aim for short distance strikes," she said, pulling her axe from the tree and moving her grip further up the handle before swinging again, hitting almost the exact same spot as where she had hit before.

"Holding the handle lower down gives you better range but won't be as accurate." She demonstrated the lesson by holding the handle furthest away from the steel head and swinging it at the tree, missing her mark by a long way.

"However, holding the handle this way for longer range attacks, gives you better long-distance throwing aim, like this," she spun to face me, hurling the axe in my direction. It hit the tree not far from where I was leaning, making a few of the men gasp as the axe hit the centre of the tree right next to my face. I however, did not flinch.

"That's true Igit," I said, pulling the axe from the tree and walking over to return it to her.

"Although, it does leave you without a weapon," I smirked at her, handing back the axe. She grinned back at me, impressed by my confidence.

"Which is why I am here to help with that. Phoenyx, fancy a bit of hand to hand combat training?" I asked, looking over towards him. I looked back to Igit and took her nod as a sign of approval.

"Sure," he said, following me as I walked away from the group to a quieter location in the forest. I had not realised I had come to the stream until I saw Yuki and Fortuna.

She was sitting on her usual tree stump with a bow on her lap. She moved her hands over it slowly, whispering something to it, and I saw the faintest golden glow emanating from her fingertips.

She went quiet when she heard me and Phoenyx approach. Yuki jumped up and ran over to me, and as I bent down to stroke him, he did not stop as he ran straight past me, and started brushing himself against Phoenyx's legs, yelping lightly for attention. Phoenyx bent down and stroked his fur, laughing lightly.

"How is it going?" I asked Fortuna as I approached. She had gone quiet and her head was tilted so she could listen to Yuki and Phoenyx.

"It's difficult, but I'm sure I will get it soon," she said to me.

"What were you saying? Some kind of magical spell or enchantment?" I asked. Fortuna made a funny face and burst out laughing, making Phoenyx and Yuki stop what they were doing and look up at Fortuna. They both stood and started walking closer to us.

"No, I was asking the bow if it wouldn't mind making arrows," she said, still giggling.

"Oh, I suppose I do not really know how magic works," I said, only thinking about what I had learnt from the mages back in the city. I had seen them carve runes into wood and steel, heard them chant words when brewing a potion or giving an object magic, but aside from that, my mistrust of Freyja had prevented me from wanting to learn more.

"I don't really know much either. I didn't spend much time with the mages, and I don't remember anything they taught me. All I know is that magic comes from nature, so I talk to it and sometimes ask it favours," she said, still smiling but no longer laughing as Phoenyx approached us. "Umm, what are you both doing here?" she asked me.

"I am helping Phoenyx with some combat training and was looking for somewhere quiet, but I do not want to disturb you, we will find somewhere else," I said, nodding to Phoenyx and starting to walk away.

"No, it's okay, you won't bother me, and I wouldn't mind the company," she said.

~*~

After an hour or so of throwing Phoenyx repeatedly onto the ground, trying to show him some self-defence and attack moves, I figured I had done all I could and should return him to the group and collect another.

I smiled at Phoenyx who was bent over, dripping with sweat, leaning on his knees trying to catch his breath. I noticed that during our sparring session he had kept looking over towards Fortuna, who had kept quiet as she worked her magic on the bow.

Yuki had laid on the ground, head up, with his paws crossed, watching us the entire time. If he were human, I would have said he was studying our moves. I do not think I had ever seen him so still for so long, apart from when he was asleep.

"I think I should return you to the group," I said to Phoenyx.

"Fortuna, do you mind if I come back here with another to train?" I asked her. When I looked back to where she sat, she was gently running her hands along the bow again, whispering to it. However, she looked more nervous in our presence, she was fidgeting, and her cheeks had turned a rosy pink. She stopped as she spoke to me.

"Not at all," she said, before returning to whispering to her bow.

"Okay, I shall be back shortly." I nodded to Phoenyx to follow me back to the group. I could have just asked him to fetch someone for me, but I did not want to waste time with them getting lost. Besides, I liked choosing my victims. Phoenyx paused and looked back towards Fortuna one last time before following me through the forest.

"Do you like magic?" I asked him.

"I don't really know much about it, I have never seen a mage practice before," he told me.

"Me neither. To be honest, I cannot stand mages, but Fortuna is different, she seems special," I said to him.

"Yeah, she does," he said with a frown. We did not speak any more and soon he left me to walk back to Igit's group.

Next, I walked over to Shea's group, whispering to her of my intentions first, then selecting a smaller built but lean muscled man. He was quite short, wearing what could pass as children's clothes in the form of cropped cotton trousers and a sleeveless top. He had short black hair and narrow eyes, with wrinkles beginning to appear in the edges. I guessed he was a few years older than Erik. He followed me to the stream and we immediately began the training. He did not seem bothered by Fortuna or Yuki's presence but was rather focused and determined, looking and listening to me intently. He watched my feet when I took a step to attack him, almost anticipating and dodging my advances, almost.

"You are smaller than some of the others, but this means you are also lighter and quicker," I told him. "Use this to your advantage, your enemy will not see you as much of a threat as the other larger men."

He did not take offence by my words but seemed to be encouraged by them. He was a fast learner and after I had taught him a few more moves, he was able to anticipate and evade half of my attacks. I was impressed. When we finished, I walked him back through the forest to return him to his group.

"What is your name?" I asked him.

"Ajax," he replied.

"Well Ajax, it was good to spar with you. I think with

more training you could be a lethal opponent to most."

"Thank you," he said, looking a little embarrassed, then rushed off to catch up with his group. It was a strange feeling, training men. Before now, I only ever saw them as weak, not disciplined enough to be able to learn the art of combat. It was nice to be proven wrong, and the more I trained them, the more confident I felt.

~*~

For the entire day, I had taken individuals from their groups, bringing them to the stream and dedicating at least an hour training each one. The light was now fading, and I was spent. I knew I would not be able to help all of them, there were not enough hours in a day, and we did not have many days.

I met with Maiya and discussed where the battle should take place. We both agreed we did not want the fight to come to us, we needed to take it to them to keep the more vulnerable out of harm's way. We decided that the cliff pass leading to the cave was our best option, it would allow our ranged fighters to hide and shoot from the cliffs.

The narrow pass would also help to funnel our enemy, even if they had greater numbers, they would not be able to overwhelm or surround us. Our only disadvantage was that if for any reason we had to retreat, it would be more difficult for our people to get away quickly, either climbing down the rock face or navigating through the cave tunnels. It was also quite close to the camp, with the forest being on the other side, but all other options seemed too risky. We agreed to spend tomorrow training and preparing our fighters the best we could. The next day we would leave early, to plant ourselves in position for the battle.

I returned to my hut, thankful to find it filled with the smell of mushroom soup and bread, Erik was just setting up the table when I entered. As soon as he saw me, he stopped what he was doing and rushed over, pinning me against the door with his body and kissed me passionately.

"I missed you," he said when his lips left mine.

"So I see," I said, looking up into his beautiful eyes.

"Is that mushroom soup I smell?" I said to him, smiling.

"Yes, Fortuna's special made," he said, moving away from me but holding my hand to guide me towards the table.

"How was your training?" I asked as we both sat by the table to eat.

"Actually, it was really good. Despite her temper, Maiya is a good teacher," he said. "How was your day? I saw you come and go with a few men in the woods," he said, smirking at me.

"Do not even go there," I said before he could make some funny joke about me disappearing off with other men. Or perhaps he was jealous, it would certainly explain the passionate kiss after immediately walking through the door.

"I wanted to help by giving some one-on-one lessons on

how to defend or attack an opponent without a weapon," I explained.

"I was surprised you didn't come for me," Erik said, dipping his bread in his soup.

"I wanted to, but I thought others would think I was giving you special training," I told him.

"That's fair, I don't deserve more of your time than any of the others," Erik said to me.

"Well, you are getting it anyway. We are going to the forest early tomorrow so I can give you some proper training," I said, smiling at him, while also diving into my soup and bread.

"We better get an early night then," he said, grinning at me again, and I knew it was not so we could get some extra rest. I was about to argue, I could not imagine a more perfect end to the day, naked in Erik's arms.

~*~

The next morning, like I had promised, we got up early and headed to the spot by the stream in the forest. The forest floor was full of dark shadows from the trees as the sun was not yet fully in the sky.

I had brought my swords, much to Erik's surprise. I had no doubt that Maiya was a good teacher, but when it came to Erik, I was not about to take any chances.

We reached the spot by the stream and I turned to him with a grin, eager to see what he had learnt.

"Think fast," I said as I threw my second sword in the air for him to catch. The moment his fingers wrapped around the handle, without giving him any time to ready himself, I charged forward and swung my sword. I smiled when he looked startled but lifted his blade to hit mine. The clang of metal echoed through the forest.

"Good," I said, taking a step back.

"Now let's see what else you can do." I lifted my sword, ready for my next attack. I did not charge this time, but stepped to the left of him, one foot crossing the other as I watched his movements.

He held his sword up and stepped to the right, keeping his body facing mine. I lunged forward, thrusting my sword straight to his chest, he stepped back quickly using his sword to strike mine away. Stepping forward again, this time I aimed higher, moving my sword diagonally to the right towards his neck. He quickly stepped forward into my move, holding his sword in front of his face and gripping his handle tight to block my attack. I smiled and relaxed my body, lowering my sword.

"That was good. You have a strong defence and a tight grip," I said, watching as he also relaxed and smiled at me.

"I don't think I have ever seen you look so fierce, even when we first met, but seeing you attack with a sword, for a moment I almost didn't recognise you. I thought you were trying to kill me," he said, laughing lightly.

"Well, that was the point. As much as I would like to take

things slow and teach you properly, we do not have the time, so we are doing it the hard and fast way."

"I thought we already had." He winked, displaying a wickedly handsome grin. I laughed in reply. Trying to keep things serious was going to be difficult.

"Maybe it is best you think of me as your enemy while we train," I said to him, trying to hide my smile and look more serious.

"I'll try Truda, but I also can't help feeling like this could be our last day together, that something bad might happen," he said, now looking at me intently with subtle sadness in his eyes.

"We cannot afford to think like that Erik, all of our energy needs to be focused on tomorrow's fight, we can win," I said to him. "Now I have seen you have good defence, how is your attack?" I asked him. Erik looked at me with a grin before charging with his sword aimed high.

Chapter 27

TRUE HEIRS

After Erik and I finished our training, we met with the others in the forest, and I left Erik to return to Maiya's group. I had been impressed; he had obviously learnt a lot with Maiya in a very short amount of time. I gave him a few more tips and pointers with footwork and strategy.

He was strong, but slow, so would need to be very watchful of his opponents moves and which direction they were to attack because one wrong blow and he would not be able to compose himself in time to defend against the following strike. His hand-to-hand combat was pretty good too, but again his speed was his weakness. I did not want to tell him that I had bested him while holding back. The truth was, if he were to go head-to-head with any trained elf, with a weapon or not, he would have lost.

The rest of the day was much the same as before, the warriors trained the men in their groups, a few switched to other groups that they felt they would be stronger in. I finished training the last fighter of the day and returned him to his group before heading back to the stream to Fortuna and Yuki.

I saw her jumping and splashing in the shallow water with Yuki as I approached. She had a beaming smile on her face, Yuki was making little excited yelping noises, as they both splashed around like children.

"Fortuna?" I said with a smile, curious and mesmerised to what was going on.

"I did it Tru, I did it!" she exclaimed. I looked towards the bow, now leaning by the tree trunk where she usually sat.

"You mean the bow?" I asked, raising my voice with excitement.

"Try it out," she beamed, stepping out of the water to be closer to me. I walked over and picked up the bow. It was not very impressive to look at, no carvings or jewels, only plain wood. Briefly glancing over to Fortuna, who nodded excitedly, I held it in position and aimed at the tree the opposite side to where we stood.

Sure enough, after a few moments of squinting, my eyes focused on one particular spot. A red ember began to ignite near my fingers, the flames grew and stretched out into an arrow shape just as I released the string as though to hit my target. The arrow made of flame left the bow, flew through the air and hit the tree, right where I had aimed. Fortuna waved her hand and curled her fingers, lifting a small bubble of water from the stream, flinging it on the flame arrow to put out the fire.

"Flame arrows?" I asked with a grin.

"I thought they might be more useful, and they won't burn the user, only the target," she said sweetly.

"Fortuna, this is perfect, we cannot thank you enough," I said to her. This would certainly give us another edge that the cities warriors would not expect.

"This is my home Tru, my friends, my family, I will do all I can to protect them."

"So will I," I said softly, realising the truth. I had more to lose here, more reason to fight for the camp, than I ever did as General Truda in the city.

"Then I had better go and get to work on the rest of the bows," said Fortuna cheerily, heading back to her tree stump and picking up the next to work with. Starving, I decided to head back to the camp to get some food.

~*~

After dinner, Erik and I went to the armoury hut to help check through gear and weapons. Phoenyx was sitting quietly in the corner, sharpening some knives with a stone. He looked up and smiled briefly before going back to focusing on his task, he did not seem in the mood for conversation, perhaps he was nervous about tomorrow.

Just then, Fortuna's white fox Yuki ran in, straight over to Phoenyx and jumped in his lap. Fortuna followed shortly after, pausing in the doorway. Phoenyx looked up at her, about to say something as he petted Yuki's white fur softly. But before he had a chance, I saw Fortuna's expression sadden and after another moment, she quickly left the hut. Yuki jumped away from Phoenyx, looking at him one last time before leaving the hut to follow Fortuna.

"What is the matter with them?" I turned and whispered to Erik.

"It's complicated, do you want to go for a walk?" Erik whispered, looking over to Phoenyx who had resumed sharpening the knives, now looking agitated and angry at something.

I nodded towards Erik and we stood and left the hut, walking along the bridges and past other huts, in no particular direction. He held my hand as we walked closely side by side, stroking my knuckles with his thumb as he liked to do. It sent shivers through my body and I wished we were alone somewhere more private.

"So, what is going on with Phoenyx and Fortuna?" I asked.

"It's a complicated love story," he told me, and then spun me around so that I was facing him. I laughed as he did and let my face lean into his chest.

"More complicated than ours?" I said while blushing slightly.

"I am afraid so."

"Let us go sit by the waterfall," I said, wanting to sit together in privacy so we could talk. We sat down at the end of the bridge that overlooked the camp and directly in front of us was the huge waterfall, our special place.

"So?" I asked Erik, wanting to hear the story that was apparently more complicated than ours.

"Well, Nyx has developed strong feelings for Fortuna and by the looks of her behaviour around him, I would say she feels the same."

Looking back, I could remember plenty of moments when they had acted strangely around each other, so it made sense this could be the reason.

"I do not see how that is more complicated than what we went through," I said to him, looking up and smiling. Erik held my hand and sat, pulling me down with him.

"That's because I haven't finished telling you the story," he told me, lifting me into his arms so I now sat on his lap. I sighed and let my head rest into his shoulder, and he kissed my forehead lightly.

"So, as you know, Nyx was sold to the Pleasure House in the city, where he was no doubt used for certain things with your kind, then he was gifted to the princess." I grimaced as I thought about what Phoenyx had said to me in the palace, that being in the Pleasure House was nothing compared to how he was treated by Princess Callidice.

"So, she is nervous because Phoenyx has been with others, is that it?" I asked, thinking of my own feelings of jealousy, knowing how Erik had been forced to be with others.

"That may be part of it but not the whole reason, although I only know this because I overheard a conversation between Maiya and Cobal, Nyx doesn't know," he finished in a sad tone.

"Know what?" I asked him.

"That Fortuna is Callidice's sister," he told me.

"WHAT!" I yelled, jumping in surprise and climbing off his lap. I paced in front of him as I processed what Erik had just told me.

"So, you can see why she might be a bit hesitant, not wanting to get involved with her sister's personal Guan."

"Phoenyx does not know?" I asked as I stopped pacing and looked at him.

"No, and he's really struggling with it, he wants to get close to her, but she just pushes him away," Erik replied.

"That I can understand. I remember how I felt when I had heard you were paired with someone else in the breeding programme before me, and that was before my feelings had developed.

"I remember that day, you were so angry, at the time I thought it was because you didn't want to get caught." He reached up and took my hand, pulling me back into his lap.

This time I straddled him, a leg either side of his waist.

"I suppose the situation is more complicated for them because Callidice is her sister," I said.

"That pretty much sums it up," Erik said, stroking his hands down my waist to the bottom of my spine. My hands started stroking his chest as he pulled me in for a kiss. It was long and deep, our bodies rocking and moving with each other, and in that moment, I really wished we did not have clothes on.

I broke the kiss, distracted by Fortuna's troubles, not just that she clearly had feelings for Phoenyx, but the fact that she was queen Callidice's sister. Wait a minute, that meant Fortuna was royalty, and must be the first-born princess, conceived when Queen Cassandra had first entered the breeding programme.

"I have to go speak to Fortuna!" I exclaimed, wriggling out of Erik's lap.

"I don't think we should be meddling in other people's love lives Truda, if it's meant to be it will happen," he said, frowning.

"I am not going to talk to her about that," I told him. "If she is Queen Cassandra's first born, then she is a princess and should be on the throne instead of Callidice."

~*~

After leaving Erik, I went in search for Fortuna. It did not take me long as she was wondering down by the stream

350

that she liked, bare foot, talking to the butterflies and trees, her fox was asleep between the roots of a large tree.

"Fortuna, why did you not tell me?" I asked her as I got closer.

"Oh, sorry Tru, I finished with all the bows, Shanor took them to the armoury hut."

"I am not talking about that. I am talking about the fact that you are Queen Cassandra's first-born daughter!" I said, my voice raised.

"Oh," she said and then after a brief pause and a sigh, she continued.

"It's not something I really like to remember. I like to pretend that I was born here, in this forest," she said to me without turning as she sat on the floor with two butterflies on her palm.

"Have you not thought about what this could mean for the rebellion? You are the rightful queen," I said to her.

"No, I'm not, my sister is. I lost the princess title the day they cast me out as an unwanted blind thing," she told me, looking sad. "Maiya and Cobal are leaders, you're a leader Tru. I am just a crazy little mage who likes talking to animals and trees," she said.

"Have you always known?" I asked her sympathetically, walking close and sitting next to her on the ground.

"My visions told me. I don't know why they didn't want me, why I was left for dead in that desert. All I know is that I don't belong there, I belong here," she finished saying, smiling as she lifted her hands so the butterflies could fly from her fingers.

"I saw him coming too, you know," she said, watching the butterflies dance into the wind.

"You mean Phoenyx?" I asked.

"Yes, I saw him many times in my dreams, like I had seen you. He was in the dreams with me." She looked down, a sad expression reaching across her face, "he doesn't understand why I push him away, and I can't tell him."

"Have you tried?" I asked.

"Tru, I don't even know where to begin, my visions saw things, painful things, between him and my sister, she hurt him, abused him, how can I tell him that I am related to that monster?" she said as a small tear fell down her cheek.

"You are nothing like your sister Fortuna, you are like no elf I have ever met before."

"I just don't know how to tell him," she said with a sob.

"A very wise elf once gave me a riddle about following my heart." I leaned forward and wiped the tears from her face. "I would say now is a good time to follow your own advice."

~*~

After leaving Fortuna to consider her options, I returned to the hut. Preparations for tomorrow had been made, and all that was to be done now was rest, to get ready for tomorrow's battle. I had been thinking of a way to talk to Erik out of going, and now Fortuna had given me a good reason why. I smiled at him when I entered, he was sitting on the cot, reading. I walked over and sat next to him.

"I need to ask you to do something and you are not going to like it," I told him. Erik sighed and folded his book closed, putting it on the floor.

"Don't even think about it Truda, I am coming with you tomorrow," he said quickly.

"No, I need you to stay here and protect the camp." Slightly frustrated that he knew me well enough to predict what I was going to say.

"You need me on the front lines fighting with you, I don't want you keeping me out of the fight to keep me safe!" he exclaimed, now raising his voice.

"This is not about me keeping you safe, this is not about us. I need you here to protect Fortuna, she is our future," I said, hoping he would understand my reasoning.

"Then have Nyx stay behind to protect her, you know he would want to," Erik argued.

"Phoenyx is not strong enough, you are the strongest one here aside from the elves," I replied.

"Don't do this Truda, I want to fight with you, to be there for you if you need me," he said in a plea.

"Having you with me will only make you a distraction, I will not be able to focus if I am constantly worried over

353

your safety."

"So, this is about keeping me safe!" He suddenly shouted, standing to face me.

"No, it is about you being in the best place to help defend the base if it comes to that," I said as I looked up at him. He did not look convinced by my words. "Fine, it is also about protecting you, but do you not see that you will also be distracted, worried about my safety?" I said, now standing up next to him, wanting to get on a better level.

I saw him sigh and lower his shoulders. He knew I was right, that he would not be able to focus in battle, and would be constantly searching for me, to check I was okay, just as I would be with him.

We were silent for a moment, both of our heads down, not knowing what to say. I had not wanted to argue with him tonight, we had not had much alone time together in the last few days, and now here I was, ruining another precious moment because of my need to keep him safe.

"I feel like you're leaving me again," Erik finally said, sounding sad. I snapped my head up to look at him, he was still looking at the floor. Raising my hands up to his face, I lifted his chin to force him to look at me.

"I am not leaving you, do you hear me? I am with you now, forever. I love you Erik," I said in a demanding tone, stepping closer to him. I wrapped my arms around his neck as he pulled me in closer to kiss my lips. Erik moved his kisses down my neck and to my shoulders, he then got down on his knees. He sat on his calves on the floor and placed his hand behind my left knee, gently bending my leg towards him. He lifted my foot and rested it on his thigh.

He kissed my knee and slowly started stroking up my thigh. My breathing became heavier as he worked his fingers down, until he reached my boot. Untying the front lace and carefully lifting my leg, he slid the boot off my foot, and after moving my leg off his thigh he repeated the process with my other boot.

Once both were removed, he stood, and stroked up either side of my waist and arms until he reached my neck. There he let his hand slowly wander down to the heaving top of my breasts, now desperately trying to get free as my heavy breathing was pushing out my chest. He looked again into my eyes as he started untying the string that held together the front of my bodice. His every movement was slow and gentle, looking into my eyes the entire time.

Once the straps were completely untied, Erik opened my bodice and pulled it off my shoulders, letting it fall to the floor behind me. Erik removed my cotton undergarments, leaving my breasts completely naked and free to his touch. He slid his thumb over my left nipple and then teased it until it went hard in his fingers. He did the same to my other nipple, my head arched back as I moaned at his touch.

Kneeling, he pulled down my leather skirt and

undergarments until I was completely free of clothing. Erik stood in front of me and stepped closer, my nipples grazing his chest, he reached with his hands and cupped my face, tilting it up so he could gaze into my eyes.

"And I love you," he said, before kissing me again. We stepped back slowly towards the cot, supporting my back with his arm he gently let me fall back as he climbed on top of me, crushing me with his weight.

As Erik kissed my lips, my neck, my breasts, I felt his hand travelling down between my thighs. I moaned the moment his fingers entered me, stroking gently, rubbing his thumb along my nib while he moved his fingers in and out at a steady rhythm.

After a few more minutes, Erik broke our kisses briefly to remove his top and pants, leaving him naked and lying on top of me again. I moved underneath him, wet and ready, raising my body to connect with his. I could feel he was hard as I slowly started rubbing myself against him. Erik, kissing me once again, lowered his hips and entered me, moaning as he filled me.

I wrapped my legs around his waist allowing him to push further, his shaft was now filling me up. My hands were holding onto his arms, with my fingernails digging into his skin as we moved together. My moans were smothered by the kisses he would not stop giving me, making me feel more wanted, more loved than I had ever felt in my entire life.

It was not long before we cried out together, shaking and burning with the fire we had just set ablaze. Erik collapsed beside me, pulling me into his arms again, not wanting to lose the contact.

"Okay Truda, I will stay behind tomorrow to protect the camp," he said while stroking my back. I looked up so I could see his face.

"Thank you, it means a lot to me."

"If it were my choice, I wouldn't leave your side ever again, but I trust your instincts and if you say our chances are better separate tomorrow, then I will agree," he said, looking down to me and kissing my forehead.

"It is for the best, I promise." I leaned into him closer, letting my head rest on his broad chest as we both fell asleep.

Chapter 28

GOODBYES AND BATTLE CRIES

When we woke early the next morning, neither of us said anything to each other. We stayed in each other's arms, holding each other tight until I heard commotion outside the hut. The camp was preparing, and I knew that we had to get up to get ready.

I sighed, kissing Erik's chest before turning from him and rising out of the cot. Walking over to my clothes, I began to get dressed, choosing my leather pants and a one-shoulder hide top. On top of that I put on gold shin guards and a gold breast plate, kindly given to me by Maiya, knowing that I had left my battle armour back in the city.

Erik walked behind me, gathering his clothes. He had also been given some better items more fit for a warrior, including some leather pants, a belt with a broad sword in its sheath, some leather gloves and shoulder pads.

He had also been given a mighty wooden and metal shield. I watched him as he dressed, looking at the new man he had become. It was true that Erik was always much more than a Guan but looking at him now, I knew it was not just me that had changed. Finding each other, ending up in this rebel base, now fighting for our lives, it had made us better, stronger, and more alive than we had ever been before.

A light tap sounded on the door.

"Come in," I said, as I strapped my dagger to the top of my thigh. Castor's little face peered around the door before he stepped inside.

"General Truda, I found this and remembered you had it at home to take with you for battles. I thought you might want to use it now," he said, holding out a small silver tin to me. I looked at him puzzled before taking the small tin from his hand and opening the lid, smiling when I saw what was inside.

"What is it?" Erik asked, leaning over to see the contents.

"Battle paint," I said to him with a smirk as I slowly brought my hand forward so Erik could see the blue woad dye.

"Thank you, Castor, this means a great deal that you would find this and bring it to me," I said to him sweetly.

"I was hoping it would bring you luck," he said before bowing his head slightly.

"We will not need luck Castor; we are going to win today."

Castor smiled and ducked out, closing the door behind him. I picked up my sword, using it to see my reflection like I used to. Dipping two fingers in the paint, I ran them diagonally across my face from my forehead down to my cheek, creating one thick blue line. I turned to Erik and smiled.

"May I?" I asked him, as I walked towards him still holding the pot of paint. He did not speak but nodded and watched as I dipped my finger in the paint, and brushed the coated fingertip over my lips, until they were completely covered. Then I stepped in front of Erik and kissed his chest, directly over his brand, the number twenty-three. I wished my kiss possessed the magic to erase the brand forever, that, and all other traces that Erik had ever been a slave. Today would hopefully signify the end of it. Today the slaves were fighting back for their freedom, and I was going to help them.

~*~

Everyone had come to the edge of the forest to say goodbye to the warriors. Maiya and Cobal stood in front of all of us as they said their goodbyes, exchanging whispered words to each other and smiling. It was sweet to see that the past had obviously brought these two closer together over time, with a deep friendship like no other I had ever seen.

Maiya glanced from Cobal to the group of warriors that stood in front of her, then glanced at me as she began to speak loudly.

"Today we will face our enemy, like we have never faced them before. They will be strong, they will be fierce, but we will catch them by surprise. They won't be expecting us to hit them head on, they won't see the Guan's from this camp as a threat, that will be the biggest mistake they ever make!" She finished, lifting her sword up high and grinning towards the faces in the crowd. Loud cheers exploded from the group as everyone pumped their fists and weapons in the air.

"Now let's move out!" Maiya shouted and started walking through the forest with the warriors following closely behind her. Erik and I hugged briefly before he rested his forehead against mine.

"Promise me you will come back," he whispered to me.

"I promise," I said to him as I quickly leaned up and kissed him, then before he could kiss me more deeply, I turned to walk with Maiya and the others.

As I walked, I looked to my left and saw Phoenyx and Fortuna, it looked like he was trying to talk to her but as he reached his hand out towards hers, she flinched and stepped back. Phoenyx gave her a pained glance, then turned to walk with the other warriors as everyone headed towards the cave. I quickly walked over to Fortuna, who I could now see had covered her face with her hands and was crying.

"Fortuna, are you okay?" I said quickly, rushing over to her.

"I couldn't do it, I couldn't open up to him and now he is going to go into battle thinking that I don't love him," she said, sobbing into my chest.

"I will talk to him. I will not tell him everything. I will just give him hope, enough to keep him focused," I said to her, stroking her hair lightly.

"You will?" she asked, looking up and wiping her tears.

"Of course I will, but you know this means you have to open up to him when he gets back?" I said to her, wiping away her last tears.

"Yes, I know, and I will, I'll find a way to tell him everything."

"Then you go look after my heart, and I will look after yours" I said to her with a smile.

"Okay, but Yuki goes with you, he will be my eyes and ears," Fortuna said. The little fox bounced in between my feet, his bum in the air and growling as though he was trying to show he was ready for battle.

"That is fine, but he stays out of the fight," I said, giving Fortuna one last hug. I watched as she walked over towards Erik, then Yuki and I turned and walked through the forest towards the cave entrance. As I walked forward, I gave Erik one more glance over my shoulder as he stood watching me walk away.

It was not until we had started making our way through the tunnels that I caught up with Phoenyx, who was clearly very angry, walking with fast, frustrated strides.

"Phoenyx!" I called. He stopped and turned to look back

towards me, he half smiled, as though he was only making the effort for my benefit.

"Hi Truda, you know I don't mind if you call me Nyx."

Just then, Yuki bounced in front of me and charged at Phoenyx, scratching and rubbing at his legs for attention. This made Phoenyx laugh as he bent down to pet the little fox.

"You shouldn't be here little guy," he said sweetly to Yuki as he ruffled up his soft fur.

"Fortuna wanted him to come, so she could watch over us," I said to Phoenyx. He looked up at me with a puzzled look.

"You do know she uses Yuki to help her see?" I asked.

"Yes, I know. I figured it out." His smile turned into a frown as he stood up and started to walk away again.

"Phoenyx, I mean Nyx, wait," I said, keeping up with him and waiting for him to turn to look at me again before I spoke my next words.

"Do not give up hope, she does care for you."

"She has made her feelings about me perfectly clear," Phoenyx said to me, looking both angry and hurt at the same time.

"It is complicated, I understand that, but so were Erik and I…" I began, but Phoenyx shook his head, cutting me off.

"It isn't the same. I have been dreaming about her for months, she was the only light I had to hold onto when everything for me went dark in the city. I didn't even know if she was real," he said, looking at Yuki who had sat next to him and was staring at him with the biggest sad eyes.

"Then I found her, she is real, and she can't stand the sight of me," he said, looking at the little fox so hurt and confused. I stepped forward and placed my hand on his shoulder, making him lift his head to look at me.

"You are wrong about what she thinks of you. Look, you have both been through so much and come from different worlds, it will be hard, and it will take time."

"I would wait if she asked me," he said with a glimmer of hope in his eyes.

"Then consider this her asking for your patience," I said, squeezing his shoulder before giving him a quick pat on the arm as I smiled and started walking forward to catch up with the rest of the group.

"Really, did she say something to you?" Phoenyx asked me as his pace quickened again to get ahead of me.

"She told me she regrets not telling you the truth and is afraid of what will happen if she does," I said to him, before stopping to tell him one last thing.

"But she wants to tell you Phoenyx, and she will once we survive this battle," I said, nodding my head to let him know this was a matter of fact.

"Then let's get this fight over and done with," Phoenyx said with a grin.

~*~

Once we had navigated through the cave tunnels, Maiya and I walked on ahead to pick the best spot for our people. We made sure our ranged shooters were perched and hidden within the large cliff edges, giving them plenty of cover, they would be difficult for ground soldiers to reach. Shanor stayed with them, not wanting to face her sister in the battlefield, crouching behind the rocks, ready to follow Maiya's lead to give instructions to the ranged fighters to fire when the time came. We stopped further ahead, finding a narrower section of the path that led to the caves. The perfect spot to force the queen's warriors to try and tunnel their way through to us in small numbers rather than a full force ambush out in the open desert sands.

"This is the spot everyone, get into position and rest while you can," Maiya called out to the group behind us. "Shea, walk to the edge of the cliffs and keep watch, come back when you see them approaching the path," Maiya said. Shea tersely nodded before jogging off towards the edge of the desert.

"Are you ready for this?" Maiya asked me.

"I am always ready for battle," I told her.

"Even against your own people?"

"This is not about sides anymore Maiya, your people, my people, it is about fighting for what is right and I will help defend you because that is what is right," I told her.

"And you're willing to kill your friends over this?" she asked. I did not have an answer. Could I really kill or seriously hurt people I cared for? It was not their fault they were fighting on the wrong side. Not so long ago, so was I.

"Well, just know General Truda, that I will be watching you, and if you let one of them live and they hurt one of us, I will kill you myself," she spat. I glared at her in disbelief. After everything I had done, it still was not enough for her to see me as anything more than her enemy. It would never have mattered which side I fought for because I would always be that. I walked away, spotting Phoenyx and Yuki sitting further down the path, deciding distance between Maiya and I right now was definitely a good thing. I slid down the rock and sat opposite them and smiled.

"I hope you don't mind me asking, but why hasn't Erik come with us to fight?" Phoenyx asked, stroking Yuki who had fallen asleep in his lap.

"He was given another important charge, to protect the camp, help the last line of defence if we fail," I said to him. I missed him terribly and wished I was in his company right now.

"He is very lucky to have you," Phoenyx said to me smiling, making me look up from my daydreaming. He must have seen right through me like Erik did. The truth was, I told him to stay behind to protect him, to keep him out of harm's way for as long as possible.

"The rebels already have my sword and soon, no doubt, the blood of my friends. I could not give them Erik too," I replied honestly with a sigh. "Besides, I fought to get him here, I think I have the right to tell him to stay."

"And what about his right to fight for what he wants?" Phoenyx asked. I looked at him puzzled, is that what he thought I had done? Forced Erik to stay behind against his will, treating him like the Guan he used to be? Is that what Erik had thought I had done?

"Sorry Truda, forget I said anything. I think that is my own pain talking," Phoenyx said to me, now looking entirely guilty, to which I just smiled. But it was too late, he had said the words and, in this moment, I wished for nothing more than to tell Erik I was sorry and that next time I would give him the choice. Just then Shea came running around the corner and whispered to Maiya.

"They are here, everyone in position," Maiya said, turning to us.

~*~

I stood towards the front next to Maiya and watched as a few dozen warriors could be seen walking across the edge of the desert towards the mountain cliff. I was not shocked to see Shanon and Imelda leading them. Gazing up briefly to Shanor, I sympathised as she watched them approach, witnessing her sister's betrayal with her own eyes.

"We let them come to us," said Maiya. I looked behind and smiled at what they must have seen walking towards us. Our ranged warriors remained hidden, leaving only a handful of elves, including Maiya and myself, now visible to the enemy. It was only when we could clearly make out their faces, that they paused.

"You are all branded traitors to the Kingdom of Nysa, surrender and return to the city to face the queen's judgement!" Imelda yelled.

"Shanor, now!" shouted Maiya, and I looked at the surprised faces in front of us as Shanor stood with her company of archers behind her. They began to fire their magical flame arrows, causing Imelda's tight lines of warriors to disperse, separating to avoid the unexpected attack. It was in this moment I nodded to Maiya, who briefly grinned at me before we both charged forward, our swords raised ready. The elves behind swiftly followed, their weapons of choice visible to our enemy. Quickly glancing behind, I saw Phoenyx and Ajax lead the other human fighters that we considered strong and skilled enough to join us in the front lines. I looked towards Maiya, who was now being charged by Shanon. I smiled to see Captain Imelda look at me with rage burning in her eyes. She ran directly for me, stopping only a few steps away.

"You never believed in me, never thought I was strong and yet, look at me now Truda. I am General, and you are a traitor."

"You could never take my place Captain Imelda, you are too weak minded and inexperienced," I said, holding my sword up, pointing it towards her.

"Then let's see, shall we?" she sneered back.

"Yes, we shall." I charged, swinging my sword across to the right, aiming for her neck. She quickly raised her sword, blocking its path. She hissed and gritted her teeth as she swung the sword low, towards my knees. I jumped, the blade of her sword only just missing my toes. Before my feet had even reached back to the ground, I saw her swing her fist towards me, which I barely managed to dodge as I regained my balance.

She clearly wanted to prove that she was better than me, she wanted more than anything to beat me, and was not holding back.

"Years of living in your shadow, always being treated like second best, well now is my chance General Truda, my chance to show them how weak you have become."

I did not reply, anything I would say would only fuel her anger and hate, and she was not my enemy. Not really. She had been fooled by the city's lies like I had. She had the true spirit of a strong warrior, all she wanted was to prove her strength and worth in the eyes of those in power, to gain their love and respect. Respect that I had not given her.

I stood tall and lifted my sword. If she wanted a good fight, then I was happy to give her one, if only to remind her of her place, which was always below me.

Just as I was prepared to charge her again, I heard a male cry in pain. I looked behind me and saw Phoenyx fighting another elf, she had sliced his leg and he was now crouching

369

on the floor, waiting for the blade to come down on him again.

Suddenly, I saw Yuki darting under people's feet, rushing to get to where Phoenyx had fallen. Using bodies in various positions of battle, he climbed his way up to head height and jumped towards the elf about to swing her sword across Phoenyx's face. Yuki's claws dug into her shoulders as he scratched and bit at her, forcing the elf to drop her sword and step back, screeching for help. I had never seen the little fox look so feral before and I wondered if it was entirely Yuki, or if Fortuna was coming through to help in the fight.

Phoenyx grabbed the fallen sword and regained his footing as he stood next to Yuki, ready again to fight. I smiled at the pair.

Imelda, obviously frustrated at my distraction, gruffly charged at me again, holding her sword up high to bring it down with all her strength. I side blocked her attack, using my sword to block hers, sand shimmered around as we disturbed the ground with our fast-moving feet.

Twisting my wrist sharply, I pressed my blade against hers and pushed, knocking the sword out of her hand. She grunted in frustration as she swung her fists towards my face. I moved my head and instead lifted my leg up high as I kicked her hard in the chest, knocking her to the floor.

Just then I heard an awful screeching sound, and a fox's wail as I looked behind me to see the talons of a big black raven, who was attacking Yuki in the eyes. It was crying, blood soaking the white fur on his face as he hid between Phoenyx's legs. Phoenyx was swinging his sword to try and frighten the creature away, which I knew would be no good.

I recognised that raven, it was Freyja's evil creature, Jetta, that now tormented little Yuki and Phoenyx. Ducking down, I grabbed Imelda's sword and started to sprint towards them, a blade now in each hand, ready to clip a certain bird's wings.

But my path was blocked, as two other elves now stood in front of me, their weapons raised. Using both swords, I thwarted their attack, trying to focus as I kept glancing ahead, concerned for Phoenyx and Yuki.

Shanor, witnessing my struggle to reach them, decided to act. With her bow still in her hand, she leapt forward, sliding her body down the rock face as she ran to their aid, firing her flame arrows at Jetta, causing the bird to squawk in fear and fly off. I grinned, as Shanor stood next to Phoenyx, fighting by his side, helping to defend him.

Incapacitating my attackers, inflicting wounds that would render them unable to fight, but allowing them to live. I looked around and was struck with a moment of sheer panic, as I clocked Terra, Lelane's partner, walking slowly forward on the opposite side of the battlefield, aiming her crossbow directly at Shanor. I began to run, but she was too far away. I knew I would not be able to reach her in time. Scanning around, I saw Maiya and Shanon, still fighting head to head, their blades clashing against each other.

"Shanon, stop Terra!" I screamed. Shanon paused, glancing over to me and then, directing her gaze at Terra, her eyes opened wide in panic when she also realised who she was aiming at.

"Shanor look out!" Shanon cried, now desperately running away from Maiya towards her sister. But it was too late, and we both watched in what felt like slow motion as the arrow left Terra's weapon, flying through the air, until it pierced straight through Shanor's throat.

Spurting blood in Phoenyx's horrified face as she turned to grab him for help. Panic filled his eyes as he held Shanor in his arms, looking helpless as he guided her body carefully to the floor.

"Shanor. No," I whimpered, unable to make my voice sound any louder. My body froze, and I watched as Shanon continued running forward, her body not failing her. Collapsing on the floor beside her sister, she pulled Shanor from Phoenyx's arms and cradled her.

I moved slowly forward, my feet shuffling as though the ground was laced with sticky tar, preventing me from running to them.

"Truda, look out!" I heard Maiya's cry, but could not see where she shouted from, nor could I react in time before I felt the pain in my back.

"Second best no longer," said Imelda through gritted teeth. I started to stumble and turn to face her, seeing the now bloodied dagger in her hand. I only just caught the shape of her other fist, before she hit me, and everything went dark.

Chapter 29

MY CAGE

The pain woke me, and it took a moment for my eyes to adjust before I recognised the dark and dingy floor I was now lying on. I was back inside the city, in the prison by the coliseum, and I was not alone.

A shadow loomed in the corner of my cell and I began to sit up slowly to position my body to defend myself however I could. A scream escaped my lips as a burning sting began to throb on my back.

"Take it easy," said a familiar voice, as someone slowly stepped towards me until I could see her bruised and beaten face in the light.

"Kayla?" I asked.

"Yes, it's me. They let me treat your wound but didn't give

me much in the way of supplies," she told me, bending down to help me sit up.

"I am surprised they allowed you to help me at all."

"I think they want to execute you in the coliseum," Kayla said, frowning sadly. Well, that made sense. I was the ex-general of the city, traitor to the royal family. They would not want me to die in some cell, they would want me to die some spectacular death in front of a crowd.

"Do you know what happened, did they bring anyone else back?" I asked, desperate to learn anything from the battle that would tell me if my friends had lived or died.

"No, they only brought you back. I heard that they were winning, and the rebels retreated," she replied sombrely, also looking worried about her friends. Studying Kayla's face, I could see she had a black eye and a nasty cut lip, along with various other scratches and marked skin on her cheeks and neck. She looked terrible, clearly physically punished after being caught, and taken to the prison the moment that Shanon had returned.

"I am sorry Kayla, this is all my fault," I apologised sincerely.

"I don't blame you General Truda, you didn't do this to me," she replied, smiling sweetly at me.

"You know she isn't the general anymore, so you should really stop calling her that," said a creepy, all too familiar rough tone from the shadows. It was a voice I had thankfully not heard for many weeks since my absence from the city, until now.

Freyja, stepped towards the barred door, grinning at me sitting on the floor with a gleeful menace, she was enjoying my current predicament. Her deformed winged pet, perched on her shoulder, reminding me of the battle, of poor Yuki. Flashes of Shanor's slumped body in Phoenyx's arms appeared in my mind. Oh god, Shanor, I thought to myself. Then, closing my eyes, I momentarily pushed back those thoughts, focusing on the deceitful mage in front of me.

"It has been a long time Truda, how far you have fallen," she said, grinning.

"I suppose this gives you great satisfaction Freyja. It is a shame you were never capable of putting me here yourself," I said, looking at her with my head held high.

"It wasn't like I didn't try. Who would have thought that it wouldn't be my poisons, or my hired assassins that would bring you down, but that of your own doing," she said, stepping closer to the cell.

"So, I was right, it was you. You tried to poison the breeding potion, that is why you were looking around the Breeding House for evidence that I had thrown it away, because you knew I had not been drinking it," I said, now standing to face Freyja, hearing the shocking truth. Kayla grabbed my arm and helped lift me so I could stand tall.

"I had my suspicions yes, which was confirmed when my assassins said you didn't appear weak or faint when fighting, they should have been able to defeat you easily," said Freyja, clearly proud that she was able to tell me now of her plan. I suppose as I was soon to die, it would make no difference of what I knew of the past.

"We have never liked each other Freyja. I just never knew your hate ran so deep that you would try and have me killed," I said with shortness of breath as it was becoming more painful to stand and keep my back straight. I needed to rest but I did not want Freyja to have the satisfaction of seeing me looking so weak.

"You were just an obstacle my dear Truda. I needed you and the queen out of the way so that Princess Callidice would assume the throne and I could restore order to the city."

"It was you, you killed Queen Cassandra!" I yelled. I had not been here to protect her, and she had been killed by the black mage that I had suspected to be treacherous from the start. I had failed her, failed my mother's memory.

"I slipped the queen the same potions of weakness intended for you, except hers was a stronger dose, weakening her body every day. She died within a week," Freyja smirked.

I leapt forward in the cell, reaching through the bars to try and grab her. I ignored the searing pain in my back and the wobble in my legs as I struggled to remain standing, my arm outstretched with my fingers millimetres away from reaching her face.

"You are weak, you always have been. The mages of this

city have long protected and given the elves long life, strength and speed. Yet we are merely advisors, it is always the warriors who control and command the Kingdom of Nysa. Don't you see Truda, we are the higher power, descendants of the original mages thousands of years ago, and you should be our servants, just like those male Guan scum." Freyja spoke her words through gritted teeth as though she had been keeping her feelings hidden for so long that the rage had consumed her.

"The mages are not strong enough to protect the city, never have been, that is why the warriors hold command."

"You have no idea of what I am capable of," she retorted.

"I know that if you were to face me, one on one, instead of cowering behind your assassins, you would be struck dead with my sword, before you could even finish a chant."

"You are limited by your own arrogance Truda. You will never understand the power we mages hold," she said more calmly, feeling confident in her position with the bars between us, safely out of my reach.

"And what of the princess, your now chosen queen with no magic, will she be your next target?" I asked, glaring at her through the bars.

"Queen Callidice is young and selfish, as long as I can keep feeding her dark desires, then she will remain loyal to me."

"And if she does not?" I asked, knowing what the answer would be but wanting to hear the words from Freyja.

"If she doesn't, then she will no longer be useful and that

will be the end of Queen Cassandra's bloodline, leaving the path open for the mages to take full control of the city," she said, shrugging and smiling.

"You, Freyja, are a snake, and one day I will be granted with the gift of no longer having to listen to the sound of your slithering tongue." Freyja laughed deeply in reply and walked away.

"That gift will be granted to you tomorrow Truda, because tomorrow will be your execution." Her words echoed down the tunnel, just before the shadow of her body could no longer be seen on the floor.

~*~

I did not know what time it was, but I knew it was late in the day due to the darkness that now filled my cell. Kayla was no longer with me as a guard had taken her away and locked her in another cell further down the hall. I could not talk to her unless we shouted, which would not have been tolerated by the prison guards.

I was laying on a pile of hay with a torn blanket under my head, the pain in my back prevented me from getting any sleep. Kayla had done her best to help heal me, but I knew they had not given her many supplies and much of my wound was still exposed. Blood had trailed down to my legs and I felt dizzy, when I reached to touch the bandages, they were soaked through with blood. Using the blanket, I tore it in large strips and tied it across my back and over my left shoulder, screaming with pain when I pulled the bandage tight before making a knot on my chest.

I lied down on my stomach, hoping to slow the bleeding by lying as flat as possible and closed my eyes, but I could not sleep, the pain was too much. So, I laid still and waited for the light to come through, letting me know that it was morning, and I would be killed soon.

Just then I heard footsteps that stopped outside my cell, I tilted my head and looked up.

"Acqueline!"

"Was it worth it?" she asked me, no emotion in her voice. I wanted to sit up, but the second I tensed, I felt the searing pain down my spine. Inhaling sharply, I relaxed my body again and turned my head, resting it back on what remained of the folded blanket as I looked towards my friend.

"Was what worth it?" I asked her, trying my best to hide the pain from my voice.

"Betraying your people, saving a few slaves, fighting with the rebels," she said, her voice steadily growing louder with anger.

"I did not betray our people Acqueline, we were lied to, the rebellion is not what we thought," I started to say.

"You were supposed to protect us, protect her. Instead, you left us, left the queen to die," she snapped.

"If I remember rightly Acqueline, it was your job to

protect the royal family, so do not hold me responsible for your failures," I snapped back, instantly regretting my words as I saw her shocked and hurt expression.

She did not know what I knew, that Queen Cassandra had been poisoned. There was nothing anyone could have done, without knowing Freyja's evil intensions.

"Acqueline, I am sorry. I did not mean that, you are right. I neglected my responsibility, but you have to believe that I was doing what I thought was right, and you would too if you listened to the truth."

"I don't want to hear it Tru, all your lies, you left us, abandoned your city, abandoned me, and for what?" she shouted. Clenching my fists, I forced myself to sit up despite the pain. Once on my hands and knees, I slowly pushed off the floor so I could sit up on my legs.

"I did not abandon anyone, I was lied to, set up, almost killed! Did you not have that potion analysed? Surely that is all the evidence you need?"

"There was nothing wrong with the potion, the results came back normal Tru."

"Then you were lied to, or the potion was switched."

"Do you hear yourself? This is ludicrous!" she yelled.

"What do you want from me Acqueline? You will not hear the truth, do you want me to lie? Do you want me to say I should have acted differently? Because I will not," I said to her, trying my best to ignore the throbbing in my back.

"I don't… I don't know," she stuttered, as her eyes began to glisten, and she turned to hide her face away from me.

"Acqueline, listen to me. In all the years you have known me, have I ever given you reason of doubt, have I ever made any decision that you did not only agree with, but whole heartedly supported?" I asked her, standing slowly as I spoke and stepping towards the bars, holding onto the iron rods for support.

"No, you haven't," she said, looking back to me.

"Then I need you to listen, let me tell you everything and then I will let you decide if you agree with my actions or not."

~*~

Acqueline stood quietly and listened to my story, not once interrupting me or asking any questions. I saw her face change as though showing her emotion at certain points that she did not like to hear, but apart from that, nothing. She let me tell her the entire story.

From my first encounter with Erik, to the punishments he had received after I met him. I told her what happened after we escaped, and what happened when I reached the rebel base. I told her about the people I had met and the stories they shared with me about the truth of the rebellion, that the rebellion leader was father to the twins. I told her about Phoenyx and all he had gone through. I told her about Fortuna and her true origins. I even told her about little Yuki and the first time I had seen him in my dreams. I told her about Freyja and the truth of Queen Cassandra's death. Lastly, I told her what I had witnessed on the battlefield, Shanor's death, before I was knocked out and brought here, not knowing what had happened to my friends after that.

Once I finished, she remained quiet, but I could see in her eyes that she was taking everything in, and struggling with the emotions she now felt. I did not know if she hated me or could now see the truth as I did. She walked closer to the cell and reached inside her pocket, pulling out a small vial filled with a clear liquid.

"Drink this," she told me, holding back all emotion in her voice again and reaching her hand forward to give it to me.

"What is it?" I asked, taking the small glass bottle from her hands.

"It will deeply lessen your pain, so you will no longer suffer with your injuries, and you won't feel anything when they..." She stopped speaking.

"When they execute me," I said, glumly.

Acqueline nodded, and after glancing towards me one last time, she walked away from my cell and headed back down the corridor. So that was it, that was the conclusion to sharing my full story with my long childhood friend and sparring partner. Whether she believed me or not was unclear, but I now knew she was not in support of my actions and would leave me to die.

~*~

A short time had passed before I heard footsteps stopping in front of my cell. Two guards stood in front of the prison door, accompanied by Imelda, her angry eyes baring into mine.

"Unlock the door and make her wear these," she said, as she passed some clean leather garments and armour to one of the guards.

"I would advise you not to put up a fuss Truda, we don't want to make your injuries worse," Imelda said to me.

"Of course not, that would ruin the show, if the great General Truda did not die on display," I mocked. She glared at me as the guard unlocked my door and both walked into the cell.

They began removing the torn blanket strips and my dirty blood-soaked clothes. They did not bother replacing my old bandages but instead began to roughly dress me in the new leather garments and armour. I was grateful to Acqueline for giving me the potion as the pain was barely noticeable, and I was able to smile menacingly at Imelda who was frowning. At least I was able to keep up appearances of playing the tough act.

Once they had finished dressing me, they scraped back my hair and tied it off my face, wanting me to look as presentable as possible for the occasion.

I was now ready for my execution.

The guards led me out of the cell, holding me on either

side by my arms as they followed Imelda and led me out of the prison.

As we approached the gate, I could hear the crowd, shouting and talking with anticipated excitement. Imelda opened the big black gate as I was walked through onto the open ground of the coliseum.

It took my eyes a moment to adjust to the brightness of the sun on what appeared to be a beautiful day, clear bright blue skies, tainted with only the odd white cloud. As we approached the middle of the arena, I saw the new Queen Callidice approach the edge of the balcony to address her people.

"Behold the traitor of the people!" shouted Queen Callidice, and the crowd began to shout and boo.

"Not only have we discovered that the ex-general of the city betrayed us by joining forces with the rebels, but we have received recent evidence that she is responsible for my mother's death, the beloved Queen Cassandra!" she shouted, not even glancing my way, instead only looking over all of her people.

"What?" I said as I looked up and wanted to shout against her words, but before I could, Imelda used the hilt of her sword to quickly bash my skull in almost the same spot as she had done on the battlefield.

I could not feel the pain that was sure to be there, but my eyes blurred, and I felt dizzy, close again to passing out, only just able to remain conscious.

I looked around me, and through blurred vision I could see Freyja standing behind Queen Callidice as she spoke, no doubt the person behind the lies of the queen's death. However, it would not have mattered to Callidice if she knew that it was Freyja who had killed her mother, she likely would have been more than happy to direct the blame to me anyway.

To my left I could see Kayla. She was kneeling with another guard next to her, she was to be executed after me from what I heard the guards talking about earlier.

To my right I saw Acqueline, she was staring at the queen with disbelief in her eyes, listening to her words and letting them puzzle around with her thoughts. Then she glanced over to me, before looking to the ground, not able to hold my pleading gaze. Was she remembering the events that she knew? Was she now taking in what I had said? Was she putting all the pieces of the puzzle together and realising they did not fit?

"Now we cut off her head and destroy all memory of the ex… General… Truda!" Queen Callidice bellowed.

I fell to my knees as I felt Imelda kick at my joints, forcing me to drop and then looked as she held her broad sword, standing to the side and beginning to line her blade to my neck.

This was it. This was my end.

Chapter 30

THE END

I looked up one last time to the blade in Imelda's hand and then, accepting my fate, I looked to the ground. I thought about all I had done to bring me to this moment and knew I would change nothing, because I regretted nothing.

I wished I could save Kayla from her death that would follow mine. My only hope was that everyone else I cared for was either here safe in the city or hidden.

Maiya would lead them from the rebel base away to safety, her and Cobal would take the people to find a new home where they would be free. Most importantly, I was sure of Erik's safety and survival. I had sought out to free him from the bonds of slavery and led him to a place where he could live out the rest of his days in peace, to grow old like Cobal had. I closed my eyes, blocking out the boos and cheers from the crowd and waited for Imelda's blade to cut off my head, except the sound of a whistling blade through the air never came, and the screams of the crowd quietened.

I opened my eyes to see Kayla staring upwards. I looked over to Imelda and she was doing the same. In fact, as I looked at everyone around me, all necks were craned back.

Through blurred vision, I looked up to see what they saw. Fast moving black clouds were hastily covering the blue sky, then came the rain, heavy droplets that felt like needles trying to pierce the skin. A flash lit up the arena, followed by a deep rumble that could be felt beneath my feet on the ground. When the rumble sound stopped, the ground did not stop shaking, it got worse. Loose stones bounced on the floor as the ground rumbled and vibrated. Tiny cracks started to appear in the floor that trailed outwards like a tree's roots until it reached the coliseum stone walls. Another flash spread across the sky, followed by a louder rumble.

The ground continued to shake, and I saw as Imelda and others started to lose their footing. The walls of the coliseum began to crack and split through the seating area where the crowd now ran in fear, trying to find a way to escape.

We all looked to the black prison gate as it fell from its hinges onto the ground, waves of dust dissipating in the air as it crashed into the sand. That is when I saw her.

"Fortuna?"

She stepped through into the coliseum, her arms raised, her fingers pointing towards the sky, and I watched as she swung one of her arms down to the ground and instantly a lightning bolt struck in front of Imelda's feet, forcing her to take a few steps back from me. I could not believe my eyes, Fortuna was controlling the weather. Not only that but the ground cracked with every step she took as she channelled her magic.

Behind her, following closely, was Phoenyx and little Yuki. Behind them I saw Maiya, Shanon, Shea, Igit, Ajax and Erik! He ran as soon as he saw me, dropping to his knees and pulling me into his arms.

"That's the last time I let you go anywhere without me," he said as he kissed my forehead. This was the moment that Callidice and Freyja moved forward on their balcony, anger covering their faces.

"General Imelda! Kill Truda and the intruders at once," shouted Freyja, pointing at me and Erik. Her raven flew off her shoulders and, while showing and clenching his talons, he swooped down towards us.

"You won't touch them!" shouted Fortuna, dropping her arm down swiftly again so a bolt of lightning hit the raven, cooking him in mid-flight. He was dead within seconds, dropping to the ground with a thud, only a few feathers remaining on his fried body.

Freyja screamed and picked up her staff. Whispering into

the red jewel at the top, it began to grow a ball of fire. She let the flame grow and then jerked her staff forward, shooting the burning orb at great speed towards where Fortuna stood. Fortuna simply waved her hands in a circular motion and collected the immediate drops of rainwater until it appeared as a rippling wall, putting out the flames the moment it made contact.

"Guards, stop them!" shouted Queen Callidice in frustration.

But as I looked around, no one moved, not even Imelda. All eyes looked towards Fortuna and her small party of warriors and they remained frozen. As it would seem, the rebels did not need great numbers to defeat the cities army, because Fortuna was all the army they would ever need. What remained of the crowd that had not fled stared at Fortuna in awe.

"Who are you?" cried Callidice in frustration towards Fortuna.

Fortuna ignored her and walked slowly towards Erik and I, the earth still cracking as she stepped but the rain began to slow as she neared me. Kneeling down she smiled and gently pulled me in for a hug.

"Are you okay Tru?" She asked me so sweetly and innocently, as though she had not just walked through the city, conjuring a storm to which she could wield and control to strike with lightning.

"I cannot believe you came," I said, directed at both Erik

390

and Fortuna.

"How could we not, after everything you have done for us," she said.

"Would you believe us if we said this was Maiya's idea," said Erik.

"What really?" I replied.

"She knew what Fortuna was capable of if she put her mind to it, and after you were captured it seemed to be all the motivation she needed to tap into her full potential," he told me, making me laugh lightly.

I had been given the clues to Fortuna's power from the moment I met her, from the way she could use magic without being given proper instruction, even her own apologetic comments about her moods affecting the weather. She was a pure descendant of the mages who had so much power to be able to wield the elements, the ancestors Freyja admired enough to commit murder for.

"Who knew all I had to do was get captured by my own people and held for execution before Maiya would finally warm up to me," I said, making us all laugh. I looked towards Maiya who stood a few metres away, she looked at me and nodded her head with a smile on her lips.

"I said who are YOU!" screamed Queen Callidice. Her anger had increased while we all shared our moment of reunion.

Fortuna stood and walked towards the balcony, little Yuki

now walking next to her. I noticed a little brown leather eye patch covering the eye he had lost thanks to Freyja's now dead raven.

As she approached them, she aimed her head towards the balcony so they could clearly see her face as she spoke.

"My name is Fortuna. I am the first-born daughter of Queen Cassandra, born in the city of Kven and rejected by the Mages Temple," Fortuna said, proudly and with confidence.

~*~

"That cannot be, there is no way she would have survived," said Freyja in shock.

"And I suppose you would know as it was you who cast me out," replied Fortuna. I looked up in shock.

"She was an abomination, blind, weak and pathetic. If I hadn't gotten rid of her, the queen wouldn't have had another daughter and she would be left to rule the people. I was saving the city from more future failures," spat Freyja, directing her words to the people around her.

Freyja had been responsible for Fortuna's abandonment? Did Queen Cassandra know? Were these the decisions that haunted her, ridding the kingdom of a blind child so that she could give birth to a warrior fit to rule? Perhaps this was how someone like Freyja, an untalented mage, had ended up on the council in the first place. She had obviously dug her claws into the royal family a long time ago.

"Well, I did survive and here I am, to finally take my rightful place amongst my people, as the rightful queen of the Kingdom of Nysa," Fortuna bravely said, loud enough for all who remained in the coliseum to hear.

"Even if what you say is true, I am queen now and you will not take my crown from me, the people won't accept you!" stomped Callidice in a temper.

"Guards, kill the imposters, I command it now!" shouted Freyja.

"You do not command us mage," said Acqueline as she stepped forward holding her bow up high aimed at Freyja on the balcony. Glancing over to my friend I smiled, she could finally see it and was unravelling the poorly woven lies. She pulled her string taught, ready to release an arrow at any moment.

"How dare you Acqueline, you will be treated as a traitor and killed with the rest, GUARDS!" Queen Callidice shouted. Yet no one moved, out of fear or disbelief for the events that were unfolding. It seemed like the true colours of a black hearted mage and a spoilt cruel child were coming to light, and all the people could see it. That, and they may have been too afraid to challenge Fortuna.

"It seems to me the people of Kven are starting to realise that they have been lied to, you no longer have hold over them little sister," said Fortuna.

Phoenyx, holding his axe, walked up behind Fortuna and

Queen Callidice's face turned red as she watched Phoenyx take his place by Fortuna's side.

"I will have you all killed, starting with that one! He will die the most painful and horrible of deaths," she screamed, pointing at Phoenyx.

It was too much for Fortuna as she shrieked suddenly with rage, making Callidice flinch and step back in fear. The rain once again began to fall more heavily as the droplets now turned into little stones of ice. The sky rumbled, and flashes of lightning forked through the black clouds.

Phoenyx stepped forward, trying to calm Fortuna as the ground started to crack and shake again. The earth began to split right in the centre of the coliseum. But it was no use, she could not hear him, as a whirl wind of air and ice swirled around her. The crack widened, slowly travelling towards the balcony where Queen Callidice and Freyja stood.

They could only watch with horror as the cracks climbed up the walls around them. It left them no time to react as the floor crumbled and broke, forcing their bodies to fall and be crushed by the remaining stone from the balcony that fell after them.

Witnessing their end, Fortuna froze, the cyclone surrounding her body dissipating. Beginning to cry as she covered her face with her hands, realising what she had just done. Erik helped me from the ground, and we walked over towards Fortuna and Phoenyx, who stood by the giant rubble of stone. As we got closer, I could see parts of the now lifeless mangled bodies, which had been forced to bend in unnatural ways due to the weight of the rocks that had crushed them.

Phoenyx held Fortuna in his arms as she turned away from the graphic sight. The storm had stopped, and the thunder had quietened, but the rain had returned, matching the tears that now ran down Fortuna's face.

"Shhh, it's alright now," he said to her as he gently stroked her blonde hair.

"Do not cry for them Fortuna. If they had had their way, we would all be dead and the Kingdom of Nysa would have been left for them to ruin," I said to her.

"I know," she muffled. Pulling her face away from Phoenyx's chest she looked over to me, still being held in his arms.

"It's just I have never killed anyone before," she said looking around her as others stepped forward to join us.

"Tru?" said Acqueline as she stepped next to me timidly, glancing towards Erik, not knowing how to respond to him, or the fact that I was being held up by his strong arms.

"It is okay Acqueline, you have nothing to fear from us, I am still your friend and always will be," I said to her.

She stepped forward and hugged me, forcing Erik to stand back a moment as she wrapped her arms around me, gripping tightly.

"It is a good thing you gave me that potion," I whispered into her ear, making her jump and step back from me. I momentarily lost my balance before Erik was behind me again wrapping me in his arm as support.

"I'm sorry Tru," she said, looking guilty and worried for me.

"Honestly, I am fine, I just need rest," I told her.

"What happens next?" Acqueline asked.

"Now we show our people a better way," I said as I looked around her towards the group of people she used to think of as rebels.

"And you think this will be easy? Where do you even start?" asked Acqueline as she too looked towards the people.

"By putting our faith in her," I said as I smiled and looked towards Fortuna who was now talking to Maiya and Shanon.

Shanon glanced over to me, and I saw the guilt in her eyes, she blamed herself for her sister's death. It was obviously the reason she now stood by Maiya's side and had returned with the rescue party. Shanor's death was the sacrifice we had to live with to end the fighting.

"That won't be easy for everyone," said Acqueline, looking between me and Erik.

"No, I do not suppose it will be," I said. Then, looking towards Erik, I smiled. "All I know is that not too long ago, I was the queens general, who believed in only one way, until I met an extraordinary man who gave me his heart and shared his wisdom, showing me a better path. The true path to not only our survival, but to also end the conflict and bring peace to all our people... and that path is love."

Epilogue

Months had passed since the day Queen Callidice and Freyja had been killed, a full year since the first day I was told I was to enter the breeding programme.

How different life had become.

Fortuna had been named queen of the Kingdom of Nysa, and for the first time in our history, we also had a king. Fortuna had finally confessed her love for Phoenyx, and they now both sat together on the throne, ruling the city of Kven. It had helped the union of our people. All Guan's had been released from their servitude and were to be treated as free men to choose how they wanted to live their lives.

It was a difficult adjustment to our way of life, something that we were still smoothing out, but I was confident that in time we would go down in history as the generation that changed the fate of our future for the better.

Acqueline remained the head of the Royal Guard, Shanon becoming her second in command, supporting her and aiding in the protection of the royal couple. Shanon was never the same again, as she struggled more than most over the death of her sister. Maiya had been named General. I had been offered the position first but declined after it was discovered my injuries had caused some permanent damage, I would never be fully healed.

Instead, I had been named head of the Training House and was charged with instructing the next generation of young fighters, both elves and human.

I was also a member of the new council, as was Erik, Cobal, Maiya and Acqueline. Peril had chosen to stand down as she struggled with the truth of Freyja and Callidices's betrayal, as well as losing the title of Breeding House master since the principle of the place no longer existed.

Erik and I were on our way to a council meeting, which were held every morning at first light. With so much to do and talk about, it was the best way for all of us to be kept informed at the city's delicate transition into a new way of life.

We knew there were a few people who did not like or agree with freeing the men and we were worried that a rebellion of a different nature would arise. As we walked through the throne room hand in hand, the first smile I saw was Acqueline's.

"Good morning Tru, good morning Erik," she said to us both. I was more than pleased that it did not take Acqueline long to warm up to Erik, not that I was surprised, as I knew she would see his strong and kind heart as I did.

We sat around the table all talking amongst ourselves. Castor had decided to remain with Cobal, who had adopted him like the child he never had, giving Shanon a new little brother to train and tease.

I smiled over to Maiya, who had become good friends with Acqueline and I. We often sparred together in the Training House and I would try and hold back my smugness, as I would still often defeat the pair of them, despite my disadvantage.

Suddenly, the royal chamber door opened, and Fortuna walked through holding Phoenyx by the hand. As he stepped closely behind her, they walked forward together as he sweetly looked at her with so much affection in his eyes. We all saluted as they sat in front of us.

Fortuna had found many books hidden in her mothers bedchamber, including the books detailing the start of rebellion. We did not know why Queen Cassandra had taken them, but I wondered if it was to hide past actions that she did not agree with herself. I longed for her to be here, so I could ask her. Not just about why she had hidden the books, but also would she have agreed with what we had done. Would she be proud of her daughter, our now amazingly powerful queen?

"Good morning everyone," said Fortuna, a smile on her

face.

"What is the first thing on our agenda today?" asked Phoenyx, squeezing Fortuna's hand.

"Well, what would you like to discuss first? We still have the repairs, the lack of housing, communications and trade with the people who live outside the city," said Maiya. When we freed the Guan's, we also gave the people a clear choice, no-one, elf or human, was prisoner to the city of Kven, many had decided to leave, some rumoured to be retreating back to the hidden base within the forest.

"Not to mention that we still have yet to decide what to do with Imelda," Maiya remarked.

"She should just be killed," said Acqueline.

"I do not believe that is the best way forward," I argued.

"But she almost killed you Truda," Erik stated.

"She was only following orders," I told him, squeezing his hand.

It would be wrong to kill Imelda for serving her kingdom and would not set the right example for the way forward. After all, we had not punished Terra for killing Shanor, although we did have to hold Shanon back from beating the living day lights out of her. We had all suffered enough loss, it was pointless to create more chaos for the sake of revenge.

"Then perhaps we should start the meeting with some happy news," said Fortuna, looking over to Nyx who smiled sweetly and nodded excitedly.

"What happy news?" asked Maiya.

"We have just had the test which confirms I am pregnant," Fortuna said with a beaming smile. We each stood and gave them our congratulations, hugging them both.

"Do you know if it is a boy or a girl?" asked Cobal.

"I have dreamt of a boy, and he will be the first child of the union," said Fortuna, proudly.

~*~

Later that day, I was once again home after another full day at the Training House, a home I now shared with Erik. After the meeting, he had left to go and help lead the repairs. In the early days, he had just started helping to keep himself useful, which of course had only landed him the job of organising and sorting all of the repairs in the city.

His latest project was to be named 'Tobias's House'. I, of course, had chosen the name, telling Erik it was my way of being able to honour the path that Tobias had set me on. Once complete, the house was going to be a safe haven for all the young human children who had been freed and did not have a home that wanted to accept them. It was also to be a place of learning, one that even little Castor would attend, and finally be able to learn how to read.

Erik usually came home covered in sweat, dirt and dust and I would scold at him to have a bath before he came anywhere near me, which usually meant he would tackle me lovingly to the floor and ravage me until I was then also covered fully in sweat, dirt and dust.

This is how he greeted me when he came home today, the perks of this were that we could bathe together and stroke each other's bodies clean with soap and oils.

I was lying in the bath with Erik, my back resting on his chest as I was leaning in between his legs. My eyes were closed as he was gently massaging citrus oil into my shoulders and across my breasts.

"It was nice to hear of Fortuna and Nyx's news today," Erik said to me as he continued to caress my shoulders.

"Mhmm," I said as I felt myself drifting off to sleep from the bliss of the lovemaking we had just had and the tender touch of Erik's strong hands massaging my skin in the bath.

"Which got me thinking," he started. "I know you told me once that you didn't want children, and just wondered if you still felt the same way?" he asked me, which made me alert from my moment of relaxation. I sat up and turned to him quickly, making a wave of water tip over the bath edge onto the floor.

"You want to have children?" I asked, feeling a sudden panic.

"Not right now, and if you say that you don't, then that's okay. I just wanted to know how you felt," he said to me, looking nervous.

"I do not know, it is not something I have ever really

thought about," I said honestly, then looked into his eyes, feeling his love for me hit me like a heat wave. Breeding for me had only ever really been something we did out of necessity, to keep our numbers at a good population or to breed more slaves if we needed them. I was also a different person back then, a warrior and not much else. Erik had brought more to my life by filling my heart. He showed me there were more important things to life and I wanted to share every moment of it exploring all of those things.

"If the love that we now share created a life of its own, then I am sure it would bring me more happiness," I said, smiling at him.

Erik sat forward and grabbed me by the top of my thighs, using the water to lift me closer towards him until I was straddled across his lap. He kissed me then roughly and my arms fell around his neck.

"Then we'd better get practising," he said, making me laugh as I leaned in closer to kiss him.

Thank you so much for purchasing this book I hope
you enjoyed reading it.

I am a new author, from the United Kingdom,
passionate about graphic design, reading and writing.
I love tea, chocolate and dogs! Manumission is my first
novel, and I'm hoping to release many more stories
in the coming years. You can show your support by
joining my writing social media pages, or sign up for
a montly newsletter via my website to hear about my
many upcoming projects.

R. A. HATTON

🌐 www.rahatton.com
🅵 R.A Hatton Author
📷 @r.a.hatton_author